ON THE EDGE OF DESTINY

BOOK 3

THE VAMPIRE NAVY SEAL SERIES

S.B. ALEXANDER

Cover designed by Hang Le
Cover copyright © 2021 by S.B. Alexander

On the Edge of Destiny
Book three: The Vampire Navy SEAL Series

First Edition: December 2014

E-book ISBN-13: 978-0-9887762-6-5
Print ISBN-13: 978-1-954888-12-8
Large Print ISBN-13: 978-1-954888-14-2

1

If today were my last day, then there was no place I'd rather be than nestled in the arms of the most gorgeous vampire, Webb London. I'd never imagined a world where my heart—and, quite possibly, my soul—connected to another so strongly as it did to him. I was drunk from his touch, his kiss, his presence, and I didn't want our date to end.

But reality trumped the world I lived in, and life knocked on the door. It was time to leave.

Reluctantly, I slid back into the limo. I had three hours before I lost my glass slipper. Midnight loomed, and Dad was expecting me.

Threading his fingers through my hair, Webb

kissed my temple. "I had a great time today, Jo," he whispered. "Did you?"

"I did." I sneaked my hand under his shirt, tracing circles around his navel.

Any chance he gave me I explored his body, learning every curve, dip, and valley above the waist. I had an inkling my bloodlust was going to take a back seat to my craving for the sexy vampire.

As the limo rolled down the coastal highway, I reminisced about the magnificent day that Webb and I spent together at his secluded house on the coast in Maine. It was my first date ever, and I'd had no idea what to expect. Most of the girls in school went out on dates to movies or out to eat. My best friend, Darcy Rose, had shared her experience with me. Her first date had been with a boy who had taken her to see one of the Harry Potter movies. At first she'd been nervous. They hardly talked on the way to the theater, but after the movie ended they went for pizza and discussed what they liked and disliked about it. According to her, the movie was a great icebreaker.

I couldn't think of an icebreaker that released some of the nervous tension I had except maybe time. As the day progressed, I became more comfortable with Webb. We took advantage of the sun and sand as we walked along the beach, dipping our toes in the surf. Maybe the soothing sounds of the waves helped to relax me. When we weren't outside, we snuggled in front of the windowed doors, which overlooked the Atlantic Ocean. I'd learned Webb had built the house four years ago as a place to relax and find peace.

The moon lit the way as we continued our trek home, towards what I'd hoped were better days. A light tickle at the base of my spine, however, warned me to be cautious. Why? I didn't know. I was still growing into my vampire body. Yet my sixth sense grew stronger and more acute every day.

George, a family friend of Webb's, was driving. He'd picked up Webb and me from the military base earlier that afternoon. The little amount of time I had to chat with him, I'd found he loved the game of basketball. I wasn't surprised, given that he was tall and lanky.

The soothing hum of the tires caused my eyelids to droop. I tried desperately to stay awake. I wanted to spend every last minute with Webb.

"I don't want to go back," I mumbled as my fingers roamed north over his toned abs.

Sure, I wanted to see Dad and my brother, Sam, but I didn't want to deal with whatever lay ahead. We had actually gotten through a day without any craziness—no phone calls, no explosions, no fires to put out, and no one kidnapping me or trying to kill me.

He groaned, gently pulling back my hair. We locked gazes for a second before his lips devoured mine, far from gentle as our tongues collided. He broke away, breathing heavily.

"What you do to me," he whispered.

I blushed as I kept my eyes locked on his.

"You have no idea how much you affect me, do you?"

I kind of did. We'd been inseparable the entire day. Still, I wanted to hear his words, so I gave a slight shake of my head, my stomach fluttering in anticipation.

Suddenly he lifted his head, his eyes widening. "George? What's wrong?"

What could possibly have Webb spooked? I sat up.

To my horror, the limo was barreling down a steep incline.

"Sir," George said. "The brakes..."

The headlights illuminated a warning sign. *Slow down. Ten miles per hour.* I glanced at the speedometer, and my body turned to ice.

We were traveling at sixty miles per hour, and the needle was ticking higher.

"Emergency brake," Webb called.

I checked my seat belt. It was already fastened.

To the left, the ocean whizzed by, as did the high mountain range outside my window on the right.

"It's on, sir," George said frantically.

"There should be a runaway for truckers before you reach the curve," Webb said without a hint of fear or panic in his voice.

How the heck were we going to survive? This was a limo, not a NASCAR vehicle.

His hand grabbed mine. I leaned back and closed my eyes.

What a freaking way to end a date.

My eyelids flew open as the car banked around the curve. George's hands clutched the wheel so hard, his knuckles glowed white.

"Now, George!" Webb shouted.

George turned the wheel hard, and the limo barreled up the hill where it stopped for a brief second before rolling backward.

"Straighten out. We'll go up the embankment behind us and slow some more. Then we can get out," Webb said, still without any trace of panic.

George did as Webb instructed. The car rolled down before creeping a bit up the hill behind us.

I gripped the seat belt, ready to free myself and jump out, when I spotted a glow in the distance. I dialed my vampire vision, zeroing in on several pairs of eyes gleaming in the night. I couldn't tell if they were animals or...

I didn't get a chance to figure it out before a rumbling noise pierced my ears.

"Jo. George," Webb said calmly. "Get out and run up the hill behind us. Whatever you do, don't look back."

A large boulder up the mountain crunched over the gravel, making a beeline straight for us.

"Out. Now!" Webb growled.

I punched the release on my seat belt, but either my hands shook too much or the flippin' belt was stuck. I tried again. Nothing. Panic grabbed me.

Halfway out of the car, Webb turned, glancing between the seat belt and me. The rock clipped the front corner of the limo. My head bounced off the leather seat. Webb fell from the car out of sight.

The boulder rolled down onto the pavement, breaking through the concrete barrier between the road and the ocean, and disappeared into the night.

Time stood still. I dared a peek out the window. The vehicle sat at a slight angle, facing the road.

Holy hell! Much more movement forward, and the limo would likely plummet into the Atlantic.

Webb suddenly appeared and grabbed the door, nudging the car forward.

"Rip off the belt and jump. Now!" His inky black eyes were wide with fear. "I'm not losing you tonight."

And I wasn't dying tonight, especially not in that ocean. I'd recently had a close call when the boat Ben Jackson and I were on sank during a freak storm.

Tearing the belt from me, I opened the door. I took in a breath, ready to leap, when the limo started sliding down the gravel incline, fast approaching the road.

Jump, tuck, and roll had been what the gym teacher had taught me in gymnastics class. So this should be easy. Not.

"Jo. What are you waiting for? Get out!" Webb barked from somewhere, panic in his voice.

I tucked my chin, covered my head with my arms, closed my eyes, and jumped. My hands hit gravel before my entire body slammed against the ground. I rolled as though I were a snowball, barreling down the hill and gaining momentum. Pebbles embedded in my skin. Larger rocks jabbed me in the legs, back, and stomach.

I opened my eyes. The gaping hole in the concrete barrier grew closer, and at the rate I was going, I'd probably plow right through and into the Atlantic Ocean. I had to find something to stop me.

"Jo, grab onto the pole," Webb shouted.

Pole? What was he talking about? I didn't see anything except death.

As I hit smooth pavement, a bright light lit up the roadway. Didn't people see a bright light just before their life ended?

I rolled once then twice before I relaxed my body, prayed, and braced for whatever fate had in store for me.

The light grew brighter before the sound of an engine roared in my ears. I was either going to roll through the broken barrier behind the limo and into the dark depths of the ocean below, or the car speeding toward me would claim my life.

Out of nowhere, a strong wind hit me, followed by a whooshing sound. All the air left my lungs.

"Stay still," Webb whispered.

How could I move? His weight kept me pinned to the ground. While I loved the vampire's arms on me, even his body on top of me, which was a new position for him, I couldn't freakin' breathe.

"Um...can't...breathe," I managed to squeak out.

A loud crash echoed. A bright orange light graced the sky followed by pillows of smoke. Was it the limo or the other car that fell to its death?

Webb eased up slightly. "Are you okay?" he asked, sweeping his gaze over my face, his hands furiously searching my body. His heart was beating uncontrollably.

"I will...be...when I can breathe...better."

"Oh. Sorry." He lifted up slightly.

I gulped in large amounts of oxygen, and the tightness in my chest slowly dwindled.

His hands were still checking every inch of me.

"I tried to roll over so you wouldn't take the impact. I'm sorry. I didn't have a good hold on you. You sure you're okay?"

"I will...be." I sucked in more oxygen.

"Stay here. I need to check on George." He jogged down to the road.

I sat up as George met Webb.

"Are you two all right?" George's brown eyes were wide with fear.

Webb opened his mouth to respond but quickly shut it when a woman appeared behind George.

"I'm so sorry. I narrowly missed you and that car." She stabbed her thumb toward the ocean.

"Can you give us a ride into town?" Webb asked.

"Sure. But I need some help. My car stalled for some reason after I skidded to a stop. It's a ways down the hill." Her brown hair glinted in the moonlight as she flicked her head to her left.

I stood up, brushing the dirt and rocks from me.

"George. Help the lady, please."

"Yes, sir. Hang tight."

George and the brunette made small talk as they both disappeared.

Webb walked back to me, pain painting his handsome features. "Are you sure you're okay?"

"I'm breathing." I looked into his molten onyx eyes.

Webb's eyes shifted between the most amazing cobalt blue and black when his emotions changed.

"Why aren't we going?" I asked.

"She's human, and I want to make sure your

thirst is okay before we get into the car." His heart beat wildly.

"Hey." I reached up and touched his face. "What's wrong?"

He cocooned me in his arms. "You scared me. I don't know what I would've done if I'd lost you." He again ran his hands over my entire body before easing back and sweeping his gaze over me for the tenth time.

"I'm fine, Webb."

His forehead kissed mine. "You would tell me if you weren't?" Apprehension threaded through his words.

My throat closed with emotion. So, I gave a slight nod and blinked my answer.

He sighed heavily, and his heartbeat began to slow. Mine followed suit. It seemed our hearts were in sync.

"What happened?" I asked.

"I don't know." He pushed his strong hand through his shoulder-length brown hair.

A crescent moon dotted the sky, and smoke lingered in the air. I imagined the crashing waves put out the flames from the burning limo.

"Do you think someone messed with the brakes?" Given the way my life was going, I had to be suspicious of everything.

"The thought has crossed my mind."

George was a longtime family friend, so I couldn't imagine it would be him. However, stranger things had happened. Like how Webb's sister, Kate, had switched sides and was now sleeping with our archenemy, Edmund Rain. Plus only a day had passed since Kate staked her brother with a cobalt sword, missing his heart by only an eighth of an inch.

As if he knew what I was thinking, he said, "It's not George."

"How do you know?"

"I just do." He scanned the area.

"Not good enough. If someone is trying to kill us, we need to look at everyone. Even you know this."

I didn't want to play the Kate card, but if I had to I would.

He grasped my shoulders, hard. "George...has been loyal to me for many years." Anger supplanted the worry on his face. "Besides, why would he tamper with the brakes then get in the car with us?"

He had a point, I guess.

"Webb, you're hurting me." I didn't know if he realized his grip was like a vise.

His left hand slid down to the small of my back

while his right hand cupped my cheek. "I'm sorry," he said. "I didn't mean to."

I leaned into his palm. "It's okay."

I wanted to shoulder some of his pain. I didn't want to see him hurt any more than he wanted to see me hurt, whether physically or mentally.

He peppered kisses down my neck, his fangs grazing the skin.

I shuddered at the sensation. When I did, an image materialized of me sucking on his wrist the night in the woods. My body quaked at the remembrance of how his blood tasted, sweet and sinful. How he reacted, melting into me, moaning in pleasure as I sated my hunger.

I mewled as I tilted my head to give him better access.

He growled.

My fangs dropped. I desperately wanted to taste his blood again. As I licked my lips, I stilled. What was I doing? What was he doing? Our laws dictated new vampires could only drink from another vampire if it were an emergency, meaning if I were hurt or needed blood. Neither was the case at the moment. But was he hungry? Was it legal for him to drink from me?

"Webb?" I breathed.

"Yes, angel," he said in a husky voice.

"Are you hungry?"

I didn't want to get in trouble with the Council of Eternal Affairs. They were the vampires who governed the laws in my world. Regardless, I would do anything for Webb, even though my head was on the chopping block for the death of my nemesis, Blake Turner. He'd been a product of Edmund Rain's sick plan of converting ordinary humans into vampires.

"I'm not." He jerked up his head as if I had thrown ice-cold water on him.

"If you are, I don't mind."

His expression flickered with confusion or something I couldn't figure out. Did he think he would hurt me if he bit into me? He smiled as though he had found the answer to whatever was plaguing him.

"Why are you smiling? Seriously, if you're hungry—"

His finger grazed my lip. "I'm fine. It's..." His gaze penetrated me as if he were searching my soul.

Now I was confused. "What? I know it's not legal for new vampires like me, but can you drink from another vampire?"

"I'm not bound by the law like you are. Soon enough, you will not be, either." His eyelids dropped to half-mast. "My struggle right now...is my desire...to taste your blood. And, beautiful, it has nothing to do with my blood thirst." His seductive voice caressed every inch of my body, inside and out.

My lips formed a silent O. I'd remembered how sensual it felt when I drank his blood.

"Exactly," he said in response to my facial expression.

Heat stung my cheeks while a butterfly winged through my abdomen.

"Don't be embarrassed. It's life and part of being a vampire."

I thought back to when I witnessed Edmund sinking his fangs into Kate. I felt as if I'd interrupted some private make-out session.

"Webb?" George called from the road.

"We'll talk more later. We need to go."

Oh, my was all my brain kept repeating.

He took hold of my hand, and we walked to the car. Well, Webb walked, and he pulled me. I was still in zombie mode, trying to get my brain unstuck. How would it feel if he drank from me? My cheeks were going to be red and hot the rest of the night.

When we were strapped into the back seat of the car, the fragrant strawberry scent inside snapped my brain back to the present, reminding me the woman driving was human.

Webb threaded his fingers through mine as the lady turned the wheel and gave the car a little bit of gas, then we were moving. I let out a sigh, grateful we were alive. After the boating accident and fighting Edmund and his gang, I was beginning to think I had nine lives.

"What was wrong with the car, George?" Webb asked.

"Not completely sure, but the engine seemed to be flooded. It took a few tweaks, and then it started."

"Thank you, George, for your help," the lady said. "And again. I'm so sorry about what happened." Her voice was soft but shaky.

She looked to be in her thirties. A studded clip secured her brown hair into a chignon. She had pale skin, which I imagined might be from her almost killing me or herself.

"By the way, I'm Lauren. I've met George here." She flicked her head toward George, who was sitting in the front. "And you are?" She checked in the rearview mirror.

I slid a sideways glance at Webb. "I'm Webb, and this is Jo," he said.

"So what happened?" she asked. "One minute

you were in the road, and the next you were gone. Like in a flash."

"We're not sure," Webb replied. "We lost the brakes on our car."

I didn't think that was what she was asking. Webb had swooped me up at vampire speed.

"You don't even have a scratch on you." She looked at me in the rearview mirror with a suspecting look.

"What were you doing up here?" Webb asked.

Way to change the subject.

"My dad owns one of the homes up on the hill," she said. "Webb, you must be the gentleman who owns the magnificent house not far from his? I have to say. You look awful young to own that home."

There were two other homes that sat along the coast about ten miles from Webb's home.

Webb and I exchanged glances. I was surprised she directed the checking question to Webb and not George. Sure, her father probably told her. But Webb didn't spend a lot of time at his house. He lived on the naval base ninety-nine percent of the time. Plus he'd told me it had been awhile since he had been up here. To me that meant Webb had little interaction with her father.

"Actually, I own the house," George answered.

She eyed him briefly. "Oh," she said in a surprised tone.

She seemed to know George was lying.

"Well, my dad is getting old," she offered.

"Who is your father?" George asked her.

She's fishing for something. Webb's voice sounded loud and clear in my head.

"Robert Pride." Her eyes stayed on the road ahead.

"Both of those properties are vacant right now. Their owners aren't here yet for the summer," George said.

"My father will be up in a couple of weeks. "I came up to unwind. It's quiet up here."

Silence ruled.

The lights of the town came into view as Lauren maneuvered the last curve on the winding road.

"There's a diner up ahead on the left. Do you mind dropping us there?" Webb asked.

"No, not at all. I'll stop a minute with you before I make my way back to Boston," Lauren answered.

We rolled into the diner, and a neon light flashed Open in the window. All of us exited the vehicle.

"You should be okay to make it back to Boston," George said. "But now that we have more light, let me take one last look at the engine."

"That would be wonderful," Lauren said. "I need to use the facilities." She snatched her purse and headed inside.

"George." Webb followed him to the front of the vehicle. "Did she say anything to you when you were helping her?"

George popped the hood of the Lexus and buried his head underneath, fiddling with a few things.

"Just small talk. She's a bit shaken up," he replied. "I'm not sure she is who she says she is. A Robert Pride does own one of those homes, but I wasn't aware he had a daughter."

"Is he a vampire?" I asked.

"No. He's not." He stopped what he was doing. "And he doesn't know most of this town is made up of vampires. The folks who own those two homes up on the coast are only here a few times a year."

"When you left the house earlier, where did you go?" Webb asked him.

"I came down and sat with Trina for a bit and had some pie. Then I got gas and a few things at the store. Afterwards, I worked in the yard. The only time the limo was out of my sight was when I was in the diner and in the store."

"Mmm. When you finish, can you round up Stan from the sheriff's office and alert him to what happened tonight? I need to call in." Webb reached into his pocket for his phone.

"No problem, sir." George bent forward and resumed tinkering with the engine.

Switching my attention to Webb, I followed him across the parking lot to the edge of the diner. "Are you calling my father?"

"If we want to get back tonight, I think it's wise. He is expecting us."

I'd overheard Webb telling him before we left we'd return by midnight, and we were at least three hours away.

Webb talked on the phone as I leaned against the building. The area outside was quiet. A gas station sat across the street. A trucker was filling up. Two blocks down, a marquee for Tam's country store lit up the darkness.

My mouth was parched, and water sounded good, although George had mentioned pie. For some reason, the thought of something sweet tickled my taste buds. Food had not been appealing to me since I became a vampire. Dad had said we needed to eat human food, protein mostly, and although I did consume a few of my favorite meals like hamburgers and pizza, they didn't have the same lure to me anymore.

I pushed off the building only to be stopped by Webb. I swatted away his hand as he continued to listen to my dad.

"Um. I need some water." I glared at him.

"Hold on, Commander." He pressed the phone to his chest, covering the speaker. "Wait until that woman comes out. I don't trust her." He planted a soft kiss on my nose then resumed his conversation with my dad.

How could I refuse? *Smart vampire.*

He draped an arm over me, and I snuggled into him. My senses tuned in to Dad's voice.

"Lieutenant, do you think it was on purpose?" Dad asked.

"Not sure. I can't check it out, either, since the limo is in the ocean. My instincts tell me this wasn't an accident."

I jerked up my head as Webb pulled me tighter. He must've known how I was going to react.

"Well, stay put for the night," Dad said.

I stiffened in his arms. Stay overnight with Webb? Alone?

My heart sprinted.

Webb rubbed a hand down my back, as though he were telling me we'd be fine, just the two of us.

Silence reigned over the line.

I envisioned Dad biting the inside of his cheek. I glanced up. Webb's eyes waffled from blue to black then blue again. I flushed, remembering our recent conversation about how he wanted to taste my blood.

"Commander?" Webb probed.

"Sorry. Tripp walked in," Dad said. "Mr. Jackson is here. We'll talk tomorrow. By the way, how much blood did you take for Jo?"

"I brought a few extra containers in case of an emergency. If it's not enough, I'll check with Dr. Vieira. He'll advise if she'll be okay with what we drink."

"Can I talk to my daughter?" Dad sounded bothered by something.

Webb handed me the phone.

"Hey, Dad."

"Pumpkin. Are you okay?"

"It was a little scary, but I'm fine."

"Will you be okay for a couple of days?"

"Wait. You're asking *me*? I should be asking you that." I wanted to laugh and run at the same time. I was nervously excited at the idea I'd be spending time alone with Webb. Nevertheless, I couldn't believe my father, the old-fashioned vampire, was allowing me the freedom.

Dad laughed into the phone. I couldn't tell whether or not he was nervous. "First, Jo, I can't keep you chained, although part of me would like to." He laughed again. "Second, you're growing into an adult, and I need to let you make decisions. Finally, Webb knows I'd cut his head off if he did anything."

I didn't want to know what he meant by "anything." Dad must've put the fear of God into Webb before we even left the base today.

"What's going on with Mr. Jackson?" I moved on to something less awkward.

"I'm not sure," Dad replied.

Mr. Jackson was becoming more curious about Sam and me. I couldn't blame him. One minute we were living with him, and the next we had all but vanished. Lately though, his concerns were more about his son, Ben, Sam's best friend, who always seemed to end up in our medical facility. He'd had a few encounters with Edmund Rain and the team.

"Don't worry about Mr. Jackson. Before I forget, the council pushed out the hearing another few weeks, so I'm working on getting you a tutor for the summer," he said.

"Why are they postponing it?" Not that I wanted to go back to school right now. The whole incident with Blake Turner was still raw, and I didn't want any reminders.

"Something came up on their end. No need to be concerned about it," he said. "Look, pumpkin, put Webb back on. Be careful, and I love you."

I smiled. Mountains had moved, it seemed, for me to hear those three words from Dad. We had just shared our feelings about our father and daughter relationship a few days ago.

"I love you, Dad." I handed the phone back to Webb.

"Yes, Commander."

Lauren walked out of the diner and over to George.

Webb said, "Yes. Don't worry. She's safe," then he pocketed his phone. "Everything okay?" Webb asked Lauren as we met her at her car.

"Fine. Why?" She dropped her phone into her purse.

She seemed to take forever in the ladies' room.

"I want to make sure you're okay to drive back."

"Thanks for your concern," she said, eyeing Webb.

What the heck? She was checking him out. I didn't blame her for looking. Still, a tinge of jealousy zinged through me. I almost growled but caught it in my throat. I didn't want to call attention to us, given that Webb was suspicious of her.

George closed the hood. "Everything pans out. It was probably a fluke." He wiped his hands on a towel.

"I should be fine. Boston isn't far anyway." She got into her car, started the engine, and rolled down the window. "Mr. London, here's my card. If you ever need anything, please don't hesitate to call me."

Webb didn't flinch when she said his last name. I didn't remember him telling it to her. He just took the card and quickly read it before glancing up at her.

"I don't think we'll be needing a lawyer, Ms. Dryer," he said with no inflection.

"If you ever do, you have my number." Then her gaze flicked to George. "Thanks for all your help. I'll tell my dad to look you up when he's here."

George nodded. "Be careful driving."

With the good-byes out of the way, she drove off.

"How did she—?"

"Don't know, Jo."

I racked my brain, trying to figure out how Lauren knew Webb's full name. We'd only told her our first names.

Her last name was Dryer, not Pride like her father.

I shrugged it off. The difference in her last name could be from adoption, marriage, or even divorce.

"I didn't say anything," George added before we even looked his way.

"Well, let's not worry about Lauren right now. Did you happen to get ahold of Stan?" Webb asked George.

"I did. He should be here shortly. He was out at the Millers' farm. They had some cattle killed recently."

"Let's go see Trina." Webb slipped Lauren's card in his jeans.

The bell dinged when we entered the diner. A couple stood at the register. Webb nodded at the pair as though he knew them. Then a short stocky man rose from his seat, taking money out of his wallet. Webb guided me to a stool at the counter, and the three of us settled in as the patrons paid their bill. No sooner had the couple and the short man left than did the waitress turn the Open sign to Closed and glided over to us.

"Webb, darling," she cooed, throwing her arms around him. "I haven't seen you in ages. Where have you been?"

Webb stood and embraced the petite blonde. "Trina. Nice to see you." He kissed her on the cheek.

She had a perfect white smile and deep green eyes. Her short hair was pulled back with a wide headband, exposing her smooth, high forehead.

"Trina. I would like you to meet a friend of mine. Jo, this is my dear old friend, Trina."

She rested her fists on her hips and looked me over, her eyes growing wide. "She's lovely, Webb. Wherever did you find her?" She ran her fingers through the ends of my hair.

Why did people do that when they met me? My headmistress, Ms. Lawrence, did the same thing when she first laid eyes on me.

Webb glanced around before saying, "Jo, Trina is a vamp."

I rolled my eyes. Well, I'd known that, since her green eyes had flickered toward black when she first spotted Webb. Plus she certainly didn't have the delicious, sweet scent of a human.

"So, Trina..." Webb kept looking around.

"No worries, young man. Aside from the love of my life in the back, no one else is here."

I guess I didn't have to be jealous of the woman.

"Did you see the brown-haired lady who was in here earlier?" Webb resumed his position on the stool next to me.

"The human? Yes. She was arguing with someone on the phone in the ladies' room. I couldn't make out the whole conversation, but she repeated your name a few times." She wiped the countertop. "Do you know her?"

"No" was all Webb said.

"So, she didn't ask you about Webb?" George asked.

"George, old man, you know better than that. She didn't, but if she did, I wouldn't share any information about any of my friends."

"I had to ask," George said.

The concern in his voice led me to believe he wouldn't betray Webb.

"What happened, anyway?" Trina propped her elbows on the counter. "Someone said they saw an orange glow up on the coast."

Webb explained what happened while Trina served apple pie à la mode to George and me. I found it curious that she didn't give Webb a piece.

"Have you seen that woman in here before tonight?" Webb asked.

"No." She filled a cup with coffee and placed it in front of George.

The bell dinged, and in walked a tall, dark-haired man with a badge and a smirk.

"Gee, London. How many times do I have to tell you this is a quiet town? We try to keep a low..." He let out a whistle as his brown eyes swept over me. "Who's the beauty at your side?"

Webb growled, jumping to his feet.

"Easy, London. I know she's off limits." The man with the badge held up his hands.

I swiveled on the stool toward him while Webb decided to lean against his stool with his back to Trina. He and the sheriff exchanged handshakes.

Then the sheriff offered me his hand. "Hi. I'm Stan, the local sheriff around here."

"I'm Jo." We shook.

"Pleased to meet you, Jo," Stan said. "Be careful. He's one of the most possessive vampires I know."

I'd thought Webb was being protective. Yet the more I said the word *possessive* in my head, the more it started to make some sense.

Then again, what alpha male wasn't? Heck, my

father exemplified the word and seemed to be proud of it. "You haven't met my dad."

Stan laughed, letting go of my hand. "If he gets too smothering, you let me know."

"Stan," Webb barked.

"Cool your jets, London." He rolled his eyes.

"You're a vampire too?" I knew the answer. I was just trying to break the tension between the two.

Stan nodded. "Now. What happened?" he asked, shifting to an all-business demeanor.

Webb explained to Stan that he'd been on the beach most of the day with me, and George added in where he saw fit. While the men chatted, I bit into a piece of the apple pie and lost all sense I was a vampire. My human memories flooded back. None of our foster parents had been big on giving Sam and me sugar, especially before bed. But that hadn't mattered to us. We would still sneak into the kitchen late at night and steal dessert.

As I closed my mouth around the next spoonful, I wondered... Who was Lauren Dryer? How did the brakes fail? Was someone trying to kill us? How did she know Webb's last name? Did she know vampires existed? As the delectable treat melted on my tongue, the questions likewise vanished.

By the time I scarfed up the last of the pie, Stan and Webb had finished their conversation. I suddenly became queasy. I guessed my vampire system wasn't used to sweets. Placing a hand on my abdomen, I stood.

"What's wrong?" Webb asked.

"Not feeling good." I blew out a breath.

He looked at the plate then at Trina before his eyes landed on me.

"Are you going to throw up?" Stan covered his mouth as though he were, too.

Acid rose in my throat. "Bathroom." My body became warm, and the room began spinning.

"This way," Webb said in a strained voice.

I followed him around the counter and down a small hall into the ladies' room. I threw open the stall door before dropping to my knees.

"I shouldn't—" I lost every bit of apple pie.

"You're right," Webb whispered as he held my hair behind my head.

How sweet was he to help me when I was puking?

After I heaved the contents from my stomach, Stan drove us back to Webb's place. I relaxed against Webb as the police cruiser rolled up the coast. Dizziness still lingered, so I closed my eyes. In the front, George repeated his day's routine to

Stan. Both speculated about what could've happened to the brakes.

Webb didn't contribute to the conversation. Not that I wanted to read minds like my father, but right then I would have loved to be in Webb's head. His heartbeat was rapid. I couldn't imagine he was nervous. Was he thinking about the sleeping arrangements, like me? He only had two bedrooms. One was his, and the other belonged to George, since he stayed at the house most of the time, helping Webb with the upkeep of the property.

Stan pulled into the long driveway and let the engine idle. "George, buddy, why don't you crash at my place? I'll let you borrow one of my trucks in the morning."

"Not a bad idea," George said, turning and looking at Webb. "My car is in Boston. Is that okay with you?"

"Sure," Webb responded. "Jo and I will be staying for a few days. I want to check out the accident site tomorrow. Maybe we can fish the car out of the ocean."

"There are a lot of rocky areas off the side of the cliff," Stan said. "More than likely, it's sitting on the rocks. However, I doubt you'll be able to find much, especially if it went up in flames. But I agree. We'll take a look tomorrow."

We said our good-byes and slid out of the cruiser. We waved as the headlights faded from the driveway. When darkness replaced the light, my heart jumped into gear. Now what?

"No need to be nervous," Webb said as he unlocked the front door. "I'm not going to bite."

I laughed nervously. Maybe I wanted him to.

Once inside, an awkward silence stretched between us. Webb sauntered into the kitchen. I didn't move from the small foyer. It was as if someone had injected lead into my feet. Or maybe it was the ten thousand needles pricking my stomach. After all, a sexy-as-hell vampire and me alone all night spelled all kinds of heart-racing, mind-twisting thoughts.

He said something, but the buzzing in my head drowned out his voice. I closed my eyes, trying to calm my nerves, and his hand touched my cheek. "Hey?"

The closeness of our bodies only served to increase the jittery little beasts poking sharp pins into my tummy. My lids slid open, and his eyes latched on to mine.

"I told you I don't bite." He traced my bottom

lip with the pad of his thumb. "But I do kiss." A smirk tugged at the corners of his mouth.

My heart did several jumping jacks. Nope, I wasn't going to make it through the night.

"You take my bed, and I'll sleep on the couch." He must have sensed my trepidation.

"I...can...sleep on the couch." I swallowed. "Or I could sleep in George's room tonight."

I couldn't take Webb's bed. This was his home.

His thumb moved to my cheek. "No way. George's room isn't clean. No arguments on this." He placed a soft kiss on my nose before taking my hand. "Come on. Let's get you tucked in."

I released a long, pent-up breath, and the pricking sensation in my stomach slowed. "Webb, I can stay on the couch." I didn't move.

I'd slept in worse conditions in foster care. I even slept on the floor once. It had only been temporary, since one of the other foster kids was scheduled to leave the home the next day.

"I insist. And if I have to carry you up to my room, I will. Your choice." He raised one eyebrow.

I stared at him. I could protest, but his don't-argue-with-me look told me I wouldn't win, and I just wanted to get through this freaking awkward moment.

"Would you stay with me?" my mouth said ahead of my brain.

My blood stopped flowing.

His eyes darkened to vampire black.

I lost my vision for a split second before my own eyes shifted while my heart fell to the floor. I mentally whacked myself a few times. What was I thinking? I wasn't ready for this. Sure, I'd slept next to him in his hospital bed, but that was a place where Dr. Vieira came in to check on him, and even my dad sat in the room, talking to him while I slept.

This was different, very different. It was him and me. Alone.

2

I had a restless night. Webb had declined my offer to stay with me. I tried to reassure him it was just to sleep, nothing more.

"As much as I would love to," he'd said, "it would be best for me to sleep on the couch."

I hadn't argued or questioned his decision. He seemed a little nervous himself, and I'd recalled my dad's words. "Webb knows I'd cut his head off if he did anything." Part of me was disappointed, yet another was relieved. I wasn't prepared for more than kissing.

A soft knock sounded through the door.

I sat up, adjusting my blouse. I'd slept in my clothes last night. Yep. Call me crazy. I had a hang-up about sleeping in my underwear in Webb's bed.

"Come...in." My voice cracked.

The door opened, and Webb's woodsy scent wafted in along with the imposing vampire.

"Good morning, beautiful," Webb said. "Sleep well?"

Between his scent and his voice, I could barely speak. I swept my gaze over his entire body, my tongue glued to the roof of my mouth.

A black Henley stretched across his broad chest. Jeans hung low on his hips. His long lashes fanned out at half-mast as his blue eyes latched onto mine with such intensity I swear the vampire wanted to devour me. My inner voice told me to run for the hills. My heart told me not to.

I shook off the drunken dizziness that always seemed to hit me when Webb walked into a room. I hadn't experienced feelings like this before. Actually, I'd never had so much attention from anyone. Boys didn't give me the time of day in school.

"I did. What about you?" I asked, thankful I'd formed two complete sentences.

The mattress dipped as I combed through my locks.

"Come here." He tucked his fingers in the waist of my jeans.

I sucked in a sharp breath at his touch.

A smile ghosted his lips while he urged me toward him. As if I had a choice. Even if I wanted to run—which I didn't—the hold he had on me, and the look in his eyes was enough to reduce me to nothing. With his help, I inched my way to him.

"You slept in your clothes," he said, our noses practically touching.

I nodded.

He brushed the backs of his fingers ever so lightly against the exposed skin underneath my shirt.

My eyes widened. A shiver crawled up my spine as a warm flutter slid down my belly. What was happening to me? Yesterday, I'd spent the entire day alone with Webb, holding hands, cuddling, kissing, and talking, and I didn't feel this nervous, scared, or excited. Was it because we were alone in his bedroom and I'd slept in his bed? Or was it something else?

His soft kiss brought me back from my thoughts. "You're thinking too much this morning, and the sun isn't even up yet," he said against my lips.

With vampire speed, he gripped my waist and placed me on his lap. I was now straddling the hulking vampire.

His hands coasted down my arms, and he swept his gaze over my face as though he were trying to get into my brain. I slanted my head. He smiled, and his lips grazed over mine.

In two heartbeats, we were in a heated kiss. I groaned his name in protest—only because of morning breath. He took possession of my mouth, obviously misunderstanding, so I gave in and buried my hands in his hair. My nails scraped along his scalp.

His hands stopped on my hips while his vampire eyes drifted shut. A low growl sounded in the back of his throat. After a moment, he grasped my wrists, pulling them down while he broke away.

"I've been wanting to kiss you since I woke up hours ago," he said in a velvety voice.

"Why didn't you wake me up then?"

"Because you're beautiful." He traced circles on my lower back.

I scrunched my eyebrows together. "What kind of answer is that?"

A wolfish grin was etched on his handsome face as his lips grazed mine. "One that you'll have to accept for now. Let's go for a walk on the beach. We have some time before George gets here."

I pouted, sticking out my bottom lip. I wanted to keep kissing.

"No. That look isn't going to work on me," he

said as he pushed to his feet, lifting me off him before setting me down.

A girl had to try.

He opened the wall of curtains, exposing
French doors that led out to a deck overlooking
the beach. A faint blue tinted the sky in the distance. The sun would be up soon.

"Why don't you freshen up? The bathroom is
right here." He waved a hand at the open doorway.
"I'll meet you downstairs." He crossed the room.
"Don't take long. I want to watch the sun rise."

"Uh... What about clean clothes? I didn't bring
a change or anything."

"We'll go into town and pick up a few things
for you." The door closed behind him.

I took in the warm, inviting room, this time in
daylight. The walls were painted a muted gray.
White woodwork framed the perimeter of the
ceiling and baseboards. Splashes of blue, gray, and
white complemented each other, creating a
calming atmosphere. A natural wood dresser sat
against one wall, while an oversized upholstered
chair faced the ocean view.

I traipsed into the bathroom. I decided to forgo
a shower until I got clean clothes. Instead, I
plucked a washcloth from the basket on the sink
and washed a few important body parts. I swept a

brush through my hair then pulled it into a ponytail with a band I had around my wrist.

I checked myself in the mirror one last time. Silver eyes stood against my sunburned cheeks. Apparently spending all day in the sun yesterday had an effect on me.

Now if only I had a toothbrush. I glanced around and spotted a tube of toothpaste. I squeezed a small amount on my finger before sliding the pasty stuff along the tops and bottoms of my teeth, then rinsed my mouth a few times. It wasn't the greatest way to get the crud off, but it would sure help with morning breath.

As the word *morning* slid through my brain, my throat began to burn. At the thought of blood, heat rushed through me.

I had to stop thinking about the taste of Webb's blood. Otherwise, I wasn't going to last here with him for the next few days.

Satisfied I was at least presentable, I left in search of my flats. I spied them nestled in front of the chair in the bedroom. After slipping them on, I found Webb in the kitchen, sipping from a mug. One sniff, and my fangs descended.

He set down his mug on the counter and retrieved a bottle from the fridge.

"Here." He kissed me on the lips as he handed me my breakfast. "Enjoy."

I wasted no time. The blood cooled the fire in my throat. I loved the stuff. My fangs retreated as soon as I finished.

"So on the phone yesterday, you told my dad something about what you drink. What type of blood is it?" I didn't think it was the flavored stuff, but I wasn't sure. I rinsed out the bottle.

He joined me at the sink as he downed the last of his own breakfast before washing out the cup and placing it in the dish rack. "The blood the sentinels, including your father, drink comes from one of our suppliers. It's not flavored. It is, however, filtered for any impurities like chemicals, manufactured substances, fructose, and preservatives." He wiped his hands with a paper towel. "Come on. The sun is almost up. Let's go sit on the beach."

Well, that answered what type of blood my father drank.

The doors leading to the deck, according to Webb, were pivot doors—four of them—and all were glass. Two of them were ajar, and salt air trickled in.

Webb grabbed the flannel blanket from the barstool as I trailed behind him.

"So the blood you drink is human, right?" I asked, stepping onto the massive deck.

"It is. The blood banks have to dispose of older blood, sooner or later."

"And I'll be able to drink that type eventually?" Without thinking, I grabbed his hand as I climbed down the last step to the sand.

"I imagine," he replied. "Your father doesn't like the flavored blood. I don't, either. It's not healthy. They put too many artificial ingredients in it."

I liked the flavored blood. "But we're vampires. We can't get sick."

"Jo. You know our systems can't tolerate some things."

Case in point, my recent puking stint after I ate the apple pie. I let the subject drop.

Holding hands, we walked toward the water. Webb settled on a spot several feet from shore, where he spread out the flannel blanket. The horizon had a tint of orange. It wouldn't be long now before the sun peeked out.

He made himself comfortable on the multicolored blanket, kicking out his jean-clad legs and bare feet while he rested on one elbow. I toed off my shoes, sat down, and folded my legs underneath me. It was nice just to stare out at the serene ocean and listen to the soft caress of the waves and nothing else. The air was surprisingly warm for this time of morning, especially near the ocean. Or maybe the heat stemmed from the vampire next to me.

"You're thinking too hard, Jo." His husky voice tickled my ears.

I slowly swung my gaze to him. I hadn't realized my hand was in his.

"You want to talk about it?" he asked.

That moment might be the perfect time to talk since George wouldn't be here until later. "How do you think the boulder moved last night? I mean, it was big, and the limo didn't hit it."

"The force of the limo barreling up the hill could've caused the rock to move."

Maybe he was right. Besides, if someone did sabotage the brakes, how would they have known we would end up at that particular spot?

"So I know you don't think it was George, but what about..." I met his blue gaze, hesitant to bring up his sister Kate.

His eyebrows knitted.

I glanced out. Waves crashed along the surf. "Do you think Kate or Edmund had any part in this? She does know you own this house, right?"

"Look at me, Jo." His voice had a sharp edge to it.

I followed his command, meeting his vampire black eyes. My pulse quickened as I did. I didn't want to upset him.

"How would Edmund and the Plutariums have known we were here? I didn't decide to come up here until I had you in my arms in the medical facility. I didn't tell anyone except your father. Sam didn't even know. I did that for a reason. We still have a mole inside our group."

"They could've been waiting outside the base then followed us."

"True, but George and I didn't see anything suspicious on our way here. Your theory is plausible, but I have a hard time believing the Plutariums would show themselves only a day after we fought them at the mansion. Knowing Edmund, he wants to regroup before he does anything else."

"So if it wasn't the Plutariums, including Kate, who else would want us dead?"

"Until we can see the limo, I'm not going to speculate. It doesn't do any good to jump to conclusions. The brakes could've easily failed from wear and tear, Jo."

He had a point. So why did I feel it had been something different?

Webb sat up. "Come closer, Jo."

I scooted over to him. Our thighs barely touched, and electricity zinged up my leg. Did he feel it, too? I glanced at him and sucked in a breath. He was looking at me through hooded eyelids. Suddenly, the world around me vanished except the beat of his heart—or was it mine?

He slid his hand onto my thigh, and I laid mine on top of his.

The wind seemed to shift as the sun rose. We both turned our attention to the reason why we were out here. Orange brightened the sky as the ball of fire rose. The waves crashed along the shore, and a few seagulls cawed along the ocean's edge.

"I'm glad you're here, Jo. I'm also relieved nothing happened to you last night."

He wrapped an arm around my waist, and I rested my head on his chest.

"I'm glad nothing happened to you too," I whispered.

His fingers skimmed down my arm then back up as he kissed my hair.

The sunlight glinted off the water.

"Incredible," I said. "I've never seen such a beautiful sight before."

"I have, and she's sitting right next to me." He

tugged me closer. "You do things to me I've never thought were possible." His lips hovered over mine.

I almost pinched him to be sure he was real. The vampire soldier stole a piece of my heart every time he batted his blue eyes at me or whispered words I'd never imagined anyone saying to me. I closed my eyes, trying to prevent the tears from surfacing. I didn't want to cry, but my heart was filled with so much emotion...

"Open your eyes." He kissed my nose.

I lifted heavy lids and met his gaze, which was heated with desire. One heartbeat later, he pressed his lips to mine. The tips of our tongues touched ever so lightly, and we both explored. He nibbled, suckled, and kissed, and I did the same. I wanted to stay in this spot with him forever.

His cell phone rang, ruining the moment.

Breaking away, he plucked it out of his jeans. "Hey, George. Yes, Jo and I are down on the beach. No, we're fine. Sure, I'll see you in a couple of hours." He threw the phone on the blanket. "Where were we?"

The blue in his eyes sparkled. The first time I saw his sister, Kate, she'd walked into the hall in the women's barracks on base with the same sparkle in her blue eyes.

I still couldn't wrap my mind around Kate trying to kill him. I wanted to make sense of it. Was he ready to talk about it? "Webb?"

His body tensed, apparently at the sound of my voice.

"What's wrong?" I touched his hand.

He searched my face. "Your tone. It sounds like you're afraid of something."

I was, simply because I didn't know how he was going to respond.

"Can we talk about Kate?" I held my breath.

He tensed. "I'm not sure what you want to know."

I threaded my fingers through his. "Why would Kate side with Edmund?"

I avoided the dreaded question of why she wanted him dead. Maybe if we understood why she switched teams, we'd uncover the reason she wanted to kill him.

His grip tightened on my hand, and I winced. "I can't honestly find any reason, other than she's in love with him. My sister tends to fall hard for someone she loves and will do anything for him." His eyes glazed over. "Our dad was one of the leading Mafia bosses in Boston. He hired a sharp young man who became his number one lieutenant. Well, Kate and he fell in love. And he convinced her to run away with him and get away from the Mafia business. Our father found out and went... Well...he got upset. He and Kate argued. During the argument, she managed to threaten my father with a cobalt dagger. She was no match for him." His delivery was deadpan.

I didn't flinch when he squeezed my hand harder, even though shock coursed through my body. She'd tried to kill her own father?

"Anyway, her love for Edmund is driving her actions."

"If she threatened your dad..." I couldn't finish the sentence. If I did ask the obvious, I would essentially suggest Webb should've known. Right?

"Then what, Jo? I should've known she was capable of betraying me?" Anger coated each word.

I pushed away the bite in his tone, chewing my lip as I thought about Sam. How would I react if my brother tried to kill me? As soon as the question scrolled through my brain, I let out a sigh. Without question, I would never believe Sam to be capable of harming me. However, I knew all too well how volatile a father-daughter relationship could be, which was way different than a sister-brother one.

We both sat in silence. His hand was still tethered to mine, but his grip had loosened.

I refused to believe anyone would kill her own kin because of love for someone else.

"Webb," I said over the crashing waves.

With vampire speed, he spun me around so I was straddling him—a position that was becoming the norm for us.

"She's my sister, Jo." There was pain in his voice.

"Yeah, and that's the point. She's your family, Webb."

He framed my face with his hands. "Listen to me. Kate and my father had a very explosive relationship. But Kate and I didn't. We'd do anything for each other. This is hard for me to grasp." He pinned me with a hard glare.

Maybe Kate was bipolar. I didn't have the answers, and no matter how many times we speculated about why she drove a sword through his chest, we weren't going to find the reasons.

"Would you kill your own sister, Webb?"

I'd asked the question once before, and he hadn't been able to answer it at the time. However, he'd since had time to mull over Kate's actions.

"Would I intentionally? No." He gripped my shoulders. "Would I in self-defense? Maybe." He let go of me then looked away. "It all depends on the circumstances."

I had so many mixed emotions regarding the conversation. Never in a million years or in this lifetime could I or would I kill my brother. Never. Ever. Not for anyone. Not even in self-defense.

"Hey, breathe." His tone changed, his choleric mood seeming to blow away in the wind. "We're not going to solve this today. We're not going to understand what Kate is thinking. I do, however, want to have a chance to talk with her."

"Sam told me you did talk with her at the mansion, and you two got in a fight."

"True. But I want to talk to Kate without Edmund present."

"How?"

"No idea right now. I'm sorry if you're angry and upset over this. I'm being honest with you. When you ask me something, I'll always be honest." His voice gentled. "Okay?"

The sunlight highlighted the sadness in his eyes.

"I'm sorry for bringing up Kate. I don't want to see you hurt."

"Thank you" was all he managed to say before his phone rang again.

We both glanced down. My dad's name flashed as the caller ID.

He picked it up. "Yes, Commander?"

I grabbed his shoulders, pushed to my feet, then walked down to the shore. A soft breeze blew off the ocean as I rolled up my jeans and dipped my toes in the surf. A prickly sensation stung my skin as the ice-cold water flowed over my feet. I inhaled crisp ocean air. I hated to see Webb hurt and angry. Even more, I hated Kate for what she'd done to her brother. I vowed to myself I would do anything to protect Webb. How? I wasn't sure.

DAYLIGHT BROUGHT on a whole new image for the small town. The grocery store parking lot bustled with people. The gas station had a steady stream of cars, funneling in and out. Cars and trucks packed the lot at the diner. This place seemed busier than the city streets of Fall River.

George had picked us up not long after Webb had finished his conversation with my dad, who'd called to check on us. I wasn't surprised. I'd asked Webb if Dad had said anything about Mr. Jackson, and he'd said no. The topic hadn't come up.

We were on the way to a Target located in the next town so I could purchase some personal items. After our shopping spree, we were scheduled to meet Stan at the crash site.

At the store, I jumped out of the car. Several humans walked by. Some were walking into the store. Others were headed to the cars.

George stopped me. "Wait, Jo," he said.

I turned back, and Webb sat in the back seat of the truck, not moving. Stan had loaned George a spiffed-up four-door Toyota Tundra.

"What's wrong with Webb?" I asked as George corralled me.

"He's talking with Stan," he said. "Webb wants you to wait for him."

Odd. I hadn't heard the phone ring.

"He called Stan," George responded to my thought.

I almost choked. "Can you read minds?" I asked.

He laughed. "No, ma'am. That task is only reserved for your father. I'm so glad I can't, either. There are twisted people in this world. Anyway, your expression told me you didn't believe me at first."

I let out a sigh. Wouldn't that suck if George could read my mind?

Webb climbed out. "Jo, are you okay?" he asked, searching my face for something.

"Huh? Why wouldn't I be?"

He did a quick survey of the busy parking lot.

"There are humans here, you know."

"Yeah, and your point? Are you afraid I'm going to attack one of them?"

The idea had crossed my mind. The sweet human aroma wafted around me, tugging at my resolve. Regardless, I had to keep my inner vampire at bay. Ben had almost become my dinner at sea. After the past couple of days, I'd decided to do everything in my power not to get myself into trouble, which meant keeping my bloodlust in check. I was confident I could. I had to, if I didn't want to face my dad's wrath—or worse, the vampire government—for infractions against a human.

"Seriously, Jo. I want to make sure—"

"Webb, chill. I'm fine. I'll let you know if I need help or I can't handle it. Can we go now? I would like to at least get out of these dirty clothes sometime today," I said snarkily.

I hadn't meant to be so sarcastic, but frankly, I was tired of everyone babying me or not trusting me. Granted, I'd brought on most of my own problems by being a whiny teenager. Still, if I were going to sink my fangs into a human, I would've already done it five minutes ago when a woman brushed past me, smelling like coconuts.

George and Webb just shrugged, then Webb growled.

"Stay close," he said, wrapping my hand with his.

So we were going to walk into the local Target holding hands. Oooookay.

"George, we won't be long," Webb tossed over his shoulder.

I laughed. "You afraid you might have to pry me from some human in the store? Is that why we're holding hands?"

He stopped short. "Jo, don't you get it? I love your touch, your skin on mine." He gave me a cocky grin before his gaze lowered to my lips.

Though his statement made my heart trip, his tone was nervous.

As soon as the doors slid open, thousands of scents hit me like a tornado. I pressed my lips together, willing my fangs to stay hidden.

"Having a hard time?"

I scrunched my nose at him. I would've stuck out my tongue, but I feared my fangs would show. Yes, they were down. I took in several breaths as we zipped over to the women's section.

The last time I'd been shopping was with Mr. Jackson when I'd still been human. He'd kindly purchased clothes for Sam and me after our fight with our foster dad, Cliff Birch.

Once I found the underwear section, I quickly

picked out what I needed. I flushed ten shades of red while Webb watched. I again longed to be in his head. His gaze roamed the fabric in my hands then the length of my body. A tingling took root in my tummy.

"Do you mind?" I glowered.

He gave me a crooked grin.

Asshat.

With my underwear selection done, I selected a pair of jeans in my size, forgoing the dressing room. If they fit, great; if not, oh well. Then I found a red blouse and two V-neck T-shirts. Next we zipped over to the toiletries section, and I swiped a toothbrush. With everything in hand, Webb and I made our way to the registers. He whipped out his wallet. The woman at the register batted her eye-lashes at Webb while he counted out the bills. When he handed her the money, her fingers lin-gered on his a little too long. A sound escaped me, and Webb's head shot up. The woman who'd been gazing at Webb with heavy lids now glanced my way, eyes wide.

Webb squeezed my arm as a feathery sensa-tion tickled the back of my neck. Then his voice filled my head. *Close your mouth. Your fangs are showing.*

I glared at the woman, deciding if I wanted to

punch her or drink her blood. Neither happened. Webb grabbed the bags then dragged me from the store.

We were at the door when a male voice blared from the intercom overhead. "Need assistance at register two."

Satisfied, Jo? You made the poor sweet lady pass out, Webb said.

I grinned from ear to ear. *Serves her right.*

Webb didn't say anything else as we got into the truck. George just shook his head. I imagined Webb had told George what had happened via telepathy.

Before long, we were on the road and headed up to the crash site to meet Stan.

"At least I didn't snack on the woman, Webb," I finally said as he drove. George sat in the back seat this time.

"Not today you didn't, but the day is still young." He looked at me then back at the road.

Without even thinking, I punched him in the arm. The vampire didn't flinch in the least.

George just laughed. "I like her, Webb."

Webb grinned from ear to ear. "I think I do too," he said in a serious tone.

"What?" I squeaked as a soprano. "You *think*? If I remember this—"

"Jo," Webb warned, sliding his hand over the console in search of mine.

I sat on my hands. As soon as his fingers touched my arm, electricity zapped me, and I jerked. "What was that?"

"Energy. Lots of energy. When we get back, I need to teach you how to use some of the energy in you."

"Huh? It's not me. You have enough electricity in you to kill a person."

"Does she have any of the elements, Webb?" George asked.

"She does. She doesn't know how to harness them yet. She has the ability to manipulate water, air, and maybe earth. And I believe she has the elemental magic, as well."

"No shit!" George exclaimed. "She's a *new* vampire. How is that possible?"

"No idea," Webb replied. "My guess? Genetics."

My dad was considered the most powerful of all vampires, and I'd learned recently he could do something with elemental magic, whatever that meant.

"Webb, you said I had the earth element, not air." During our raid on the mansion, I'd created tornados in the basement, stirring up the dirt on the floor. Now that I was thinking about it, tornadoes were air.

"I know, and I've been meaning to discuss that with you. I wasn't thinking straight."

I didn't think any of us were thinking straight, especially him when his sister was about to drive a sword into him. "So is anyone going to explain to me what elemental magic is?"

We'd also learned Edmund had some unique powers the sentinels weren't aware of, and one of them was energizing an invisible wall of air. Yes, with electricity. How? No clue. I'd been told the only one who could break an electrically charged wall was my dad...and now me.

I was still trying to wrap my brain around what I could do with water. For example, I was able to change water into ice. All these abilities only came easily when I was angry, though.

Now the element of fire wasn't on my list of abilities, but I was intrigued on how that would work. Would fire shoot out of my hands?

Webb snagged my hand and traced circles on my palm with his fingers.

"We'll talk later. We're here." He turned the truck onto the gravel incline and parked next to Stan's police cruiser.

I scanned the area. "Where's Stan?"

George opened the back door. "Probably on the rocks below."

I jumped out. "What? How did he get down there?"

My question was answered when I peered over the cement barrier. The rocks leading down to the ocean were situated like stairs.

The charred, mangled limo lay on its side with the wheels facing the ocean. Low tide helped keep the vehicle above water.

Webb stood at the opening where the boulder and the limo had gone through. "Stan?" he called.

Stan tilted up his head. "Come on down. All of you."

He was crazy. I wasn't going down there.

"Jo?" Webb had his arm out.

"That's okay. I'll wait here," I said as I glanced down. George had already descended.

"I'm not leaving you up here. So if you don't go, I'm just going to carry you," Webb said.

I raised one brow. "I dare you."

He smirked, but it didn't reach his eyes. "Take my hand. This is not an option."

I growled and shook my head.

"Jo?" His voice dropped, and his eyes narrowed before his expression softened. "I promise you won't get hurt. Please trust me."

I huffed and obeyed. We crossed the rocks, although I didn't look down. Not that I was afraid of heights, but one wrong step, and I'd be ocean diving for sure. Webb checked out the underside of the car while Stan and George chatted, pointing to areas of the limo.

I stayed away, sitting on a rock. I loved watching Webb. The way he moved, the way his muscles bunched every time he ran a hand through his hair—which I'd come to realize was a nervous habit of his—and the way the sun highlighted his masculine features. Letting out a sigh, I rested my elbows on my knees with my face in my hands, enjoying the view.

"Jo?" Stan snapped his fingers.

Tearing my attention away from Webb, I lifted my head. Stan peered down at me, wearing a pair of tattered jeans with a tan button-down shirt with the word *sheriff* on one side and his name on the other. A tan ball cap covered his head, complementing his uniform. His hair was cut military style so all that peeked out were his long sideburns.

"Yes?" I asked.

"Boy. You really like him, don't you?"

I glanced back to Webb, not acknowledging Stan's comment.

"Be careful. I've known Webb a long time. I've seen him with a few lady friends over the years. He's not the type of vampire to settle down, especially not after the crazy one." He spoke in a low tone and kept glancing over his shoulder to make sure Webb wasn't listening.

My senses went on alert. Crazy one? Lady friends? Out of the two, the "crazy one" bothered me. "Who's the crazy one?" I had to ask, even though Webb's past wasn't any of my business.

"Sorry, darling. Not my place to spill those beans," he said. "Now, why don't you join us?" He held out his hand.

"I'm comfortable right here." There wasn't anything for me to look at on the limo. Plus it was nice to sit and look out at the water. White caps broke along the surface as the wind picked up.

"Jo?" Webb waved his hand, motioning me to come down.

"You'll be fine," Stan said.

Reluctantly, I took his hand and made my way down with Stan's guidance. Waves crashed against the rocks, splashing water towards us. The tide was coming in. I stepped onto a flat rock next to Webb. Stan jumped over two rocks to stand by George.

"So what's so important?" I asked.

I wasn't sure why he wanted me down here. I couldn't tell the brake line from the gas line.

"I want to show you something." He held my hand as he pointed to the front wheel. "You see that line there?"

"Yeah." The wind whipped my ponytail around.

"That's the brake line for that wheel. If you look at the others, all four of the lines were cut."

"What? When? How?" I bent over to look at the one on the front wheel. As I righted myself, I lost my balance.

Webb's arm snaked out, and he caught me.

"You just insist on getting hurt," he said. "Let's go. We're not going to solve this by looking at it. And the tide is coming in. The car will be submerged in water soon."

He didn't have to tell me twice. I climbed with vampire speed, still pondering who would sabotage the limo and when they'd done it.

3

Webb, George, and I drove back to the house. The sun crept downward as afternoon pressed in. George excused himself and went to take a nap. He'd complained he hadn't slept at all last night. I knew how he felt.

Webb's phone trilled in the quiet room. "Yes, Commander?"

Gee, my dad was phone-stalking us. Following George's lead, I curled up on the couch while Webb talked with Dad.

"Yes, sir. We'll head back tomorrow. I'll borrow George's car." Webb chuckled at something Dad had said.

Why were we going back so soon? I didn't have anything to do on base. Plus it was the weekend. I grabbed a pillow, burying myself underneath. I was about to scream in frustration when large hands lifted my legs. I peeked out.

Webb sat down, placing my legs on top of his thighs.

"Why do we have to leave?" I asked, pouting like a whiny toddler.

"Your father needs me back to work. A lot has happened since yesterday."

I sat up. "Like what? Is Sam okay?"

Why I asked about my brother, I wasn't sure. I hadn't spoken to him since I'd left. This was the second time in our lives that Sam and I had been apart for this long. The first time had been when the Plutariums kidnapped him.

Webb ran a hand up and down my legs. "He's fine. We've had a pesky intruder along the perimeter of the base. Plus everyone is working non-stop to clean up after the explosions, and... your father wants you back. We're going to a fundraiser on Sunday evening."

"Fundraiser?" My eyebrows had to be twisted in all sorts of directions.

"Victor Costner, a prominent figure in the community, is hosting a black-tie gala. Before you ask, yes, he's a vampire." He tapped the underside of my chin. "Close your mouth. It's not a big deal."

I could care less about Victor Costner. "He has a daughter named Alia Costner, right?"

"Yes. She was instrumental in helping design the library. One of her father's businesses is a well-known design firm in Fall River."

"She was my math teacher at Durfee High School. She's the lady who Ms. Lawrence recommended to my dad to help me with my powers. Apparently, she has some magical abilities or something." I'd learned recently she wasn't even a full-fledged vampire. She hadn't been interested in making the change for some reason.

"That I don't know," Webb said.

"So I'm going to this fundraiser?" I held the pillow to my chest. "Why?"

I'd never been to a black-tie event or a dance.

"Your father was invited by Ms. Costner. He's been trying to get her as your tutor. Also, her father asked the sentinels to guard the event alongside the guardians."

"Why?"

"Not sure. Your dad will fill me in when we get back tomorrow. Let's take a walk down on the beach. I want to use the last of our time together to see if we can harness some of the energy you zapped me with today. This is the perfect area to practice since I don't have any neighbors."

I could think of better things to do with our time together. Regardless, spending any time with Webb was perfect to me, even if it meant practicing my powers.

I swung my legs over him and rose with the help of his strong hand. He planted a long, wet kiss on my lips that had me almost falling backward. "Not fair, vampire. How am I supposed to walk down to the beach after that?" I teased.

He turned and whisked me off my feet. "You don't have to walk. I'll carry you."

"Webb, I was kidding. I can walk. Put me down," I said weakly.

"Nope. Any chance I have to grab your butt, I'm going to take it."

I slapped him on the arm. "Perv."

He waggled his eyebrows. "As long as I get to touch you, you can call me anything you like." He grinned, a glimmer in his eyes.

"Crazy vampire."

He laughed.

I bounced in his arms as we made our way to the beach. "Webb, what about the brakes on the limo? If we're leaving tomorrow, how are we going to find out who did it?"

"George and Stan will keep their ears open."

"What about that lady, Lauren? Do you think she's responsible?"

"Not sure. I'll look into her background when I have a chance. While I'm quite suspicious of her, she didn't seem capable of trying to kill someone. She was quite shaken up."

"Yeah, but stranger things have happened," I muttered, my voice vibrating in time with Webb's feet digging into the sand.

We didn't go as far out this time, since the tide pushed in. He eased me down in a spot where the sand met vegetation.

"Okay, I want to see what you can do," he said, turning me to face the ocean.

He pressed his chest into my back, arranged my hips with his hands, and nibbled on my ear. My head went fuzzy, and a frisson of heat slid down my belly. An icy wind could've blown us over, and I was certain I wouldn't have felt it.

I swallowed hard. "Um...a few pointers, maybe, on how to get started? The last time I used my powers, Sloan helped."

"He didn't help at the mansion. *You* manipulated air into little tornados, and *you* broke through the invisible wall Edmund erected." His hot breath tickled my neck.

I laughed inwardly. The vampire wanted me to

concentrate on practicing my powers when all I could think about was him.

"How? Was it elemental magic?" I asked.

"I think so," Webb said against my ear. "You've shown some strong abilities, but usually vampires who have elemental magic are those who can manipulate all four elements. I know you have water and air, but what about earth and fire?"

"If you are asking if I could start a fire by using whatever it is that's in me, you're nuts. As far as earth, I haven't noticed anything. I'm not even sure how a blue light came out of me to break through the invisible wall. Care to explain that one?" I asked.

"Let me start with the basics. In our world, alchemy is a precursor to our powers. The term has different meanings, but for vampires, it relates to the elements and transforming or altering the state of the element. Like you did with water into ice."

"How?" I leaned into him.

"That's harder to answer. Each vampire is different. Some don't even have any elemental powers. Others, like the sentinels, have only two or three. Still, we're able to change or manipulate air, water, earth, and fire by the energies we absorb from nature. For example, being out in the sun allows us to absorb energy. Some of us can absorb a lot of energy. Others only absorb a little. The reason for that depends on your DNA structure."

"Is the blue light a result of the stored-up energy inside me then?" I shifted in his arms.

"More than likely." His hand slid to my stomach. "Your father is one vampire who stores a ton of it, which allows him to manipulate all four elements. This is one of the reasons he is considered the most powerful of all vampires."

Edmund had told me he dreamed of me being very powerful one day. After what Webb had just explained, I was beginning to believe I was following in my father's footsteps. "I remembered you telling me my father was considered powerful because he was able to read minds."

"I did. It was the easiest explanation at the time. He is the only one in our world who can read minds. Remember, you were human. If I told you every little detail, would you have believed me?"

I shook my head.

His hands slid under my shirt. "Sometimes learning as you go isn't bad in our world. You would've never believed you could change any of the elements, right?"

"I guess so." I shifted against him. I still had a

hard time believing I was a vampire, let alone had the skill to alter nature.

I tensed against a horrible thought.

"What is it, Jo?"

"If Edmund could energize a wall of air, does he have all four elements?"

"Possibly." He kissed my temple before releasing me.

I shivered, not only from his touch, but from the knowledge of how powerful our enemy might be.

"Let's see what you got now that I've explained all this to you." He knelt down. "First step is to learn how to use your powers when you're not angry." He lifted a handful of sand, letting it spill between his fingers. He did it again, and again...

It was like watching an hourglass being tipped, over and over again.

The sand in his hand grew into a ball and levitated an inch above his palm.

I blinked a few times to be sure I wasn't hallucinating. Several seconds later, the ball of sand still hovered in the air.

I dropped to the sand beside him. "What the..." I squeaked out.

A smile played at the edges of those luscious lips.

"Remember what I said. It's all about the energy within you." The ball of sand glistened in the daylight as he held his hand still. "Now think back to when you absorbed the energy to get the dirt to spin into funnels." He tossed the ball of sand, and it splattered against the ground.

"Yeah, but that was my telekinesis." Wasn't it? Come to think of it, that night I'd had my hands clenched into a fist and felt an odd sensation swirling inside me, as though electricity had been snaking through my body.

"Yes and no. Your mind controlled the movement of the cabinet doors. The funnels, though, were your ability to use the air element."

I bit my bottom lip.

He grabbed my left hand and flipped it so the palm faced the sky. He drew an imaginary circle in the middle with the tip of his forefinger. At first, it tickled, and then a bolt of electricity shot up my arm. I yanked my hand away, but he stopped me.

"Don't. Feel the energy from me," he said.

Yeah. I wanted to but not this type.

"Hold still." He repeated the process, pressing harder against my palm, as though he were pushing all his excess energy into my skin.

My left arm vibrated before he removed his finger.

"Now. Dip your hand in the sand and pick up a handful. Then visualize and use the energy in you to form a ball. It takes practice and concentration at first. Once you master the process, it comes easy, like tying your shoe."

While I thought manipulating the air and water belied all sense of what I knew about the universe, I was fascinated. I closed my eyes and ran my hands along the sand, dipping my fingertips into it, feeling the coolness underneath the top layer before lifting my hands at a slight angle. I repeated this step a couple of times then grabbed a handful as Webb had, allowing the sand to spill through my fingers. I tuned out all sound except the crashing of the waves against the shore.

A strong rumble-like feeling rolled through my body. As I picked up two handfuls of sand, I pictured a rotating sphere of glistening silica particles hovering over my palm.

The energy coursing through me went from the fingertips of my right hand, up my arm, then down my left one to my palm. Within seconds, the energy grew stronger. It seemed as if my body was vibrating.

I opened my eyes, and a ball of sand spun above each hand. I drew my arms in front of me, both hands touching. In one fluid motion, I lifted my arms, flicked my wrists, and pushed out, releasing the silica spheres. They soared into the ocean and crash-landed. Water fanned up and outward.

I slowly lowered my arms as I glanced at Webb. Several expressions flickered across his face—shock, surprise, envy, and excitement.

I wiped my hands on my jeans. I had no idea so much power flowed through my veins.

He gaped out at the water.

"Close your mouth, baby." I tapped his chin.

His head jerked toward me as one edge of his mouth curled.

"What?"

"I don't know whether to be more surprised at what you just displayed or the fact you called me 'baby.'"

"Wait, what? I called you—"

He tackled me to the ground and stared down at me. I flushed, heat pinching my cheeks.

"I'm sorry. I didn't mean to call you that." I grabbed onto his shoulders.

"Say it again." His voice sounded giddy.

"Seriously? You're excited about me calling you 'baby'? What about my awesome feat of wielding those sand balls?"

"We'll get to that. But first, say it like you did earlier." He stared at me through hooded eyelids.

Oh, jeepers. The vampire was crazy.

He raised his eyebrows, waiting.

"Webb, baby, aren't you going—"

His tongue plunged into my mouth. I'd never seen the vampire soldier so excited before. Over a pet name. Was he serious? It didn't matter. The warmth of his tongue and his lips caused some serious fireworks to explode inside me.

After several minutes, he broke the kiss, and we headed back to the house. A deep orange colored the horizon as the sun set and the wind kicked up.

"I'm proud of you, Jo. Your powers are only going to get stronger."

"You sure you're impressed with my abilities? Maybe it's just your new pet name." I giggled and ran ahead of him.

He caught me and swooped me into his arms. We entered the house, and he froze, his hands tightening on me. Webb set me down slowly as he looked past me. I turned to see what had his interest. A pretty lady lounged against the counter.

A black miniskirt showed off a pair of tanned, toned legs. Her short black wispy hair accentuated her delicate face—small nose, wide gray eyes with long lashes, and perfectly manicured eyebrows. Her yellow scoop-neck blouse displayed a cleavage that was hard to miss. The heels made it hard to determine her height, but I was wearing flats, and her heels put her at my height.

"Jo, can you see if George is awake?" Webb's tone bordered on a growl.

The woman stalked up to him, splayed her hands against his chest, reached up on her toes, and gave him a long lingering kiss on the lips.

I hissed, sounding like a disturbed and angry cat. I wasn't about to hide my distaste for this woman or the jealousy coursing through me. Talk about possessive. Yep, I was beginning to understand that term.

After her lips were finally away from Webb, she looked my way.

"Jo, get George." Webb's voice was hard, cold.

Not happening. I wasn't leaving this room even if my life depended on it. I clenched my hands into a fist. I had no idea who she was, but the way she bared her fangs at me, like a snake that had been disturbed on the warm concrete, led me to make an educated guess. This had to be the crazy lady who Stan mentioned.

"You need to go," Webb said to the black-haired woman. He hadn't taken his eyes off her yet.

The last time I'd seen such a look of derision on Webb was when he spat at Edmund in the basement of the mansion.

"I just got here, darling," she crooned, swinging her gaze back to Webb.

Yuck! She sounded like Edmund.

He grabbed her by the arm. "Nicki, leave," he spat out. "Whatever you have to say, I'm not interested."

So this was Nicki? The girl who Webb was supposedly in love with? Kate London's friend. Kate had said she looked like me. The only similarity between us was the color of our hair.

"But, sweetie..." Her voice dripped with polite scorn.

Webb let go of her and turned his head. "Go get George," he said to me, his eyes black as coal.

I shook my head slowly. "Not leaving," I said calmly.

Nicki laughed.

Fear slid down my stomach. Anger rose up. The two emotions equaled disaster, or maybe a meltdown. I wasn't sure.

Breathe. Breathe. Whatever you do, don't freak. You need to stay calm.

If I didn't, I was afraid of the mess I would make.

A split second of darkness ensued before my eyes flashed vampire violet. The energy I had on the beach made its way to the surface. I narrowed my eyes at Webb; his widened.

"Why don't you tell her, Webb, how we used to have good times here," Nicki said excitedly. "How we used to do—"

Webb whipped around, growling. "Can it, Nicki."

"But I want to play. You know how I like to play," she all but gushed.

Her words and tone reminded me of Edmund, for sure. Was she related to him?

Staying calm wasn't happening. My anger jumped directly to fury.

The cabinet doors opened and slammed. The lone mug on the counter vibrated toward the edge.

"Shit," Webb said.

Nicki giggled. "So I see your little toy has powers. I was watching her on the beach. I have to say, very impressive. You know you haven't introduced us at all, Webb. You don't have to. I know who she is. Kate has told me all about how weak Jo Mason is."

I dug my nails into my palm and bit down on my lower lip as my skin prickled with power. I'd been called weak by Blake one too many times when he used to bully me at the human high school. I told myself to calm down. If my powers got out of hand, I could hurt her the same way I did Blake. I couldn't afford to get into any more trouble.

Then she laughed again. The sound grated on me. I narrowed my eyes and clenched my fists tighter. She lost her smile as she backed up against the sink, rubbing her throat. Her face turned red, reminding me of how Blake looked that day at school. I turned my attention to Webb. Even his face reddened as he placed his fingers on his throat. I studied her then him.

He gave me a pleading look, shaking his head. Oh, how I didn't want to stop...but he was being affected by my powers.

I slowly unclenched my hands, dropped my shoulders, and blew out a long breath.

Nicki choked, and Webb took in a ragged breath.

Before Nicki could even take another breath, I stalked up to her, but Webb snagged me.

"So not worth it, Jo," he said hoarsely.

"Let me go, Webb," I said, struggling under his strong hold.

A familiar voice cleared his throat behind us.

"What's going on, Webb?" George asked. "Nicki. Shit."

"Get Nicki out of here, George," Webb commanded, keeping a vise-like grip around my waist. "I need you to calm down, Jo."

I bared my fangs at the woman. She freaking laughed.

"Come on, Nick." George cupped her elbow.

No argument came from her lips. She stopped in front of me, her eyes flashing to vampire black. "You'll never have him. Never in this lifetime," she said calmly. "Over my dead body. Ask his other girlfriends."

"Is that a threat?" I asked evenly.

"No threat. It's a promise." Her words sliced through me like a knife.

"And you think *you* have what he needs or wants? I highly doubt it." I squirmed against Webb's hold. "But bring it on."

"George?" Webb growled.

"I don't need his help," Nicki said. "I know my way out." She flicked her arm at George and stalked out.

George followed her.

"Jo, I don't want you to move if I let you go. Do you hear me? Do not go out that door." Webb's tone was resolute.

The adrenaline rush vanished. Between using my energy on the beach and now, I was suddenly tired, and I slumped against him. "Don't worry."

Grunting, he lifted me in his arms and carried me to the couch.

"I can walk, Webb."

"Yeah, and your point is what?" Irritation colored his tone.

We stared at each other. His eyes were still vampire black, and I imagined mine were still violet.

"I need to feed," I said instead of arguing with him.

"Don't move." He was gone in a flash.

I took one breath, and he handed me a container of blood. I chugged it down. "Thank you."

"For?" He pulled a strand of hair off my forehead.

"For keeping me from destroying your house. But I won't thank you for holding me back from punching her. I so wanted to."

"She's not worth it. Besides, knowing what you can do with your powers, it was best you didn't go there, especially with your upcoming hearing."

I shrugged as I took the last sip of blood. I didn't want to admit he was right.

The door clicked. Webb and I glanced over the couch.

George came in and took a seat on the window bench. Webb had a plush window seat built in front of one of the stationary floor-to-ceiling glass doors.

George let out a breath and scrubbed a hand down his face. "She gave me a message to give to you, Webb."

"Is she gone?" I asked.

"Her car is not in the driveway. That's all I can tell you."

"What does that mean?" I looked at Webb.

"It means she may be slinking around the house, if I know her," Webb said.

"Creepy" was the only word to come to mind.

"What's the message?" Webb asked.

"Kate wants to talk to you."

My eyes widened. What could she possibly want?

Webb leaned back against the couch, a muscle popping in his jaw. "About?"

"Kate will be at the fundraiser on Sunday." George leaned forward, elbows on his knees. "Are you going to a fundraiser?" His eyes stayed focused on Webb.

"Yes. It's being hosted by Victor Costner."

Webb's hand snaked out, and he tapped me on the leg.

I didn't know if he was asking me to come closer, but I curled up next to him. "How does Kate know you're going?"

He didn't waste any time wrapping me with his arms. His body shook slightly as he buried his face in my hair.

"Good question," George said.

Webb eased back. "Mmmph. Great question."

"Do you think someone on our side told her?" I asked. "You still suspect another person working on the inside."

"It's possible," Webb said. "Or the phones are bugged."

"You swept the base. Didn't you?"

Webb let me go and rose. "I need to call the commander. George, can you give Stan a call? Have him check around the area. I want to make sure Nicki is not hanging around."

George unfolded himself from the window bench. "You know she is, Webb. I'm sorry to have to say that. But I'll call Stan, then I'll scope the property. It shouldn't be hard to find her car, if she's still here."

"I'll go with George," I jumped off the couch. I would love to find her and finish what we started.

Webb had his hand on his cell phone. "Like hell you will!"

I stuck my fists on my hips. "Why not? I'm capable of handling myself."

He let out what I thought was a laugh, but it sounded like a grunt. "It's not you I'm worried about." He shoved his phone back in his pocket.

"What?" My voice hitched.

"I'll call you in a bit, Webb." George walked out the front door.

Webb turned to me. "Jo, your powers would kill her. I know you're not aware of the severity of what you can sling at someone, but I'm here to tell you, even I'm a little intimidated, especially after you somehow sucked the air out of this room."

I harrumphed. "You're afraid of me? Between you and my dad, you could both destroy an army."

"You could do it all by yourself."

I swallowed, remembering Edmund's prediction for the second time today. "You'll have powers the vampire world hasn't seen in all of their existence," he'd told me.

He held out his hand. "Let's go, Jo. We'll walk the property."

I didn't move. "I thought you were going to call my dad?"

"I will when we get back."

I wanted to stomp my foot like a child. Webb could be irritating when he had his possessive military mask on.

"Do I have to carry you? Because you're not staying here," he snapped.

I blew past him through the patio doors.

He followed.

We scanned the area behind the house before we circled the property. Satisfied Nikki wasn't close, we trudged up the hill on the paved road until it dead-ended on a dirt path.

"Where does this lead?" I asked.

"To a steep drop-off. I doubt she would come up here. There is no access to the house from here."

We turned and headed back toward the house. Webb was in his soldier mode, listening, scanning, and sniffing. Our species had a keen sense of smell. We searched one more time around the house but didn't bother with the beach.

George called, letting Webb know that Nikki's red Porsche had breezed through town.

We climbed the steps to the front door.

"I'm sorry about before," I said. "But you need to stop being—"

"What?" Webb asked. "Protective? I'm not going to apologize, Jo. You need to choose when you use your powers. You can't use them every time you get angry." Steel laced his tone.

Well, I wouldn't say "protective." I had a few other choice words.

"Who are you protecting, Webb? Nicki or me? If you're worried about my powers, then it's clear it isn't me."

His eyes flashed with anger. "Seriously, Jo? Do you hear yourself?" He pushed his fingers through his hair. "You really do make me crazy—and it's not the kind of crazy I would like from you. I was serious when I said I was a little intimidated. I couldn't breathe when you somehow closed off my airways. Me, Jo." He pointed to his chest. "Do you get that? When you use any of your powers, beware. They're usually not directed at one person, but many. Do you understand what I'm saying?"

Tears filled my eyes. I hadn't been trying to hurt Webb at all. That was the reason I'd stopped.

"Hey." He crooked a finger under my chin. "You need to practice, to learn control."

I was numb and scared. How was I going to learn control? Was that how I killed Blake Turner? Did I suck all the air from the bathroom that day? I was so going to jail after the Council of Eternal Affairs convicted me of murder.

"Do you hear me?" Webb's voice penetrated the shock.

I blinked away a tear and nodded. He was right on so many levels. I hated myself.

"Let's go in. When we get back to base, I'll work with you on your powers. Okay?"

Again, all I could do was nod.

George returned about an hour later and retired to his room. Webb talked to my dad while I hunkered down on the couch and berated myself the entire time. I had to find a way to make sure I didn't get angry. If I didn't, I would use my powers unconsciously. I couldn't hurt anyone, especially not those I cared about. All this time, I'd thought Sam had the anger issues, but I did, too.

I stared out the windowed doors. Dusk had settled over the ocean, oranges and blues painting the sky.

The cushion dipped, and I tore away my gaze from the crashing waves.

"Come join me, beautiful." He gathered all the pillows and piled them on the floor before kicking off his shoes and sitting down.

I crawled down and nestled between his legs. He rested his hands on my stomach while his chin sat on my head.

"How's my dad?" I placed my hands on top of his.

"Stressed. He's going to have a security company come in and do a complete sweep of the base for any type of surveillance equipment. You okay?" His lips lingered near my ear. "I didn't mean to be so harsh on you, Jo."

"That's okay, Webb. I deserved it. You're right. One of the reasons why I stopped when I did was because I saw what it was doing to you."

His hand snaked underneath my shirt.

"Webb?"

"Shhh," he murmured as his tongue found the inside of my ear. He gently traced circles around my belly button before coasting upward. "Your heart is racing," he murmured.

No, really? The vampire's magic hands were on me, and his lips were causing my insides to ignite. Of course my heart was racing.

His hand reached the underside of my breasts then slowly slid down.

"Soft. Your skin feels like I'm touching the wings of a butterfly," he whispered against my neck.

I was a goner. I almost pinched myself to make sure this wasn't a dream, but I didn't have to. The points of his fangs scraped down the column of my neck.

My pulse jumped, and I let out a soft gasp.

"Don't worry, I'm not going to," he whispered. His hands tightened on my hips. "I want you to stay with me tonight. We'll sleep here on the couch. I don't trust Nicki."

Acid rose up, killing the swarm of butterflies in my stomach. To say I wasn't jealous would be a lie, plain and simple, but it was more than jealousy. Kate and Nicki were friends, and that enhanced my hatred for Nicki all the more.

4

At some point during the night, Webb had moved me from the floor to the couch. I woke up a couple of times to find him standing in front of the glass doors, gazing out into the darkness. I tried to coax him to snuggle with me, but the sentinel in him kept him on guard. I finally gave up when sleep broke my efforts to get him to rest.

I stretched, opening my eyes to a soft light spilling in through the windows. Pink and blue streaked across the sky over the calm ocean. I sat up, glancing around.

"Good morning," George said. He sat at one of the four barstools at the kitchen island.

"Where's Webb?" My voice was rough from

sleep.

"Shower. Why don't you join me?"

I rubbed my peepers as I ambled over to the fridge. I plucked out a bottle of blood then sat down next to George.

"So is Nicki as loony as she seems?" I unscrewed the cap.

He chuckled.

I took a swig of blood.

"My advice, Jo, is to stay away from her. Nicki likes to play games. Twisted, sick ones. She's not worth your time."

True, but something suggested she was going to demand my time. "You think she was the one who cut the brakes?"

He turned to me. "The thought has crossed my mind. But"—he searched my face—"she loves Webb too much to hurt him."

My heart sank. Did Webb have the same feelings for Nicki?

George touched my leg. "Jo, I've known Webb longer than anyone. He's not one to lie, steal, cheat... You get my drift. His one flaw is he can be very possessive. But the best thing about Webb is he has a huge heart. I've never seen him look at anyone the way he looks at you."

"Does he love—" Webb's woodsy scent came before the sound of his footsteps. I turned.

His gaze latched onto mine. His cobalt blue eyes sparkled as he smiled wide.

If my heart had sunk at what George had told me, it now skipped a beat at the sight of Webb.

"Is George telling stories?" Webb asked as he stood over me. "Good morning, angel." He bent down and kissed me softly on the lips. "Why don't you shower? Then we'll get on the road."

I regarded him with open lust as he backed away. I wasn't sure I could move, let alone speak. Not after the way he said "angel" in his sweet, husky voice, nor after the feathery kiss he'd planted on my lips. My only motivation was the fact I desperately needed a shower. I downed my breakfast and ran upstairs.

I showered quickly and dressed. My new jeans fit perfectly, as did the red blouse. After gathering my belongings, I went in search of Webb. He and George were securing the doors. After they buttoned up the house and activated the alarm system, we got on the road.

As we drove out of town, I thought about my conversation with George. While he might not believe Nicki would be capable of trying to kill Webb with me, she'd said I would never have Webb.

Maybe she'd been stalking us all day, and she got into a jealous rage. I wasn't crossing Nicki off the list of suspects.

The landscape changed as we approached Boston. Cars packed the freeways, moving at a snail's pace. An image of an overstuffed car lot came to mind as I stared out the windshield. Stop-and-go was the rhythm of movement as we made our way to George's house in Beacon Hill.

Once we arrived, Webb climbed out and chatted with George. I'd thought we were switching vehicles, but Stan had told Webb to use the truck so George could use his own car.

After a few minutes, Webb slid back in. He maneuvered through traffic and onto the freeway. The road finally opened up as the city faded behind us. I didn't want to go back. I loved my brother and Dad, but I felt as though I was losing the freedom that I had with Webb at his house.

He reached over the console and laced his fingers in mine. "Do you want to share?"

The silkiness of his voice caressed my solar plexus, cutting through the despair that had settled in me.

"Just thinking how I would like to go back to your house." I stared out the side window. Sure, the military compound was my home, but the place reminded me of all the problems we'd faced with the Plutariums.

He rubbed the back of his fingers over my cheek. I leaned into his gentle touch.

"You sure your quiet has nothing to do with yesterday or the day before?" He lowered his hand onto the console.

I wasn't sure I was ready to talk about Nicki, but maybe now was a good time, before we both got caught up in the craziness of life on base. Plus, Olivia, the only female sentinel, had taught me to know my enemy, and Nicki was clearly one. "Can you tell me about Nicki?"

His face tightened as his gaze bounced from the road to me and back to the road again. "Nothing really to tell. I was at a low point in my life when Kate insisted I get out and let my hair down. So she set me up with Nicki. We went on two dates before I called it off."

"Why?"

"For one, I wasn't looking for a permanent re-lationship. Two, being a SEAL, I was gone a lot. More importantly, she's not my type. Although, for some reason, she has this notion she and I were meant to be together."

And she'll do anything to get you, too. Boy, the idea

of her cutting the brakes is looking better and better. "Is there a reason she thinks that?" I asked, voice low.

The trees along the highway whizzed by. Traffic grew heavy. The orange signs flashed road construction.

"It's hard to tell why Nicki thinks anything."

The right two lanes were closed, so Webb slowed and merged into the left lane. After we passed the construction zone, he flicked on the blinker. An off-ramp for Assonet drew closer. This wasn't our exit. We still had miles to go before we were even near Fall River. Maybe he needed gas.

"So you decided to drop me off in the woods?" I joked.

I trusted Webb completely. So why did my body tense? Maybe the red sparks in his vampire black eyes gave me reason to pause.

He chuckled then squeezed my hand. "Not a chance, Jo. Not a chance."

Webb veered off and slowed down for the stop sign before turning right and following the two-lane road for one mile. After flicking on the blinker, he drove into a commuter lot packed with cars and trucks. He navigated his way around to where the pavement met the dense brush. He backed into an empty spot.

Ooookay. Why were we here? Fear settled in my veins.

The tall trees surrounding the lot swayed in the wind as dark clouds rolled in. A summer storm seemed to be brewing. He killed the engine, removed his seat belt, then leaned over and removed mine. My tongue wouldn't move. My stomach twisted, and not in the way I wanted it to when I watched Webb.

A white beat-up car circled the parking lot before stopping behind a blue pickup truck. A lady got out of the white car and climbed into the truck.

When both vehicles drove away, Webb's strong hands were on my hips. Before I knew what was happening, I was on his lap with the steering wheel jammed into my back.

The sudden motion rendered me speechless. Sure, vampire reflexes were fast, and we usually did things in a blur when we wanted to, but he could've asked. I would've been more than obliged to hop over the console.

Running his fists through my hair, he crushed his lips to mine. My breath caught in my lungs. What in the world was going on? So we were parking to make out. Not that I was complaining, but this wasn't lovers' lane or even a secluded spot.

I smiled, and he growled, his hands cupping my face.

"Kiss me, Jo." He sounded desperate, scared. Of what, though?

My smile turned into a frown. Tunneling my hands through his hair, I trailed kisses along his jaw. "What's wrong, baby?"

He buried his head in the crook in my neck.

"Webb, talk to me. Why are we in a parking lot off the highway? You're kind of scaring me."

The vampire, the soldier, the navy SEAL never looked worried, at least since I'd known him. My mind spun with all kinds of thoughts as my heart rate kicked into high gear. Whatever was eating at him, it couldn't be good.

He leaned back, straightening his shoulders as the anguish on his face grew. I rested against the steering wheel.

He placed his hand on my heart. "It's beating really fast."

"Only for you." The words came from deep within my soul, even though I had a little anxiety.

I searched his face, trying to find something to tell me what was plaguing him. Instead, I ended up melting at the way his long crescent moon eyelashes framed those amazing heart-throbbing eyes, especially when he gazed at me with such longing that I forgot who I was. I absently traced a finger over his eyelids then his eyebrow, settling on a small scar I had just noticed under his left eyebrow.

His eyes darkened to vampire black. "Really?" His tone went deeper than surprise, as though he needed some sort of assurance that I meant what I said.

"You make my world better." The words spilled easily. "But what's bothering you?"

Time seemed to stop as we explored each other. His chest rose and fell with every breath. I didn't have to feel his heart to know it was beating as fast as mine.

"I wanted time alone with you where there are no insane people barging in, no one trying to kill us, and a few more minutes to kiss those lips of yours and touch your exquisite body."

My lips parted in surprise.

"You're gorgeous, Jo." He tangled his hands in my hair again. "You were as a human, and even more so now that you're a vampire. My heart beats faster every time I hear your voice. My stomach does somersaults when I lay eyes on you. And the one thing that gets my whole body humming is your lavender scent." He sucked in my bottom lip. "I've never been in a relationship." He kissed the edge of my mouth. "So this is new for me."

His eyes flickered with fear and excitement, and my stomach followed suit. My brain hadn't caught up to everything he'd said, but the goose bumps and butterflies sure had.

I raised both eyebrows. "But you just said you dated Nicki."

"It was a date and not a relationship."

"Is that what's really bothering you?" I slipped my hands under his shirt, loving the way he trembled under my touch.

"Our first date was great, but it didn't end well. Then Nicki showed up. So I guess what I'm trying to say is, I'm worried about us."

"I'm here. I'm not going anywhere. I promise." I didn't know the first thing about relationships either. But I wanted to build one with him. That much was certain.

Skimming his gaze over me, he grinned as though my promise was what he needed.

"What?" I asked.

"You're amazing."

Large raindrops pelted the truck, creating an ominous sound, one that faded when his lips brushed mine. His kiss was gentle until my hand traveled south over the dips of his toned chest to his abs. Then he looked as though he were a vampire possessed. Gone was the tenderness. In its place stood a predator staking his claim.

My life changed in that moment, in that truck. Without a doubt, Webb London was my future.

WE'D STAYED in the parking lot for nearly an hour without any distractions. Dad hadn't even called, which surprised me. Regardless, Webb and I kissed a lot and talked about us, and nothing more. We decided we'd try to steal as much time to see each other when we could. He had a job to do, and our time together would be minimal, especially with Dad around, dictating.

The rain had stopped, and the sun peeked through the clouds every now and again.

When we were finally on the road again, Webb didn't let go of my hand until we drove up to the security gate, and he rolled down the window.

"Lieutenant London?" Kraft nodded. "Welcome back."

"Thanks. How is everything here?" Webb asked.

Kraft was a sentinel who moonlighted as a guardian at St. Anne's Academy, the vampire school I was banned from until my court hearing with the Council of Eternal Affairs. I guessed today he was playing sentinel and not guardian.

Kraft bent his mammoth body down, looking in. His blond hair was tied back in a low ponytail, and he was wearing his fingerless gloves. The only time I'd seen all the sentinels wearing them was when we stormed the mansion. I wasn't sure of the purpose of them. Maybe it was a fashion statement.

"Jo." Kraft nodded, his mahogany eyes latching onto mine.

"Is there a problem, Sentinel?" Webb asked, glancing between Kraft and me.

Kraft had been the one to give me blood after I battled Blake Turner. When he did, I had a vision of him and a lady friend of his. I still wasn't sure what that was all about, and I didn't care to revisit it. It would just open up more questions, and given the events of the past week—heck, the past two days—I wasn't prepared to even think about my blossoming powers. Not right now anyway.

"No, sir," Kraft said. "I'm sure the commander will fill you in on the activity we've had around here. Jo, nice to see you again."

Webb nodded while Kraft stepped away from the truck.

As we waited for the gate to open, Webb asked, his tone a possessive growl, "Do you want to tell me what that look between you and Kraft was all about?"

"Um...look?"

"Jo, you're avoiding the question." Annoyance weaved through each of his words. He drove through the gate.

The branches of the trees along the road rustled in the light wind. Webb gave the truck some gas as he steered around the winding way leading to the main building.

"So Kraft looked at me. I'm not sure what you're insinuating." Was Webb London jealous?

A muscle jumped in his jaw. "Mmm" was all he said as he wound around the main complex.

We finally parked in a spot with Webb's name on it. Each vampire SEAL had their own spot reserved for them, as evidenced by the signposts. Webb's spot sat between Dad and Tripp's.

I was ready to bolt when Webb grasped my arm. "Yes?" I asked.

"You would tell me if there was anything between you and Kraft."

"Webb..." I paused, mainly because the anger in his eyes had switched to something else. What?

I couldn't be sure. "There's nothing between me and Kraft. I promise."

The line between his eyebrows relaxed as he accepted my answer. Then he brought my hand to his lips, kissing the back of it. "You ready?"

I shrugged. Was I prepared to face the future? The answer in my head and in my heart was a *hell no*. But life didn't play nice at all, at least when it came to my life.

"Angel, look at me," he said.

I lifted my gaze to his.

"We're in this together. We'll get through whatever is thrown our way."

A ray of sunlight beamed through the windows, highlighting his chiseled features.

"I know," I lied.

I wanted to believe him. There were too many unknowns. What if Kate tried to kill him again? When was Edmund going to make his next move? He did want revenge against my family, and now he also had a vendetta against Webb.

Not to mention all the loose ends. Like what about Ben and his father? My sixth sense was telling me Mr. Jackson might be more of a problem than Edmund right now. After all, Dad had his own worries about the man.

Still, the one worry that overshadowed everything was my hearing. What if I was convicted of murdering Blake? Would I go to jail?

"You're thinking too hard." The deep timbre of Webb's voice brought me back to reality.

"Webb? What do you think Kate wants to talk to you about? And why at the fundraiser?" Another issue that worried me.

"I have no idea. My guess is she knows the fundraiser is a public place where I won't make a scene, and she won't, either."

"Do you think any of the other Plutariums will be there, like Edmund?"

"Not sure. It's always a possibility."

I tensed.

He pressed my fingers to his lips again. "Don't worry. Nothing is going to happen. The guardians and sentinels will make sure the event goes smoothly."

"Why would Edmund and Kate even go? You said Edmund was lying low right now."

"Again, I'm not sure."

I didn't have a warm and fuzzy feeling about the black-tie event.

"Let's not worry. We need to get in there." He nodded to the building behind us.

We both jumped out of the truck and headed for the back of the building. As soon as we reached the sentinel at the entrance, Webb switched into soldier demeanor. His body straightened, and his face tightened, losing the softness that I'd come to love about the vampire.

"Lieutenant."

The sentinel and Webb exchanged nods as the sentinel opened the door. Once inside, another sentinel stood guarding yet a second door. Dad wasn't messing around with security.

"Wait here, Lieutenant," the inside sentinel instructed as he called the control room.

"Why?" I asked Webb.

"Our entire security system changed. Until I have access, I can't get in."

We waited for five minutes before we were cleared to enter. Webb and I headed to Dad's office first. Actually, Dad had told the sentinel to send us directly to his office.

As soon as I set foot beyond the door, cold air rushed at me along with the sterile feeling I'd come to know very well. I was home. So why wasn't I happy?

5

No sooner had I walked into Dad's office than he had me in a bear hug. I missed my dad but being back on base had my claustrophobia squeezing its way up my throat. I'd gotten a taste of freedom. Granted, I'd almost lost my life, but I still needed to experience more of the outside world whether people were trying to kill me or not.

"Pumpkin, how are you?" Dad asked. "I was worried."

From the dark circles under his eyes and the deepened worry lines on his forehead, he looked as though he hadn't slept in days.

"Lieutenant, thank you for keeping her safe," Dad said as he returned to his desk chair.

Jeepers. Dad spoke as if he'd paid Webb to

stash me away for a couple of days while he took care of business around here. I quickly discarded the idea. Webb wouldn't accept a bribe to spend time with me. No way.

Webb sat down in one of the chairs in front of Dad's desk.

Standing behind the brand new wingback chair next to Webb, I surveyed Dad's renovated office. The windows had been repaired from the recent explosion. The walls smelled of a fresh coat of paint, and the furniture had been replaced. Aside from the two wingback chairs, a mahogany wood desk replaced Dad's old steel one. Even the sitting area had new furniture.

Wow! I had only been gone two days. Whoever remodeled his office had to have worked at vampire speed. Out of all the new furniture and décor, one thing was missing.

"Where's your safe, Dad?"

"I moved it."

Dad's safe had been broken into on two separate occasions. Kate had taken his blood reserves and given them to our enemy, Edmund Rain, who sought to build an army of vampires out of humans. He had used my father's blood to change his first test subject, Blake Turner. But as a man-made vampire, Blake had one flaw—a sun allergy, which according to Edmund, was unacceptable. He wanted vampires who could function twenty-four hours a day.

Webb shrugged. I guessed Dad wasn't telling anyone where his safe was or where he kept his blood.

"I'm going to find Sam," I said. "Where is he, by the way?"

"He should be in the apartment. There's a surprise for you on your bed," Dad said, eyes brightening.

"What is it?" My own eyes widened.

He rose from his chair and walked me out. "You'll see." He gave me another hug. "It's good to have you home, pumpkin. I'll be up in a bit. I need to talk to you about the fundraiser and a couple of other things. Okay?"

I glanced over my shoulder at Webb, and he winked. I loved it when he did that. I returned the gesture with a smile when a soft tickle breezed across my nape.

I miss you already, angel. I'll talk to you as soon as I can get things in order with your dad.

Promise?

With my heart and soul.

I smiled again at Webb's words.

Then Dad kissed my forehead and went back into his office.

As I headed down the long corridor, I realized this place was different. I pushed in the door to the stairwell, trying to analyze what had changed. I'd only been back a few minutes. It couldn't be this place. No, it had to be me.

I climbed the stairs, thinking about the past few days. The way Webb held me, kissed me, looked at me. How his heart raced and how he trembled under my touch.

Still, the turning point in my mind was our time in the truck. My tummy knotted. He tore away my reticence, shattering my shyness.

I smiled at my revelation. I kept the grin plastered on my face until I saw concern flickering across my brother Sam's face. All thoughts of Webb vanished.

"What's wrong?" I shut the door to the apartment.

Sam was playing with a cell phone. He glanced at me then back at the phone. He tapped the screen before jumping up from the couch.

He adjusted the waist of his low-slung jeans. "Sorry, Sis." He threw his arms around me. "How are you?"

I hugged him back before edging away, giving

him a once-over. His forest-green eyes lacked the usual glint. His quiet behavior reminded me of those times we had spent in foster care.

"You don't seem so happy to see me." I stuck out my bottom lip.

"It's not that." He went back to the couch, looking at his phone.

"Is that yours?" I followed.

"Yeah. Yours is on your bed," he said as he typed on his phone.

Oh, that must be my surprise Dad had mentioned. Finally. I'd asked Dad for one over a month ago. If Sam and I had cell phones, we probably could've gotten out of a few pickles we'd been in. I was excited to be part of the new age of technology, but right now, I had to find out why Sam was acting different. I wasn't the Empath in the family —Sam was the one who could read and feel other's emotions. He still hadn't mastered his skills, but he had learned how to block some emotions, although he had a tougher time shielding Dad's, especially when the powerful vampire was in a fit of rage.

Still, I didn't have to be an Empath to know something was amiss. "Sam, what's going on?" I kicked off my shoes and dropped down on the oversized chair next to the couch.

Letting out a breath, he set his phone on the coffee table and ran his fingers through his shoulder-length raven hair. He smiled, but it never reached his eyes. It was the same look he'd given me just before we were shipped off to another foster home.

"Did I miss something while I was gone?" I tried to get the conversation going again without freaking out.

"I don't want you to go bonkers. Okay?" He stared at me, waiting for my answer.

I laughed nervously.

He took that as his cue to continue. "Remember how Pops kept saying Mr. Jackson was going to be a problem?" He paused. "Well, so is Ben."

"Come again." I slanted my head.

I'd last seen Sam's best friend in the medical facility.

"While you were gone, Ben showed up at the main gate, demanding to see you. Is there something you want to tell me about you and Ben?" Sam leaned forward, elbows on his knees. His tone reminded me of Dad's when he got all commander on me.

I shifted my position and crossed my legs underneath me. I'd never told Sam that Ben had asked me to the high school dance or anything else about Ben and me. I had my reasons. Mainly, I didn't want Sam killing his best friend because I might've wanted to be more than friends with Ben. Regardless, once I became a vampire, I realized my bloodlust for Ben outweighed anything else I felt for the human. Not to mention my heart was reserved for someone else.

"Well? Sis. Tell me," he demanded.

For a moment, I considered bolting out of the apartment and running off the base. I had come back to a dad who was cranky and a brother who was treating me as though I were one of his soldiers. But I knew Sam was just protective of me. So I told Sam the story from the beginning. He didn't say anything until I was done.

"So you've never kissed Ben, led him on or anything?" Sam's eyes never wavered from mine.

"No. I thought I had feelings for him, but I was confused. He's human, and I'm a vampire. Call it puberty or the change of my body, but all I really wanted to do around Ben was sink my fangs into him. But he's stubborn, Sam. Even when I was talking to him while he was in the medical facility the other day, he wouldn't take no for an answer."

Sam lowered his shoulders. "I know. Pops told me Ben said he wasn't giving up on you and him.

And I can tell you, Sis, he's not. He's certainly not the same person I knew. Or maybe I've changed. He's angry, hostile, and man, he's strong. Like, really strong."

"What do you mean?" I furrowed my brows.

"When he was here yesterday, we didn't let him in. Pops had some concerns about Ben being on base, especially after Mr. Jackson came to pick him up the other day. Anyway, I went out to the gate to talk to him. He told me that he's in love with you. I laughed. I didn't mean to. I think it was more of a nervous laugh. He threw the first punch. We fought. I was trying to go light on him given my vampire strength. Then out of nowhere, he threw me clear across the freaking road. I mean a vampire-strength throw."

I gasped. What the... How could this be?

"Dr. Vieira said Ben was human...right?" My voice cracked while my blood felt as if it froze.

The Plutariums had kidnapped Ben and pumped in several vials of a concoction known as the Human Vampire Serum—or, as Edmund dubbed it, HVS-1. The formula had been developed by Dad's brother, Patrick, a renowned genetic scientist who switched sides a long time ago. Even after several injections, the serum never seemed to work on Ben, although I did see his eyes flash red when we were both stranded in the ocean. Edmund's eyes had the same color when they shifted.

"Did you know Ben is in love with you, Sis?"

"I knew he liked me." I wasn't so concerned about Ben's feelings about me. "I'm worried about the vampire strength you said he seems to have. What if the serum is working on him? What if it just took longer for his system to acclimate to the change? You saw what it did to Blake. He was a monster."

I didn't want to see Ben changed into something that resembled evil with red eyes. We knew little about the effects of the serum on ordinary humans. Dr. Vieira had done the autopsy on Blake and said he was part human. I still wasn't convinced my powers were what killed him.

"Well, I can tell you he isn't a vampire. He doesn't have fangs or anything," Sam said.

"Did his eyes change to red?"

"I don't think so. Then again, as soon as he threw me, three sentinels swarmed him. They escorted Ben to his car. I didn't see him again."

"The sentinels didn't see anything unusual about Ben?"

He shrugged. "I didn't ask."

"Has he returned today?"

"No, but he's been texting me." Sam checked his phone.

"How did he get your number? Didn't Dad just give you the phone?" It wasn't as if I'd been gone a week or a month.

Sam glanced up. "I got it the day you left, and I called Ben. I wanted to check on him. When his father picked him up, Mr. Jackson and Dad got into an argument. He told Pops he believes we're being held against our will. So he threatened Pops. He's going to alert the military."

My mouth was catching flies. "You're kidding me?"

"Think about it, Sis. You end up in a hospital because of our foster dad, which created a whole domino game. We ran from a vampire who beat a cop into a coma. We then asked Mr. Jackson for help. He gladly went out of his way to help, including smoothing things over with the chief of police and the state social workers. One week later, I was kidnapped, and the military arrived at school to take you away. Then Ben disappears for a few days because a vampire has mauled him. We both turn vampire, and no one bothers to tell Mr. Jackson we're all right. Then Ben ends up in Dr. Vieira's care again because of the Plutariums. Really, what would you think?"

Since he put it that way, I couldn't argue.

"What's Dad going to do?"

"No clue."

"Does Dad know Ben is in love with me?" I asked. I hoped not, but as I prayed, Sam gave me an I'm-sorry look.

I wasn't certain what Dad would do with this knowledge. I knew he didn't like Ben. I'd told Ben we couldn't be boyfriend and girlfriend. He'd lashed out, grabbing me by the wrists as Dad walked into the room. He almost took off Ben's head for touching me.

"I had to tell him. I'm sorry, Sis."

"Crap."

The door clicked open, and Dad strode in.

"What's crap?" Dad's brows furrowed.

"Nothing," Sam said, shaking his head at me.

He didn't have to warn me to drop the subject of Ben.

"Pumpkin, are you sure you're okay? I know I asked you earlier, but—" Dad set his keys and phone on the small table near the door.

"What's going on? What does he mean by okay?" Sam straightened.

"You didn't tell him, Dad?" I unfolded my legs and brought my knees to my chest.

"Sorry, things around here have been quite

hectic." Dad joined us as he took a seat on the couch next to Sam.

I glanced at my brother. "Someone cut the brakes on the limo when we were coming back the other night."

Sam's eyes immediately shifted to vampire black as his brows shot up. "What? Son of a—"

"I'm fine, Sam."

"Obviously, but who could've done that?" His heart sped.

I said, "We don't know," and then shared the rest of what had happened, including Nicki's antics. The only thing I didn't share were the intimate details between Webb and me. Sam and Dad didn't need to know, and I didn't want to give Dad a heart attack. I also needed to keep my mind empty of anything I didn't want Dad to know.

Sam pushed to his feet, and in two steps he pulled me up and hugged me. "I'm sorry, Jo."

He let me go when his phone rang. "Shit." He swiped it off the coffee table.

"Problem, Son?" Dad asked.

"It's..." He bit the inside of his cheek, a nervous habit he shared with Dad. "Ben." He hit a button on the phone, and it stopped ringing.

Dad growled as silver bled through his green eyes.

The majority of vampires had black eyes when their emotions changed. Dad's shifted from green to silver. Edmund Rain's brown eyes flashed to red, and mine turned from silver to violet. No one had yet explained why to me.

A muscle ticked in Dad's jaw as he swung his gaze from Sam to me.

"How come you didn't answer it?" I asked.

Sam grabbed the back of his neck. "I don't know what to say anymore."

"Son, have a seat," Dad said, his voice dropping.

The blood slowed in my veins. I didn't like the growl in Dad's tone.

Sam obeyed as he tossed the phone on the middle cushion between him and Dad.

I hadn't realized I was still standing after Sam had hugged me until Dad looked at me and flicked his head down. I eased down onto the edge of the chair, spine straight and my hands on my thighs.

"Both Mr. Jackson and Ben are becoming more of a problem than I'd expected, especially Ben. I knew I would have my issues with his father, but we have bigger problems with the boy."

Sam and I kept our eyes on Dad as he sat forward.

He stopped talking. The suspense was killing me, and not in a good way.

I started tapping my foot. "Well, Dad?"

"I'm not sure where to begin."

Was it that bad?

"Pops, I told Jo what happened with Ben yesterday. Is there something else?" Sam asked.

"Yes. There's more to Ben you don't know. Webb had a background check completed on Ben a few months ago. Records showed the boy lashed out at Mayor Edwards."

"I knew that. So?" I said.

Back when Ben and I had first arrived on base when Sam was missing, Webb confronted Ben about his police file. Ben had attacked Mayor Edwards and was arrested, but his record was sealed since Chief of Police Garrett was best friends with Ben's father.

"There's...more," Dad said.

Both heels of my feet were off the floor as I bounced on my toes.

"More?" I held my breath.

Ben had been a nice person, seeming to care about people. Sure, he'd been moody, and he had a temper. I'd always wondered why he changed moods all of a sudden. I knew he lost his mother to breast cancer not that long ago. Since then, he hadn't been the same person. Still, what else could he have done?

Dad scrubbed his face with his hand. "When... he was fifteen, a girl accused him..."

I swallowed hard.

"Accused him of...what?" Sam asked hesitantly.

"The girl's father pressed charges for inappropriate behavior. The girl's statement indicated Ben was extremely angry that night and he'd hurt her."

"Was it...?" I couldn't bring myself to even say the word. Cliff had tried to do that to me. "Tried" being the operative word. Did Ben attempt something like that on this girl?

"The report never indicated rape," Dad answered, no doubt reading my mind.

"How did he hurt the girl then?" Again Sam was the one to ask.

Air lodged in my throat.

Posture rigid, Sam kept his focus on Dad. I hadn't seen Sam raging mad in a long time.

"The report didn't say." A deep line formed between Dad's eyebrows, and the dark circles under his eyes seemed to grow darker.

Quiet pounded in the room as the three of us sat there like zombies—or at least, I did. Sam seemed ready to explode, and Dad...well, the color drained from his tan skin.

I couldn't believe what I was hearing. Or could I? After all, Ben did lash out at me in the hospital room.

Still, that didn't mean Ben would've hurt me. The guy almost died saving my life. No way he could hurt a girl.

"When...did you find this out?" I managed to force out.

"After my conversation with Mr. Jackson two days ago, I dove deeper into their lives to understand what I was up against. The report came in yesterday. I'm stating the facts as the report outlines. Are they true? Maybe or maybe not. I've found in my line of work, humans and vampires fabricate stories to suit their own purposes. Ben's actions, however, certainly support what's in the report."

"How so? To my knowledge he didn't hurt me. He saved my life, Dad." A chill went up my spine.

"He's angry. He got into it with Sam yesterday for no reason. If I hadn't stepped in when you were talking with him in the hospital room, he might have hurt you, Jo," Dad said.

"Dad. I'm a vampire. He's human. He couldn't

hurt me." Maybe whatever the Plutariums injected him with was making him even moodier.

Sam laughed. "Are you forgetting what I told you earlier? The guy has some strength." Then Sam turned his attention to Dad. "So, Pops. What are we going to do? Doc said Ben was human. But after yesterday, I'm questioning Ben's mortality. Do you think the serum is slowly working on changing him?"

"I don't know, Son."

"Is there some way we can help him, Dad?" I asked.

Sam jerked his attention my way. "Are you freaking insane? If we help him that means he has to come on this base. And given what Pops just said, I don't want Ben in proximity to you, Sis. He was a crazy person yesterday."

"He's your best friend, Sam. Again, he saved my life. That has to count. If he is changing into something..." I shook off the thought of Ben turning into anything and glanced at Dad. "Ben is alone. He has no one to turn to. What if his father starts to catch on? What happens then? We're the only ones who can help him."

Dad stood, rubbing his chin. Electricity charged the air as he crossed the room to the table near the door and picked up his phone. He took three long strides back toward us and sat down on the coffee table, facing Sam and me.

"I haven't figured out how to handle this yet," Dad said. "We do need to do something before Ben gets out of control, especially if his father finds out his son may not be human anymore. Things could get messier than they already are."

Sam growled. "I don't like any of this. My best friend has a police record that I never knew. He's in love with my sister, which I didn't know either. And he may be a vampire now." Sam shook his head. "Sorry if I'm having a hard time grasping all this."

My heart went out to my brother. He'd always been known for his anger issues, but while a little anger edged his tone, he seemed more disappointed in his best friend.

I hopped off the chair and went to sit next to Sam. I gave him a hug. "I'm sorry." I didn't know what else to say.

"Son, I understand that this news of your friend may be hard to grasp, but let's focus," Dad said evenly. "Now, given Ben's strength, we should run more DNA testing to confirm our suspicions."

At Dad's words, I let go of Sam and relaxed against the couch. Regardless of all this news about Ben, I needed to help him. Somehow, I felt responsible for all this. When I found out vampires existed and I could be one myself, I'd asked him to stay and help me find Sam. If he hadn't, then he might not be in this situation.

"If he does come back on base, can we please keep him away from Jo?" Sam asked.

"I know you worry about me," I said as I placed my hand on Sam's back. "I know you've been protecting me all my life, but I can take care of myself now."

"Sam," Dad said. "I know you worry about your sister. If Ben agrees to letting us help him, he'll be off limits to both of you. Now whatever we do has to be done by the book. I can't have both governments all over me. For now, though, I need to address some of my emails, and I have to meet with Webb."

At the sound of his name, I almost flew off the couch. "Where is he?" I asked.

"Webb's in the control room. He's waiting for me. But before I go, one thing. Jo, Webb told you about the fundraiser tomorrow night, correct?"

I nodded.

"Good. Alia Costner—I believe both of you know her from Durfee High School—has invited us to attend her father's black-tie event."

"Why?" Webb had given me a short answer for the question.

"When I called her about tutoring you, she wasn't interested. But after I explained what happened with Blake and your powers, she said she would consider it. However, before she makes her decision, she would like to meet with you, Jo. And she thought the fundraiser would be a good venue for it. Her family raises money for various charities. This one tomorrow is to support the Illiteracy Foundation for humans. I'm sure she picked the venue so I'd donate money, too."

"Why did she say no?" I asked.

"I'm not sure. We'll find out tomorrow. It's also wise if you know Ms. Costner is a natural-born vampire who decided not to make the change. Before you ask, I don't know the story there at all," Dad said.

"You know Kate is going to be there, Dad." I knew Webb had told him, and maybe he had some insight about why she would be there.

"I do, pumpkin. Which is another thing we need to discuss, but we'll do that tomorrow." Dad stood, indicating the conversation was over. "Jo, your phone and a new key for the apartment are sitting on your bed. You two behave while I'm gone." Dad snatched his keys off the table near the door before he left the apartment.

"I need to see Tripp." Sam grabbed his phone then unfolded himself from the couch.

"I'm sorry I didn't tell you about Ben and me," I said as I looked up at him.

"It's okay, Sis." He tapped his heart twice. Our sign, which meant he loved me. Then he walked out, closing the door behind him.

What a welcome-home gift. After several minutes, I decided I wasn't going to think about Ben. I couldn't do anything for him right now, or maybe ever.

6

I'd played with my new phone, familiarizing myself with the apps. I'd also located my number, buried in the settings section. My only dilemma was I didn't know anyone else's phone numbers. I wanted to call Webb. After returning home yesterday, I hadn't seen or heard from him.

Dad had said Webb was catching up on work. I contemplated a quest to search him out, but I didn't want to bother him. He did have a job to do. Besides, I would see him tonight, although I was hoping I would get to spend a few minutes alone with him before the fundraiser.

Dad and Sam had left early this morning to pick up their tuxedos and my dress. According to Dad, Ms. Costner had a dress for me to wear for the black-tie gala. How she knew my size was beyond me. The last time she saw me, I was shorter and straighter in the hips. My new vampire body had graced me with some curves. I wasn't complaining. I loved my new physical appearance. Not to mention the toned muscles, thanks to Olivia's stringent workouts. The only thing I didn't care for was the dark purple streaks that ran through my black hair.

I was lounging on the couch, playing with my phone, when it rang. I slid the bar on the screen from left to right to answer. "Hello."

"Good morning, beautiful," Webb said. His raspy voice set my stomach tumbling in a frenzy.

"Hey, baby."

He growled and sighed at the same time.

"Something wrong?" My body warmed.

"You know I love to hear you say my pet name."

Yeah, I did. "So, am I going to see you before tonight?"

"That's one of the reasons why I'm calling. I have a few minutes. Where are you?"

"Um...I'm in the apartment." Dad didn't want me to go with him. He'd said he didn't want to worry about me, that there were too many risks, and tonight was going to be challenging enough.

That reasoning was weak at best in my book, but I hadn't argued. Dad's nerves seemed to be torn to shreds already.

"I'll be right up." The phone went dead.

Two minutes later, there was a knock on the door.

I flew off the couch and hesitated at the door. I didn't want to seem too anxious, and I had to get the butterflies in my stomach under control. I took some deep breaths.

My visitor's knuckles rapped again. I slowly opened the door. His woodsy scent trickled in.

I swept my gaze over Webb's muscular body, absorbing every detail of the imposing soldier. His black cargo uniform hugged all the right curves from head to toe. His brown hair hung loose around his shoulders.

His heart-stopping gaze scrutinized me as though he was deciding which part of me to taste first, causing my eyes to flash vampire. I would've run to him, but my legs wouldn't move. He bit his bottom lip, and I let out a soft groan. His fangs descended.

In one heartbeat, the world shifted. Sweat pearled on my nape. A single droplet started a slow descent down along my spine. I stood statue-still as the lone bead trickled down my back, cresting over each vertebra before picking up speed to keep time with my out-of-control pulse.

When he kicked shut the heavy steel door, the spell broke. He grabbed me by the waist and lifted me into his arms.

I buried my face in his hair as my hands locked around his neck. My fangs shot out as I inhaled his scent of earth and male—a powerful male. Suddenly, I wanted to taste his blood again. I had to taste his blood again.

"Legs around my waist," he commanded in a voice I wasn't familiar with.

I did as he instructed as though he weaved another spell.

His hands snaked under the back of my shirt, and I inhaled sharply.

"Where's your brother?" he asked as his fangs grazed the column of my neck.

"With my father off base."

Every inch of me tingled as he slid his hands down to cup my butt. Strength and power slammed into me as his heart pounded against his chest. He carried me to the kitchen and set me down on the counter, the cold granite surface cooling the heat radiating off my body.

He kissed his way from my ear to my mouth—where our tongues tangled, each one fighting for control. I nibbled on his tongue then captured his bottom lip and suckled, tasting more of him, needing more of him.

He groaned, low and deep, running his fists through my hair. He abandoned my lips, settling on the column of my neck. I turned to give him better access; his fangs scraped along my skin. His tongue teased, and his lips explored as though he were searching for the right spot. The sensation and anticipation was downright sinful, which made my body quiver with need. A need that I hadn't known existed.

"I want you to taste me," I whispered low.

His mouth stopped cold. He rested his forehead against mine, breathing heavily. His tongue snaked out and licked my lips. "Not yet."

"Then when?" I pouted, slipping my hands under his shirt, a place I'd come to love about the hard-bodied vampire. I relished every hill and valley along his abs. But the best part was how he reacted when my hand slid just below his navel. I loved hearing him moan and the way his body tensed and quaked.

He closed his eyes as though my touch took away all his demons.

"You haven't answered me." Mindlessly, I withdrew my hands.

His eyes flew open, and he pouted. "Put them back."

Leaning back against the cupboard, I crossed my arms over my chest. "No," I teased. I had a bit of control over the vampire soldier.

"You're playing with fire, Jo," he warned, a smile twisting his lips.

I quirked an eyebrow.

"You don't believe me," he drawled before gently grabbing my nape with one hand and drawing me closer to him with the other. My breasts smashed against his chest, soft to hard, with my butt teetering on the edge of the counter.

"Webb, it's a simple answer," I said, giggling.

"I'll make you a deal," he offered. "You put those magical hands back on my stomach, and I'll tell you when you'll be ready."

I snorted. He made me sound as if I was a piece of steak.

"Are you going to stick a fork in me to see if I'm done?" I asked sarcastically. I couldn't help myself.

"Deal or not, Jo. You decide."

Oh, what the hell. I snaked my hands under his shirt again, staring into his vampire-obsidian orbs.

Blinking long lashes, he groaned. "You make me crazy."

I rubbed his abs, his chest, before slipping my hands around to his back.

The alpha vampire was complete putty in my hands. I continued to explore, running my nails along his back and everywhere my hands could go. He purred instead of growled—a sound that left me clothed in goose bumps.

I'd kept my part of the deal. "It's your turn."

Smiling, his hands coasted up my thigh. "Thank you." Then he stepped away. "Your blood-lust should be under control in about another month or so, if it's not already. Vampire law states new vampires must wait four months before they can take blood when necessary from another vampire. But vampires usually don't drink from each other unless..." He sauntered over to me, his hands taking hold of mine. "Unless it's an emergency or there's an"—his eyes latched onto mine—"intimate connection." His voice was all kinds of sexy.

I swallowed hard, loud enough to be heard above the compressor on the fridge.

Heat infused my cheeks and shot throughout my body as though my blood was gasoline and someone had lit the match.

"You're blushing, Jo," he said.

No kidding.

"But the law applies to me, not you. I want *you* to taste my blood."

He pressed his body against my knees while his hands trailed up my legs. "Until you're free and clear of the law, that won't happen," he said, gentle but resolute.

After a long moment of silence, he lifted me off the counter then set me down on two shaky legs. "Let's talk about something else. I think we both need a break."

Wasn't that the truth? I wasn't going to argue, either. I had to process what he'd said. It seemed the intimacy of the act was as if I would be losing my virginity, and I wasn't ready for that. Or was I?

WEBB and I spent the rest of our alone time programming my phone with numbers for my dad, Sam, a few of the sentinels, the control room, and, of course, him. After we finished, he had to leave to get ready for the fundraiser. For him, it wasn't about getting dressed in a tuxedo, even though I couldn't wait to see him in one. He had to meet with the sentinels to ensure plans were set for the security detail at the event tonight.

Afternoon pressed in by the time Dad and Sam returned, hands full of garment and shopping bags. They placed everything on the chaise lounge by the window. I jumped off the couch to investigate. My jaw dropped when I peeked in one of the bags.

"You guys went shopping for shoes?" I asked incredulously, pulling out a shoebox.

Sam flicked his thumb at Dad. "He did. I waited outside. I don't do shopping."

I wasn't surprised. As a human, Sam hated when I wanted to go to the mall to look at clothes I couldn't afford to buy.

"But I thought you were picking up your tuxes. Don't they give you shoes with your tuxes?" I didn't know the first thing about renting a tux, but I watched a movie once in which the groom was getting fitted for a tux, and the store had a selection of shoes for him to pick out.

"Those shoes are for you, Sis."

"What?" My jaw dropped lower.

What planet was I on? My father was buying me shoes? Oh, I had to see what kind of taste he had.

"Before you freak, I know a thing or two about ladies' fashion."

Both Sam and I laughed uncontrollably.

My father raised then lowered his eyebrows as if to say, *Fine. See for yourself.*

I flipped the lid on the first shoebox, and my eyes grew wide. The silver high-heeled sandals were exquisite. I threw down the box and hugged my dad, who was standing next to me with a smug grin on his face.

"Thank you," I said.

"You're welcome, pumpkin. They should fit. I went in your room and checked your shoe size from a few pairs you had in your closet."

"What about the dress? Will they match?"

Dad, the old-fashioned vampire, actually rolled his eyes like some teenager. "Your dress is in this white garment bag. Yes, they do match. Also, I did check your size while I was in your room. Ms. Costner had the gown tailored yesterday to fit you. I would've had you fitted for it, but there wasn't time. Don't worry. It will fit," he said, no doubt responding to my perplexed expression or thoughts.

I unzipped the bag. A stunning midnight-blue evening gown hung inside. I eased the chiffon dress from the bag as though the strapless beauty would shatter if I didn't handle it with care. My gaze caressed every detail of the knotted sweetheart neckline that carved out the breasts, falling to an empire waist with diamond-studded beads.

The skirt had shirring just above the hips and draped effortlessly to the floor.

"Close your mouth, Sis," Sam said as he leaned against the back of the couch with his legs crossed at the ankles.

Tears clouded my vision.

"Hey, pumpkin. What's wrong?" Dad asked.

"I've...never..."

"It's okay. I know life hasn't been easy for you. This is a borrowed dress, but I can buy you one of your own." Dad wiped a tear from my cheek.

I felt like Cinderella all of sudden. I've never had anything so beautiful in my life. In foster care, Sam and I always got hand-me-downs.

"I'm going to my room," Sam announced. "I need to catch a few winks for this boring thing tonight." He disappeared.

"Pumpkin, I need to check on a few things and brief Webb on my visit with the guardians. Why don't you make sure the dress and shoes fit and rest up?"

I nodded. We only had a couple of hours before we had to leave. So Dad collected his tuxedo and went to his room. I did the same with my things and went to my room and laid out the dress on my bed.

I slipped on the shoes. Fortunately, they fit perfectly. They also had a low enough heel that I didn't need to learn how to walk in them. I'd seen some girls at the human high school who had worn heels so high they could barely walk. Satisfied the shoes fit, I tried on the gown and traipsed over to the mirror.

Tears came to my eyes. The gown fit like a glove.

Now I had a major dilemma—my hair. I had no clue how to do anything with my hair except a ponytail, and the outfit needed elegance, not screaming tomboy.

An idea tumbled out of my brain. I quickly changed back into my jeans and ran to Dad's room. I knocked. "Dad?"

He came to the door. "What is it?" he asked, walking toward his desk.

He'd completely rearranged his room. The cabinet that had displayed all the guns, daggers, and swords was now lined with books. Unsurprisingly, the titles displayed on the spines involved military and weapons. The bed had been moved to the wall left of the door, which made the room look bigger. Where the bed had been, between the bathroom and closet door, now sat his safe. Actually it appeared to be a new safe, if I weren't mistaken.

Dad sat down at a small wooden desk on the right wall adjacent to the cabinets.

"Where's Olivia?" I asked.

"Not sure. Why?" He busied himself with reading the screen on his laptop.

"I need her help." I shoved my hands into my back pockets.

"Okay. Why don't you call her?"

Crap. Why didn't I think of that? Webb had helped me program her number into my cell. I guess I wasn't used to having my own phone.

"Thanks, Dad." I ran to my room, grabbed my phone, and called her.

After two rings, she picked up. "Hello."

"Olivia? Jo here."

"Oh. Hey." She sounded surprised.

"Um, I was wondering if you could help me with something."

"What is it? You want to train?"

I laughed. Boy, that was the furthest thing from my mind right now. "No. I need some help with my hair for this evening."

I needed my best friend, Darcy. She was the fashion queen. But I couldn't expect her to rush over here, not without Dad's permission—she was human. Plus, time was of the essence. I had to call her at some point, though. I hadn't spoken to her in a few days.

Olivia laughed. "You know, Jo, I don't do much with mine."

"Yeah, but your hair always looks nice in the French braid."

Dead silence answered me. I almost thought she'd hung up. Then she cleared her throat. "Okay. I've been to a few of these soirees. I'll be up in about an hour."

I had time to shower, so I did. Thirty minutes later, I emerged from the bathroom and banged on Sam's door.

"Enter," he said.

I poked in my head. "The shower is all yours."

"Thanks." He sat up, resting his own head against the headboard.

"What did you and Dad do today, other than shopping?" I walked into his dark room.

His bed butted against a wall, in between two windows. Two nightstands stood on each side of the bed. A dresser and a desk lined one wall, and a chair sat adjacent to a closet door.

"We checked out the place where they're having the charity benefit. I ran into Ms. Costner, too. She wasn't surprised we were vampires. She said she knew."

"Wow. How could she tell?" I sat down on his bed.

"She mentioned something about scent and our eyes. Your eyes did shift the last time we were in her class."

I wasn't surprised. I'd gotten into a scuffle with Blake Turner just before her class. "Did she say anything about why she hadn't turned vampire?"

"No. We're heading over there early so she can talk with both of us before the party starts." He lifted his arm and placed a hand behind his head.

"Where is it?" I picked a piece of lint off his brown comforter.

"Her father's house. He lives up in the Highlands, in one of those humongous homes on the top of the hill."

"You mean like Ben's house."

"No. Ten times bigger."

"Speaking of Ben, has he called you or anything?" I asked hesitantly, keeping my eyes on the comforter.

Sam grabbed my hand, and I looked up.

"You can't talk to Ben or see him, Jo. You got that? I know you want to help him but let Pops." Fear laced his tone.

"Hey, I know you're scared. But how the heck

am I going to see him? He's not going to be there tonight, is he?"

"No. Why would he? This is a charity event for the illiterate kids Ms. Costner supports—which, by the way, humans will be attending. I think that is one of the reasons why Pops is freaking out. We're still new vamps, and he thinks our bloodlust might be a problem." He let go of my hand.

"He's not worried about Kate?"

"Not really." He pushed a hand through his hair. "According to Pops, she wouldn't try anything at a public event. Although he's not one hundred percent certain."

"If Dad is so worried about our bloodlust and all, then why are we even going? Why couldn't Ms. Costner just come over here?"

"I asked Pops that, too. His response was we need to learn how to live among humans, and he can't keep us locked up forever. Plus, Ms. Costner coaxed him into donating a lot of money for this charity. Look, if someone makes you mad tonight, don't get into your *Carrie* mode. Okay?"

"Ha, ha," I said sarcastically.

There was a knock on the apartment door.

"That's Olivia," I said as I stood then turned to leave.

"Jo?" Sam called.

With my hand on the doorjamb, I glanced over my shoulder.

"You're going to look pretty tonight."

I smiled wide. "Thanks, Sam." I tapped my heart twice then headed for the apartment door.

Dad came out of his room. "I have to get something out of my office. I'll need you and Sam ready to leave in one hour." He passed Olivia at the door. "Petty Officer Brock, are you ready for this evening?"

"Yes, sir."

"Good. We can't have anything go wrong," Dad said then left.

Olivia and I went into my room. She was wearing short yoga pants and a tank top.

She set her sport bag on the bed. "We'll have to make this quick, since I still have to change into my uniform. Do you want your hair up?" she asked, all business.

"I think so." I sat on the bed.

She eyed the dress then opened her bag. "Okay. Let's get started. I think your hair will look best with the sweetheart neckline." She removed a small curling iron, a brush, and several hairpins from her bag.

I shifted into a position on the bed to give her better access to the back of my head. After plugging in the curling iron, she brushed out my hair. She curled, braided, pinned, teased, and sprayed. Within five minutes, she had my hair up and in place.

"Before you look in the mirror, I want to chat a minute." She grabbed something from the front pocket of her bag before joining me on the bed. She tucked one leg underneath the other.

I did the same.

"I know you haven't trained with any weapons yet, but just in case something goes wrong tonight, I want you to have this." She uncurled her fingers, revealing a small thin rectangular metal box.

It reminded me of one of those magnetic hide-a-key contraptions, only smaller. How was a metal box going to help me?

"I know what you're thinking. This is actually a Taser." She slid back the top. "This button inside"—she pointed to it—"is what you will push to activate the Taser. It's not going to kill anyone, but it will slow an attacker down. The Taser is cobalt, and it does pack a powerful punch. You can slip it between your breasts."

"Cool. Sometimes I feel like I'm part of a James Bond movie."

She laughed. It was the first time I'd seen her

laugh or even smile. All the sentinels were rather reserved by nature.

She closed the box and absently scratched her leg. "Keep it tucked away. The banded bodice should keep it from falling out. I don't expect any trouble tonight, but you never know."

A half-inch scar marred the skin above her right knee. Where did she get that?

"Any questions, Jo?" She handed me the Taser.

"Not really. It seems simple. Can I ask you something?"

She nodded.

"Is that a battle wound on your knee?"

"It is, but not a military one," she answered softly, not with the hard soldier tone she usually used. "I pissed off a boy in catechism when I was a little girl. He chased me for, like, five miles, all the way to my house. When I got to the gate of the yard, I hesitated. That's when he drove a knife into my leg." The edge of her mouth turned upward. "From that day on, I never let my guard down. That one incident taught me a lot."

She rose from the bed, went over to her bag, and fished out a silver clip.

Her story reminded me of my own stabbing by my foster dad. I absently rubbed the scar on my face.

"You want to talk about it?" she asked.

"I try to forget about it, but it's hard when I'm reminded of that night every time I look in the mirror."

"Did he..."

"No. If Sam hadn't shown up, I'm not sure I would even be here. The creep was going to have his way with me whether I was dead or alive." Tears suddenly stung my eyes. I wanted my foster dad to pay for what he'd done.

"Have you talked to anyone else about this?" she asked gently.

"No. If I do, like now, I shift between crying and anger, and all I want to do is hunt the asshole down and kill him. And since I can't..."

"Jo. Do you believe in karma?"

I shrugged one shoulder as I traced the outline of my scar. "I've never thought about it."

"The brute will get his due. The boy who stabbed me got his. My parents wanted me to report him to the police, but I didn't. I thought I could take care of the situation myself. Then the following week, when I walked into catechism class, he wasn't there. I asked about him afterwards, and a girl in class said he'd been sent away to a school for delinquents."

I hoped karma would knock on my foster dad's door one day.

She grabbed a can of hairspray. "Why don't you see if your hair passes inspection? I'll spray it and add this clip."

Standing, I took the small mirror she held in her hand. I walked over to the dresser then positioned myself so I could check out her masterpiece. "Wow! You did a fantastic job."

I had a small part on the right side of my head, where Olivia had woven a loose French braid that traveled from the front to back over my ear. Each section of hair outside of the braid had been teased and loosely twisted before being secured with bobby pins. My straight hair was a mess of curls, all strategically pinned.

"The hairstyle is called a twisty hawk," she explained, securing the small silver clip just above my right ear where the French braid began. "I learned the style for one of the balls I had to attend when I was younger."

I was in awe.

"My mom relates this style to a Mohawk, though it's an elegant take on the style. Hence the name Twisty Hawk."

I could see why she likened this style to a Mohawk. My hair had raised curls on top of my head to the nape of my neck. "It's amazing. Thank you so much."

She applied hairspray. "Webb's heart is going to fall out of his chest when he sees you," she said in a low voice, as though hesitant to bring up his name.

We locked gazes in the mirror.

I'd never spoken to the sentinels about anything personal. Actually, this was the first time I'd spent any time with Olivia outside of training. I'd bet she knew more about my life than I did about hers, if only because the sentinels had been protecting Sam and me from our archenemy, the Plutariums. Still, I wondered if Webb had told her or any of the sentinels about him and me.

Then again, I didn't know what special abilities Olivia had. She might be an Empath, able to feel the emotions between Webb and me, or she might just be very observant.

"How do you know?" I asked.

"It's hard not to see, Jo. Remember when he came into the training room, the day you and Sam were fighting with poles?"

I nodded as I stared at her in the mirror.

"That was when it clicked for me. But my suspicions were confirmed when I visited him in the medical facility and found you sleeping in his arms."

Well, that was proof enough, I guess.

"Webb is like a brother to me, Jo. Whatever you do, please don't break his heart," she said, almost pleading. "Or else I'll have to hunt you down and kill you." She winked and smiled. "Seriously though, I hate to see either one of you hurt."

I had no intentions of breaking his heart. Although I knew we'd probably fight about things like any couple.

She turned away and began packing her bag. "Oh, and one more thing," she said, whipping out a compact. "Let's apply a little blush. That's all you need." She brushed on a small amount of pink blush.

A knock sounded on the door. "Jo," Dad said. "You need to be ready in fifteen minutes."

"No problem," I replied.

"Okay. You're ready," Olivia announced, fiddling with something in my hair. "Slip on the dress, make sure you carry the Taser, and have a great time." She retrieved her bag before heading for the door. Opening it, she turned. "Jo, thanks for asking me to do this for you. I enjoyed it." Her brown eyes sparkled. "I'm here if you need anything at all. I know that this life can be challenging, especially among all the men."

"I appreciate that," I said.

"See you tonight." Then she was gone.

I stood frozen for a few seconds, overwhelmed by our time together. I did need a girl to talk to. I loved Darcy, but our friendship was strained because of the difference in our species. I had made a new friend at St. Anne's Academy, the vampire high school, but Zea didn't live close by. Plus I wasn't sure I would see her anytime soon since I wasn't allowed back to school until after the court hearing.

I slipped into my dress, and I had begun to strap my feet into the sandals when Dad's voice sounded from the hall. "Jo, can I come in?"

"It's open." Sandals on, I walked over to the mirror to make sure everything was in place. My mouth fell open. Was that me? Holy...

"Cow," Dad said, finishing my thought. "You look amazing." His wide green eyes reflected in the mirror as he stood near the door dressed in a tuxedo with a velvet box in his hand.

Before I could process anything else, Sam sidled up next to him, messing with the bow tie on his tux. He opened his mouth then closed it. "Holy crap. Is that my sister?"

I smiled. "That tux looks a lot better than the school uniform."

Did it ever. Sam had his black hair tied back in a low ponytail, just like Dad. His green eyes stood out over the black tux and white shirt. Again, just like Dad. If it weren't for the lines around Dad's eyes and forehead, I probably couldn't tell them apart.

"We should go," Dad said. "But before we do, I wanted you to wear this tonight, Jo." He walked over to me then opened a velvet box. "It was your mother's. She wanted you to have it when the time was right. I don't know if there will ever be a right time, but this feels like one." Melancholy tinged his voice.

A necklace graced the inside of the pretty box, a blood-red ruby sparkling in the center of a square diamond. My lips parted.

"It's beautiful, Dad. But I can't wear that. It looks too expensive. What if I lose it?" I'd never owned any jewelry, let alone something that looked as if it cost a fortune.

"I insist. Your mother would be disappointed if you didn't wear it. Turn around."

"Can you tell me more about Mom?" I knew little about her. Dad had only shared pictures and said how he'd loved her.

"When we have more time." He latched the chain in place.

"Thank you, Dad." I kissed him on the cheek.

"You're welcome, pumpkin." He held out his arm. "Let's go. We need to meet with Alia before the function begins. And Webb is waiting downstairs."

At the mention of his name, my stomach started quivering.

7

On the elevator ride down, I took in a few calming breaths, attempting to tame the beasts burrowing in the pit of my stomach. I smoothed my hand over my dress, absently touching the Taser, which seemed to be burning against the skin between my breasts. My imagination was on a collision course to the freak-out zone.

Several questions contributed to my edginess, but only one had my palms clammy. Would Webb like the dress?

The elevator doors opened, and cold air whooshed in. Sam exited first. Dad offered his elbow. Without hesitation, I grabbed onto him. Anything to keep me upright.

"Breathe, pumpkin. Webb will falter where he stands when he sees you."

Sam walked ahead of us as we passed the circular reception desk in the middle of the lobby.

"Can you do me a favor?" I asked Dad.

"What is it?" Dad's gaze darted to the sentinel guarding the door.

"Please stay out of my head tonight." Even though I'd gotten used to Dad reading my mind, I couldn't have him skipping through my brain, especially when I saw Webb in the next few minutes.

"We're taking two cars anyway, Jo. You and Webb will be in one car. Sam and I are riding together."

A small bit of tension waned as I searched for my date. "I thought you said Webb was downstairs?"

Dad placed his hand on mine—the one gripping his forearm like a vise. "He's outside."

"Commander," the sentinel at the door said.

"Lane, good evening. Make sure the doors are secure when we leave," Dad ordered.

"Ms. Mason." Lane nodded, his soft bronze eyes glistening.

The warm air coated my skin as Dad and I strode out into the humid night. Light sprayed down from the lamppost on the median across from us. I didn't need light to know Webb stood to my left. I drank in his delicious woodsy scent, and my heart fluttered.

For some reason, I sought out my brother. Why? I didn't know. Sam leaned casually against a black SUV, his hair tied back in a low ponytail, his green eyes glinting my way. As though he knew my reticence, he tapped his heart twice. A gesture of ours to say we loved each other and everything would be okay.

Whether I was okay or not, desperation or anticipation made me turn. Or maybe Webb's presence pulled me to him. Regardless, when his eyes latched on to mine, my heart roared in my ears.

If anyone were talking to me, I wasn't listening. My focus fixed on the vampire standing near a sleek black car, dressed in a tuxedo that made him look...imposing, beautiful. He swept a languid gaze along the length of my body, and my pulse quickened.

Fortunately, Dad walked me over to him. I didn't think my feet would move.

A slow smile graced Webb's lips as we approached. Lips I wanted to kiss.

If Dad were reading my mind, I didn't care one bit. He pried my hand from his arm. The small sensation seemed to get the blood moving inside me again.

"Webb," Dad said, breaking through some of the fog in my head. "Have the sentinels left?"

"Yes, sir. They're on their way." His gaze never wavered from mine.

"Good. Sam and I will meet you there."

"Yes, sir." Webb took my hand. Electricity skittered up my arm before his husky voice filled my head.

You've taken my breath away before, but nothing—absolutely nothing—like right at this moment. Your radiance consumes me, your beauty captures my soul, and your presence makes the world around me disappear. You are my beautiful angel.

His words sent a shiver up my spine and fire down my belly.

"Be careful," Dad added, walking away.

"We will," Webb answered Dad.

Webb grabbed the handle of the Audi. "I want to kiss you desperately." He opened the door. His hand nestled against my lower back.

I lifted my skirt and slid in slowly.

Webb said something to Sentinel Lane before he climbed in on the driver's side. Wasting no time, he started the vehicle and shifted into gear. Silence filled the space as we wound through the base and out the main gate. After several turns and traffic lights, he flicked on the blinker and turned left into a parking lot.

Mmm! What was it with him and parking lots?

He released his seat belt and let out a growl before he leaned close to me. I followed his lead, silently cursing the console separating us.

His warm lips brushed mine as his fingers traced the curve of my sweetheart neckline. "You are stunning, Jo."

"And I'm crazy about you," I whispered.

His hand froze. He pulled back slightly, his eyes searching mine as if in search of the answer to unasked questions.

Did I say something wrong? Maybe "crazy" wasn't the word to use.

His piercing gaze continued, making me very uneasy all of a sudden.

"We need to go." His tone hardened. He strapped his seat belt around him.

I didn't move. My forearm rested on the console while I stared at him. What just happened? He went from the lovable Webb to a cold soldier, as if I'd told him I hated him. I was about to ask him what was wrong, but his phone rang.

Damn it.

He drove out of the lot, ignoring the sound. No

sooner had the phone stopped ringing than it trilled again, cutting through the quiet.

I flinched.

He answered. "Yes, Commander. No problem. Sure. We're almost there."

The tension between us skyrocketed with every turn and stoplight. What the hell? Tears would not be shed tonight. I interlaced my fingers in my lap to keep him from noticing them shake. I struggled to understand why he would react this way to what I'd said. I'd told him yesterday that he made my world better. He didn't wig out then. So why now?

My door opened, and a chill skittered up my arm. When had we stopped? I flicked off my seat belt, and a white-gloved hand reached in for mine. In one fluid motion, I swiveled, planted two feet on the brick pavement, and accepted the offer for help.

"Thank you," I said to the valet dressed in black pants and a short red jacket with a white shirt underneath.

"Ma'am," he responded as he escorted me to the two-story portico held up by classical columns.

Webb spoke with one of the valets. Two more cars rolled in behind Webb's Audi. Ladies exited the vehicles with the help of more valets. Their gowns glimmered under the muted spotlights shining on the Colonial Mansion. Music spilled out from the house as a door opened. Webb patted one of the valets on the back then strode over to me.

He extended his elbow, and I hesitated, searching his face. He lifted his eyebrows as if to say, "Well?"

The vampire was confusing me tonight. I wanted to desperately ask him what happened in the car, but this wasn't the time. So I raised the skirt of my dress with one hand and took hold of his arm with the other. Instead of going into the mansion, we headed toward a lighted path nestled between a canopy of trees.

"Alia Costner is waiting for you at the guest house," Webb said sweetly, as though whatever bothered him in the car was now gone.

As we stepped under the tunnel of trees, I couldn't take it anymore. "What's wrong, Webb?"

I inhaled, absorbing the sweet fragrance of the slew of flowers bordering the path. Lavender, lilacs, roses, lilies, and jasmine lingered in the air.

Webb was breathing but not talking. What the heck?

We'd just passed a cement bench when a shiver crept up my spine. I stopped, checking my surroundings. Water trickled from somewhere in the gardens. The warm air turned cold all of a sudden. Rubbing my arms, I looked at Webb. He too scanned the trees, flowerbeds, and beyond.

"What is it?" I asked.

"Not sure. It's probably nothing. Let's go. The cottage isn't far." He kept scanning the area as we made our way down the path.

"Are you going to talk to me about what happened in the car?" I looked around as well.

"*No*," he said emphatically. "We'll talk later."

Let it go for now, my inner voice told me. I wasn't sure I could. Tears threatened. *Don't cry. Don't cry.*

We stopped walking.

He turned and framed my face in his strong hands. "I promise we'll talk later. Okay?"

I nodded as I stared into his onyx eyes, seeking clues to his ire. Yeah, like I could read minds.

He dipped his head and planted a chaste kiss on my lips.

"Sis, Ms. Costner is waiting." Sam's voice was somewhere near.

Webb stepped back. "Go with Sam," Webb said softly.

I didn't want to go anywhere until we talked.

"Sis," Sam said. "You can see Webb later."

I reluctantly walked away.

ANOTHER SHIVER CREPT up my spine when we arrived at the cottage. Again I scanned the area. Nothing. Shaking it off, I entered the home. My senses immediately went on high alert at the cinnamon fragrance that tickled my nostrils, matching Kate's unique vampire scent. I straightened my spine. Was she here? I clenched my fists at the thought.

"Jo, dear." Ms. Costner glided gracefully toward me, smoothing out her black gown. Her blond hair was twisted up into a chignon, her bangs swept to the side. "Good to see you again." She kissed me on my left cheek then the right. "Come. Let's sit for a spell." She interlinked her arm with mine.

I found it odd that her human scent didn't bother me. Then I recalled what Ms. Lawrence had said to Dad, that Ms. Costner had the unique ability to mask her humanity.

We crossed the foyer into a sitting room. Dark browns and blues colored the fabric curtains and walls. Two loveseats faced each other, separated by a rectangular coffee table, and a stone fireplace graced the wall adjacent to the sofas.

A blond teenage boy lazed near the fireplace with a beady-eyed dog at his feet. Instinctively, my nostrils flared, and my fangs slid out.

"Jo." Sam darted out of nowhere, blocking my view of the human.

"It's all right, Sam," Ms. Costner said. "She's reacting to Biker's blood. I didn't mask his scent."

The dog growled, as if in annoyance that she didn't protect him.

"Weird," Sam said. "I didn't react like that. Then again, Jo seems more sensitive to scents than me."

"You're making Biker nervous, Sam," the blond boy said.

Sam stepped to the side.

"Jo, this is my son, Matthew." Ms. Costner waved a hand at him.

"Hi," he said.

I nodded. "Nice to meet you."

Ms. Costner guided me to one of the loveseats. Sam and the blond eased down onto the other. The dog stayed on his haunches in front of the crackling fire.

"You're nervous, aren't you?" Her blue eyes sparkled beneath her heavily mascaraed lashes.

"Something isn't right around here," I replied. The path, the gardens, and the scents floating in the air were definitely unsettling.

"What you're feeling is magic," she said. "My home and gardens are protected by a spell." Ms. Costner lifted her glass from the tables and sipped on the red liquid.

I wasn't surprised about the magic, but I was curious about the liquid in her glass. Why was she drinking blood?

"That dress looks amazing on you," she said. "I wasn't sure if your father gave me your right size or not."

"Thank you for letting me borrow it, Ms. Costner. It's gorgeous."

She placed a well-manicured hand on my knee. "Please call me Alia. So, your father tells me you're showing early signs of your powers. What are they, if I may ask?"

Sam chuckled.

"What are you laughing at?" I glanced at my brother.

"My sister is very talented," he said, adjusting his bow tie.

My gaze slipped from Sam to Matthew. "You're human, right?"

"I am. Why?" His voice was deep.

"Just curious. And are you a natural-born vampire?"

"No." He shook his head, smiling and seeming pleased.

"Jo, neither Matthew nor I are vampires. My son doesn't carry the vampire gene, either," Ms. Costner stated outright.

Dr. Vieira had once explained that genetically natural-born vampires were produced of a male vampire and a human female who had a blood type of Vel-negative, which meant that Matthew's father wasn't a vampire.

"So why are you drinking blood?" I dropped my gaze to the glass in her hand then back to her.

"Ah," she said. "The short answer is because I have to. The long answer is for another day. Now, let's talk about your powers. I need to see if I can help you."

I accepted her answer because I had to. Her authoritative tone reminded me of my dad. "I thought you didn't want to help me."

"It's not that simple."

"Just tell her," Sam piped in.

Ms. Costner withdrew her hand from my knee and tangled her fingers around the stem of the glass.

I shifted where I sat. "I can make things move

without touching them. I seem to have two of the elements. And I can speak telepathically."

"You can?" Sam leaned forward, elbows on his knees. "Just don't get in my head, Sis. You know I hate that."

I guessed I hadn't told anyone about my mind-speaking ability except Webb. *Whatever.* All I wanted to do was get out of the stuffy room. Maybe it was the magic or the cinnamon fragrance making me antsy. I had to find Webb. I had to be there when he spoke to Kate. What if she tried to kill him again? I couldn't let that happen.

"So how are you going to help me?" I turned my attention back to Ms. Costner.

"Which elements?" she queried.

"Water and air. And if I ever have fire, I just might puke."

Matthew laughed.

My sentiments exactly.

"Mmm." Ms. Costner rose, setting down her glass. "We should go. The guests will be arriving, and I have to meet the head of the Illiteracy Foundation."

"Huh? Ms. Cost...Alia, you haven't answered my question."

"I'm not sure yet, Jo. You have many powers for

such a young vampire. Your father tells me they're strong, too."

"But Ms. Lawrence seems to think you can help me learn to control them."

"Jo, the reason why I told your father no was I don't have the capability to help you. Your powers seem too strong. I would be more than happy to tutor you and Sam in your studies of math and such."

"But Sam is going back to school."

"Pops wants me to hang around the base right now. If you can get tutored, then we both can sit through the sessions together at the library." My brother smirked. He would give his fangs to ditch school or not wear the uniform he hated.

"Why would everyone think you could help me with my powers, then?"

Ms. Costner petted Biker on the snout. "Matthew, please grab my purse from the table in the foyer."

Without a word, Matthew obeyed his mother.

"Both of you," Ms. Costner started, "have grown so much from when I last saw you as humans. Sam, when I heard what had happened, I was devastated. I truly am glad you survived that ordeal with your uncle. Jo, I can't say I'm surprised at how you turned out. The last day in my classroom, I knew it was a matter of time before your life changed. But what you've grown into in almost three months' time is remarkable. And I will admit I can help new vampires get their powers under control, but only those who have weak abilities. You, Jo, don't fall into that category. Telekinesis and elements are unheard of at your stage. I mean, we haven't seen anyone in our world with telekinesis since your grandfather."

I had all sorts of questions for her: Why hadn't she made the change? How could she do magic if she wasn't a vampire? How did she know my grandfather?

Matthew poked in his head. "Mom, we should go."

I unfolded myself from the couch, and Sam did the same.

"Jo, let's table this discussion. I'll make it a point to visit you. Maybe you can show me some of your talents, and I'll decide then. Plus I want to do some research. Until then, enjoy yourselves tonight. I'm glad you're both here and your father decided to come. And I'm also glad he donated a lot of money to the foundation."

We started for the main house. Sam escorted Ms. Costner while Matthew escorted me. He lightly explained the history of the property. His great-grandfather had settled in this area from the Azores many moons ago, in a small shack. Open fields had graced the five acres of the sprawling estate.

I gathered my gown and lifted it as I walked, careful not to trip over it.

"She's pretty," Matthew said.

"Thank you." I looked up at him.

"For what?" He angled his head.

"Didn't you just compliment me?"

"No."

"You didn't just say 'pretty'?"

He shook his head slightly. "I didn't say anything, Jo."

Then who did? It sounded like his voice. Maybe Sam was complimenting Ms. Costner. No. I knew my brother's voice. Still, I dialed my hearing to him and Ms. Costner, who were strolling along the path ahead of us, talking about math.

"The slope of the line would increase," he said to Ms. Costner.

Maybe there were little faeries protecting the place, and they were talking to me.

Inwardly, I cracked up. Faeries? Ha.

Don't discount the idea. Stranger things have happened, my inner voice reminded me.

"Wow, she smells wonderful."

There was the voice again, and it sounded like Matthew's, only not as deep. My gaze darted in all directions.

"Are you okay, Jo?" Matthew asked as we passed a cluster of peonies.

"I'm fine," I lied. "Are you sure you didn't utter a word?"

"You look a little pale," he said, ignoring my question.

It had to be all the magic, making me hear voices.

When we cleared the tunnel of trees, I let out a huge sigh, relieved to be away from the magic. Maybe I wouldn't hear any more voices. "Thank you for escorting me."

He placed a hand on the small of my back. "No problem. Are you ready? My mother masked the house with one of her spells so vampires don't get a whiff of the human scents. So you should be fine this evening."

All I could think was *Cool!*

Music tickled my ears as we entered through a side door, and into a wide hallway leading into an enormous ballroom. The large chandelier created sparkling diamonds on the black-and-white marble floor. Round tables and chairs were strategically positioned around the dance floor, where couples danced to the waltz. Ms. Costner and Matthew merged into the crowd.

"So what now?" Sam asked, casually scoping out the room.

If humans were present, I couldn't tell, even when I opened my senses. Whatever magic Ms. Costner weaved, it worked. "You're asking me? I've never been to one of these things."

"Like I have?" he asked.

Okay, so we were both new at this.

"I don't see Pops," Sam said.

I didn't care about Dad. I searched for one other vampire in particular: Webb.

The orchestra on stage switched from the waltz to another slow tune.

I was about to go in search of Webb when Ms. Costner walked up to Sam and me with a very large and tall man at her side.

"Dad, meet Sam and Jo Mason," Ms. Costner said.

I craned my neck. Unlike the sentinels, Mr. Costner had short brown hair, shaven at the sides and styled on top with some styling product.

He shook Sam's hand then mine. "My daughter has told me a lot about you two. Please make sure your father donates lots of money." An arrogant smile stretched his thin lips.

"Dad, Steven has already donated. You know that," Ms. Costner reminded him.

"Um...do the...humans here know about us vampires?"

Sam looked at me as if to say, "What a great question." I hadn't thought about it until now.

"Of course not," Mr. Costner said, as though I were an idiot for asking. "And we don't want them to." Lines formed around Mr. Costner's eyes. "You two are new vampires, so behave. I'm not sure why my daughter asked you to be here." He peered down at Ms. Costner. "This might be a mistake. Don't say I didn't warn you." Then his head bobbed as he pushed his way through the crowd.

Were Sam and I the reasons he'd asked the sentinels to help with security? Did he think we would attack the humans?

"Pay no attention to my father. He's just a worrywart."

If Ms. Costner was right about her father being a worrywart, he might have a very good reason, especially if the meeting between Kate and Webb didn't go well...or if Edmund showed up.

Matthew strode up with two glass flutes in his hand.

"I hope that's not champagne," Ms. Costner said to Matthew.

"Mom, of course not. It's sparkling water." He handed one to me.

I wrapped my fingers around the stem and sipped it. The bubbles in the water danced on my taste buds as they slithered down my throat.

"Sis, I'm going to find Pops. Will you be okay?" Sam touched my arm lightly.

"She'll be fine," Matthew answered for me.

I tapped my heart twice. Sam returned the gesture.

"Matthew, take care of Jo." Ms. Costner kissed her son on the cheek and excused herself.

"Well, what would you like to do?" he asked now that we were alone.

Oh, my. Did he think I was his date?

"Do you dance?" he asked.

I choked, almost spitting out the water.

"Okay, so you don't," he said, laughing.

He was rather handsome. I liked the way his blond curls were kind of wild in some spots, especially how they wound their way around the lower part of his ears. Darcy would love him. His eyes were crystal blue. His mother's were more bluish-green.

"Nope. Never have." I swept my gaze over the room again.

Where was Webb?

"Come, I'll teach you." He grasped my hand.

A tickle skated across my nape, and not from Matthew's touch.

Holding a human's hand. Do you think that's wise? Webb's voice was firm but gentle.

How did he know Matthew was human? The magic spell was working because I couldn't smell any humans, unless he knew Matthew?

"Something wrong, Jo?" Matthew tugged on me.

Before I could utter one word, Webb appeared out of nowhere at my side.

"There you are," Webb said. "We should sit."

Not letting go of my hand, Matthew sized up Webb.

I removed my hand from Matthew's, and Webb quickly wrapped an arm around my waist drawing me close to him. The vampire was either jealous or afraid for the human in my presence, or maybe a little of both. Regardless, I introduced them.

"Matthew, this is Webb, my father's lieutenant and my date for the evening." A date who was acting a little weird.

A look of disappointment washed over Matthew. "Nice to meet you." He nodded to Webb. "I'll see you later, Jo. Maybe a dance." He smiled weakly.

Webb's hand tightened on my hip as the music stopped.

"Please, everyone," Ms. Costner said through a microphone, "take your seats. Dinner will begin momentarily."

"That's my cue," Matthew sauntered toward his mom.

Webb tugged me into the hall. "Why were you holding his hand?" His face tightened.

"How did you know he was human?" I ignored his question, only because whatever answer I gave him wouldn't soothe the poor attitude that seemed to linger from our time in the car.

"You're avoiding my question." His eyes narrowed.

Even mad and jealous, the vampire stole the breath from my lungs.

"There you two are." Dad's voice filled the hallway. "We need to take our seats."

Webb and I were in a stare-down.

"Lieutenant, whatever is eating at you, drop it for now," Dad said in an even tone.

"Come on." I feigned a smile at Webb. I didn't want any trouble. Plus, this wasn't the place to have this conversation with him.

Dad stalked into the ballroom.

"Wait, Jo," Webb said.

"We need to—"

He moved in a blur, and his lips pressed to mine. I almost pushed him away. Almost. My instincts told me to let him take what he needed for now.

"Bizarre" summed up Webb's behavior and everything else that had transpired so far today, and I still had hours to go before the day ended.

The dinner went smoothly, although I didn't touch my food. Sam examined the chicken on his plate before pushing it away. Dad and Webb ate theirs. As the waiter poured the coffee, I glimpsed Dr. Vieira sitting at Alia Costner's table. He wore a red bow tie instead of the standard black one that everyone else was wearing with their tuxedos. His dark brown hair was slicked back, and the style seemed to enhance his round facial features. He nodded to me when our eyes met. I returned the gesture with a smile then diverted my gaze to Matthew, who was sitting next to Dr. Vieira. He too nodded my way. Then he leaned into Dr. Vieira and whispered something in his ear.

Was he asking about me? I tried to tune in to their conversation, since they sat two tables in front of us near the stage. But with the soft music playing overhead and others chatting, I couldn't hear. Not to mention, Webb growled low when he saw that Matthew was looking at me. Webb was still in a weird mood. One minute he was quiet, like in the car, and the next, he was jealous of a human giving me attention. I wasn't surprised. Webb acted this way when Ben was around me, although he might be wound tight since Kate was supposed to be here.

Dishes clashed and silverware clanged as the servers cleared the tables.

I leaned towards Webb. "Have you seen Kate?" Not that I was excited to see her.

"No." He laid his arm over the back of my chair and drew closer to me. "I'm not in the mood, anyway. It's best she isn't here."

"What? Are you serious? You wanted to talk to her." I slanted my head.

"I did. I do. But not here, especially—"

"Because you're grouchy," I finished for him.

He traced circles on my bare shoulder.

An elderly human couple presented themselves. The baldheaded man was dressed in a gray suit, making him stand out among the other men in their tuxes. The lady wore a soft pink gown that complemented the gray in her companion's attire.

"Is anyone sitting here?" the man asked as he pulled out the chair next to Dad.

"No, sir. Go ahead," Dad said.

"You missed dinner," Sam said as the man waited for the white-haired lady to sit.

She gave her companion a flirty smile as she gracefully eased down onto the chair.

"We know. We had a prior engagement," the old man said as he took his seat.

"Coffee, madam?" the server asked the lady.

"Please."

The waiter filled her cup.

"You two look like you're in love." Her brown eyes were on Webb and me.

Dad's head shot up. Sam snorted, and Webb tensed. Me—well, I almost choked. Love was not in the air between Webb and me. I guess she couldn't tell the vampire was cantankerous.

"Young love. I do remember when Harry and I were like that," she said.

Maybe she saw something in Webb that I didn't. Right now, his expression screamed of nothing, zip, blank.

"But, Millie, we still are, darling." Harry kissed her on the cheek.

She cooed.

How sweet.

"So you support the Illiteracy Foundation?" I asked, deflecting the conversation to a safer topic.

"We do," said Millie. "We've known the Costner family a long time and helped Alia put the organization together."

"She's our math teacher," I said.

Dad and Sam gaped. Why? No matter.

"Oh, how nice, dear. She loves children. Every chance she gets she's at the public library reading to them. They have a wonderful reading program for the kids. Do you help out?" Her brown eyes were soft as she tilted her head to the side.

"I haven't yet but would like to." I used to read to the younger children when Sam and I lived in foster care. I enjoyed reading *Winnie-the-Pooh* to them.

"Why don't you come down to the public library on Wednesday? The audience range in age from five to eight years old. I'm sure Alia would love to have the help."

I glanced at Dad. "Why don't we do that at our library?"

"You have a library?" Millie's voice hitched.

"My dad is the commander of the military base in the city."

"I'm sorry, are you Steven Mason?" She turned her attention to Dad, beaming with excitement.

"I am. This is my son, Sam; my daughter, Jo; and Webb."

I caught a hint of human. Was the magic spell wearing off?

"I'm Millie, and this is Harry. We're pleased to meet you. I've heard about your library. Alia was so excited when she was designing that place. I have yet to see it."

"We'd love to show you around. Why don't you make an appointment with my secretary?" Dad said.

Huh? Dad hated for humans to visit the base. Or did he just hate Mr. Jackson nosing around?

"I would absolutely love to. Do you have a reading program for the children living on base?" she asked.

"We do," Webb said.

My head swiveled so fast his way I thought my neck would snap. "We do?"

"Sure," Dad said. "Ms. Simpson has a program for the little ones where she reads to them on most afternoons. The kids love it."

Sam slouched in his seat, as bored as ever. If I knew my brother, he wanted to be hunting the enemy, or anywhere but here.

The music faded. The conversations died as Ms. Costner's delicate voice said "Check."

"Ladies and gentlemen." Ms. Costner paused from her spot on stage, scanning the crowd.

Clothing rustled as some people changed the angle of their chairs to face the stage.

"I want to thank all of you for coming this evening." Ms. Costner pulled the mic closer to her. "Without your healthy donations, our organization wouldn't be able to support the many, many people who struggle for one reason or another in learning how to read. With that said, I would like to introduce Debra Broward, president of the Greater Fall River Illiteracy Foundation. She and her magnificent team have done a terrific job in touching lives and helping people of all ages learn the basics of the written word."

The room erupted in applause.

A short, black-haired woman stepped up to the podium while Ms. Costner shuffled to the side.

Debra explained her organization, sharing examples of citizens in the local community who had benefited from the program. The speech lasted fifteen minutes before Ms. Costner took the podium again.

"The music and dancing will resume momentarily, but first, I would like to recognize a few of our larger donors this evening: the Davenports, the Stroths, the Johnsons, the Masons, and rounding out the top five, Edmund Rain. Thank you for digging deep into your bank accounts. The organization and the children are grateful."

At the mention of Edmund's name, I searched the room. Was Edmund here? If he was, did that mean Kate was, too? Everyone clapped except me. Okay, Sam didn't, either.

Dad and Webb didn't seem surprised.

"He's not here," Webb whispered so low only I could hear.

"Why would he donate to this event?" Edmund was the villain. Well, he was our enemy. I'd only seen the worst of him when he tried to kill Sam and me. I was shocked at his generosity. Even more shocked that there could be a good side to Edmund.

"Remember he wants power, greed, and revenge." Webb said. "The one way to get that is to inveigle himself into the community, the government. Look like the nice guy. Make them like you. If they do, it'll be easier for him to infiltrate an organization."

"But what about the vampire government? Don't they want him for kidnapping humans?" I didn't know a whole lot about our world, since I'd only been part of it for a few months.

"They do, if they can catch him. Which is where the sentinels come in. Our team was formed because of people like Edmund. Keep in mind, Jo, anyone—human or vampire—can be bought. Money speaks to many different people. And there are a lot of people in both governments who are greedy for money and power."

"So why do you think Kate didn't show?" I asked.

He leaned in. "We need to leave. We've served our purpose here."

I tried hard to keep patient despite my anger that he ignored my question, but his moodiness infuriated me. I needed a time-out before I got into a car with him.

"I'm going to the ladies' room first." I pushed myself to my feet.

"Webb?" Dad said. "I need a word with you. Sam, please accompany your sister to the ladies' room."

I rolled my eyes. "I'm fine."

Sam stood. "Yeah, like the last time. You re-member what happened, right?"

All too well. The last time I went to the bathroom alone, I ended up drugged by Kate, taken out to a yacht in the ocean, and pretty much left for dead. Still, did I always need a bodyguard with me to go to the bathroom?

"Whatever," I murmured. I had little energy left to argue.

After wandering around, we finally found the bathrooms. I slipped inside and dropped down on a cushioned bench in the sitting area between the entrance and the bathroom. I inhaled the bouquet of fragrant lilies on the table in front of me and closed my eyes. I had just drifted off when a knock jolted me awake.

"Sis, you okay?" Sam asked.

"I'll be right out," I replied.

Well, so much for quiet time.

***

THE BALLROOM WAS PACKED with people standing in groups, chatting; some sat and sipped their drinks while others danced to the slow melody played by the orchestra. When Sam and I returned to the table, it was empty. I spotted the elderly couple swaying to the music on the dance floor, but Dad and Webb were nowhere to be found.

"Let's go, Sis. We'll walk around. We're not going to find them standing here."

Sam led, and I followed. The groups of people automatically moved one way or another as Sam and I snaked through. I'd just passed a lady in a yellow three-quarter-length gown when a tall black-haired man turned from the people he was talking to and bumped into me. I stumbled backward, but he grabbed my shoulders just before I fell on my butt.

"Excuse me." I dragged my gaze upward to lock with his.

He glared down at me as if it were my fault he plowed into me. We stared at one another for a minute before his features softened. "I'm sorry, young lady."

Sam backtracked a few steps. "Jo, let's go."

The man let go of me, smiled, then disappeared behind me. Sam and I continued our quest to find Dad and Webb. We were walking around the large ballroom when Sam stopped short.

"What is it?" I asked. I followed his line of sight, and my heart fell out of my chest. We'd found Webb, all right. His body was stuck to Nicki's on the dance floor. What the hell? When did she show up? Suddenly, I couldn't breathe. She had one hand on his shoulder while he held her other in his hand close to his chest. I blinked a few times just to be sure I wasn't imagining things. Then a blinding flash caused me to squeeze my eyes shut.

"Damn camera," Sam barked.

After a few seconds, I opened them, and white specks floated in front of me as the photographer snapped more pictures. Once the cameraman moved to his next victim, I shook off the blurriness. When I looked out on the dance floor, Webb and Nicki were gone. As I scanned the throng of dancers, a man twirled his partner, and an area opened up. Webb and Nicki waltzed into view.

The desire to kill sped through me like wildfire. I clenched my fists as the air fled my lungs. My heart rate topped the charts. Pressure pressed against my gums, my fangs itching to drop. The room and the people in it vanished. The music became a faint sound, and my body vibrated with energy.

I had to get out of here before I attacked Nicki. Another flash blinded me.

"Sis?" Sam's voice was in my ear. "Breathe. We're going to walk outside."

I blinked to erase the flecks of white. As my vision cleared, Webb's gaze latched onto mine, and I froze. Nicki smirked and trailed her hand up Webb's chest. My fangs shot out.

"Don't make a scene, Sis. And tuck your fangs in. Remember, humans are among us."

His last sentence penetrated my rage. I couldn't let humans see what I was capable of, plus I didn't want to prove Mr. Costner right. I liked and respected his daughter too much to get her into a squabble with her father. He reminded me of mine, in some ways, and the wrath of a domineering father was never good.

Covering my mouth, I barreled through the crowd and ran out. Once outside, I dropped my hand, gathered my dress in both hands, and soared past the valet, cars, and other people lingering outside, and kept running for several blocks.

I stopped and removed my sandals, thankful I hadn't fallen, given the heel size. Without the shoes, I walked at a brisker pace, continually looking over my shoulder. A light breeze rustled the leaves of the trees along the street. A dog barked, and red taillights shone as a car backed out of a driveway, stopping for a brief second.

No one was following me. I panted and slowed. Tears sprang to my eyes. How could Webb dance with her? He didn't want me to hang around

Matthew, but it was okay for him to dance with Nicki?

I wiped a tear from my face.

Out of nowhere, arms grabbed me from behind.

My shoes fell from my hand. After a second of reorienting my wits, I remembered the Taser. As I reached for it, I got a whiff of a familiar scent, and I tensed. Ben? My hand froze on my chest, and my lips moved, but nothing came out. Where did he come from? How did he know I was even here?

"I'm not going to hurt you, Jo," Ben whispered in my ear.

I didn't think he would. He did save my life, and if he was in love with me, he wouldn't hurt me. Would he?

"B-Ben?" I twisted in his arms to look at him.

His eyes had deepened to red—dark, blood-like. Even Edmund's vampire eyes weren't that color red.

I gasped.

"Cat got your tongue?" His hands tightened around my waist.

Finally. She's in my arms. The plan is working. Okay, that was Ben's voice, but his lips weren't moving. I shook my head and squeezed my eyes shut at the same time, hoping like heck I wasn't reading his mind. When I opened my eyes Ben had an evil smirk on his face, reminding me of Edmund.

"Don't think of running or using any of your vampire powers on me. It won't work."

I hadn't planned on running. I wanted to help him. But his hold on me was beginning to hurt, and if I had to reason with him, I needed him away from me.

"Ben, let go of me, then we can talk." I planted both hands on his chest.

"You don't know how bad I've wanted to see you." He sniffed my neck.

My eyes widened. *Sniffing* me? Maybe he really wasn't human anymore. Did he…

"Ben, please." I didn't want to make him angry, even though my own anger started to surface.

I need to get her somewhere where they won't find her, especially London. There was his voice again.

Ignore his voice. Get the Taser.

As fast I could, I reached into my cleavage and withdrew the Taser. Ben glanced at the tiny device in my hand before he smirked.

"What is that?" he asked. His lips were inches from mine.

"Ben, I don't want to hurt you."

He brushed his lips over mine. "You can't hurt

me, Jo. I can match your strength. Unless you think the lipstick in your hand is going to hurt me."

I smiled. I'd seen a vampire get Tasered before, and he went down as a human would when hit. The only difference, though, was the vampire's skin burned from the cobalt in the Taser.

"Are you saying you're a vampire?" I searched his face. His eyes were still red. I flared my nostrils, and his usual burned-sugar scent had turned acrid, nasty.

His grip loosened. His smirk turned into a frown as his eyes changed back to their normal brandy color. Then he released his hold on me and ran a hand through his hair.

"Let us help you," I said softly with my finger ready on the Taser, just in case.

"And what is it that you think you can help me with?" He shoved his hands in his jean pockets. "You think you can turn me back into a full-blooded human? I doubt no one in this universe knows how to change animals into humans. Not even your uncle." Disgust coated every word.

I wasn't surprised. From the day Ben learned I had the DNA to change into a vampire, he tried to talk me out of my decision to give up my humanity. He'd said he believed in a world where people grew old and had families, not a world where vampires lived and fed off of humans. He wanted nothing to do with vampires. Well, with the exception of me. When he was in the hospital recovering from when the Coast Guard pulled him out of the ocean, he'd told me he didn't see me as a vampire.

"Go ahead. Try and see if you can take me on," he said. No hint of anger or sarcasm in his voice.

"I told you. I want to help you. What did you mean earlier when you said the plan was working? What do you want?"

"I didn't say that out loud." He cocked his head to one side.

A sudden strong wind ruffled my dress and hair.

"Ben, step away from my sister," Sam said from somewhere behind me.

Son of a bitch. Her fucking brother is a pain in my ass. And I thought London was going to rescue her. I wanted to take him on. Damn, that woman didn't follow through on her end of the deal. Ben's voice was loud and clear in my head.

Ben stepped toward me as his eyes changed from brandy colored to red again. "I can promise you, we'll have our time together, Jo." He dragged the backs of his fingers along my cheek before stalking past me.

"You didn't learn your lesson, Mason," Ben spat out.

"Bring it on." Sam sneered. "You don't stand a chance."

"Ben, wait." I ran toward them.

Sam pivoted on one leg and struck out with the other. His foot connected with Ben's jaw. Ben's head bobbed back then forward. Ben lunged and threw an elbow to the side of Sam's head. Fist after fist hit Ben, then Sam. The two were beating each other to a bloody pulp, and Ben's strength seemed to match up with Sam's.

They separated, staring each other down, both breathing heavily.

"Stop, Sam! We need to help him." I inched closer to my brother.

Ben laughed. "I don't need your help. I told you that." He stared at Sam.

"Sis, go back to the mansion. Webb is on his way." He pushed me behind him.

The air thickened. The wind picked up again and began swirling and howling. Leaves rustled. Several streetlights popped, covering the area in darkness. After a second, my vision sharpened, adjusting to the dark street.

Time stood still. Leaves and other decaying plant life hung suspended in midair.

I glanced at Sam then at Ben. Both seemed frozen. Then Sam fisted his hands at his side, and he began opening and closing them, not taking his eyes off of Ben.

In slow motion, the wind picked up again, gathering all the leaves and other debris into a ball. Sam seemed to be using his powers, which he hadn't shown before now.

The ball of leaves grew bigger as Sam continued to open and close his fists. He was building a weapon of sorts. Even a ball of leaves could hurt —maybe even kill—someone if he used enough force.

If I hadn't seen my own powers in action when we fought Edmund that night, I wouldn't believe manipulating air or water could hurt anyone.

Ben stood, entranced as he reached for his neck. The glow in his red eyes dimmed, reminding me of what Blake had looked like right before he collapsed. Was Sam trying to...

Sam couldn't kill him. I was already scheduled to stand in front of the council for the death of Blake. I couldn't let Sam go through the same fate.

Before I could react, several sentinels stormed the street. Tripp tackled Sam to the ground. Instantly, the ball of debris dropped, spraying in all directions.

Ben collapsed, his eyes rolling back into his head. Olivia and Sloan ran to him. Tripp stood, pulling Sam with him.

"Sam?" I ran over to my brother.

His eyes were open, but he wasn't acknowledging me.

Tears clouded my vision. What happened to him?

"Jo." Tripp's voice was gentle. "Give him some room."

I took his advice and stepped back.

Strong hands came around me and settled on my stomach.

I screamed. "Get away from me!"

"Shhh, beautiful. It's just me," Webb whispered.

"No. Let me go."

"Lieutenant, get my daughter out of here," Dad said from somewhere nearby.

"Sam, please, if you can hear me—" I cried.

His eyes drifted shut, and then he collapsed in Tripp's arms.

"Come on. He'll be fine." Webb's voice was soft.

"Jo, he's used a lot of energy," Tripp said. "Webb's right. He'll be fine. His pulse is strong. He just needs to sleep it off. I'll take him back to base." He glanced behind me.

"Stay with him until he wakes," Webb ordered.

"Yes, sir." Tripp carried Sam away.

"Hey." Webb's lips skimmed my ear. "Sam will be fine. I promise."

His words, his voice, his touch all made me sink into him until I remembered why I was out here.

I kicked his shin with my bare foot. "It's all your fault."

He held me tighter. "I'm sorry. I'm so, so sorry."

"Get Ben out of here," Dad commanded from somewhere nearby.

"Let me go, Webb." My voice was shaky.

"No. Never."

"I said...to let me go." I gritted my teeth.

Dad walked up. Webb straightened a little but kept his hold on me.

"Young lady, why did you run like that?" Dad only called me "young lady" when I was in trouble.

"It was my fault, Commander. I—"

"You don't have to stick up for her. I know why she ran." Dad stared daggers at me.

Yeah, he was mad. The vibration in his voice was a dead giveaway. No matter. After my ordeal in the ocean, I'd decided to be an adult about things, which meant I would own up to my mistakes.

But running from the party hadn't been a mistake. Displaying my powers in a room full of humans would've been worse.

The deep line between Dad's brows softened, as though he had read my mind.

"I'm not sorry for running, Dad. My powers were about to take over."

Webb let go of me as car doors slammed; engines started and faded into the distance.

Dad let out a breath. "Take my daughter home, Webb."

"That's it? You're not going to yell or reprimand me or anything?" I asked.

"Not tonight, Jo. I get that you took the lesser of two evils. Although jealousy will get you in trouble every time," he said casually.

"What?" I couldn't believe Dad just broadcasted my jealousy in front of Webb. I wanted to cringe.

"I'm not dead, pumpkin. You two are dealing with something. What? I don't want to know. But jealous rage will always end in disaster." Dad scrutinized both of us. "Get your issues resolved before you return to base. I have very little patience with stuff like this." Dad stalked off, into a waiting Hummer.

I went to find my sandals. I had no idea how Webb and I were going to resolve anything, especially if he didn't want to talk about it.

9

Silence hung in the Audi as Webb drove. He sped through the streets of Fall River as though he were on a racetrack, heading for the finish line. I should've been frightened, especially when he almost clipped a side mirror from a parked car, but I wasn't. My body was numb as I thought about the night. Out of everything that had happened, I was worried about Sam. Did he kill Ben?

Nausea churned in my stomach. I hated the thought of Ben being a vampire or whatever he was.

Was he still human? His thoughts... Oh my God, had I actually been reading his mind? I straightened against the leather seat. Had I been reading Matthew's mind while we were walking through the gardens?

No. I refused to believe I had that power. It had to be all the magic Ms. Costner put on the place. That was it.

Relaxing my shoulders, I peeked at Webb. His gaze was fixed on the road, lips pressed into a thin line. Mt. Hope Bay passed by on my right in a blur. The lights of the military base drew closer. Hadn't Dad said to get our problems worked out before we came back?

As we reached the first set of iron gates, I said, "Webb, we need to talk."

The Audi came to a stop, and Webb rolled down his window. "Sentinel."

"Lieutenant." The sentinel nodded to the guardhouse, and the gates opened.

Webb's window slid shut as he gave the Audi gas. The next set of gates slowly opened as the sentinel standing at his post saluted as we drove through. I flashed back to the first day I had stepped foot on the base and how nervous I'd been. I held my hands tightly in my lap as a sense of déjà vu washed over me. Back then I sat next to Webb, wondering what in the world was going on with my life. He'd been quiet as I tried to ask him questions about my brother, who'd gone missing. But he wouldn't answer me.

Now, as we drove through the base, he was quiet, looking straight ahead. I stared out the side window, trying to prevent myself from crying. Maybe he didn't want anything to do with me after dancing with Nicki. Maybe he realized he did have feelings for her. All of a sudden I couldn't wait to get out of this car and run to my room and hide as I normally did when anything bothered me.

The winding road seemed to go on forever. Just as the main building came into view, Webb veered left toward the wooded area of the base.

"Where are we going?" I hated the damn woods.

He still didn't say anything.

The Audi slowed as a small A-frame building peeked out from the tall evergreens that towered over it. Was this one of the safe houses that I kept hearing about? Tripp had been ordered to take me to one the night they picked me up from the Coast Guard Cutter. Webb parked in a small, paved spot, and without a word, he jumped out, trudged up to the front door, and unlocked it. As soon as he disappeared inside, a light came on.

I sat in the car. Should I follow him? Maybe he was getting something before he took me home.

An owl hooted from somewhere deep in the forest, and I flinched. Well, I wasn't staying in the car. Ever since I heard the story of the girl who'd been killed in the Fall River State Forest back in the mid-seventies, woods gave me the creeps.

I let out a low, frustrated sigh at myself for being a little scared, but also at Webb who was driving me crazy with his quiet attitude. I jumped out, not bothering to put on my sandals. I decided I was more comfortable in my bare feet.

I scanned the area while picking my way from the car to the front door. I stepped cautiously around several branches and rocks, ensuring I didn't snag the gown or poke a hole in my bare feet. The front door was ajar, so I walked in. "Webb!"

My toes sank into soft carpeting. A soft glow illuminated the room.

Warm colors painted the walls. A comfy brown sofa sat in front of the large-screen TV. An office area with a desk, a computer, and a few filing cabinets lined the left wall.

This didn't strike me as a safe house.

"Webb?" I called again.

I ambled to the arch leading to the next room and crossed the threshold into a brightly lit kitchen. A fridge, a stove, and a table for two made up the small room. Webb stood against the sink, sipping from a mug.

"Is this a—"

"This is my home on base," he said abruptly. "We converted a few safe houses for the sentinels." He tipped back the mug then set it down.

"So why doesn't my dad have a place like this?" It would be nice to live in a small house away from the main building, where the sentinels didn't stand guard, watching every move I made.

The recessed lighting highlighted the sadness on his face. He'd confused me more in the last few hours than he had since I'd known him. Part of me wanted to run and jump in his arms. The other part of me wanted to shake the words out of him, for why he was angry or sad or whatever emotions he was holding back.

"Your father likes to be close to his work. He's always been like that. Come here, Jo."

His gentle voice certainly did match his outward appearance. Regardless, I wasn't going to jump every time the vampire changed moods. Webb and I were brand new at this relationship thing.

Still, I needed to be strong, not only for him but for us. "No. Not until you stop being an ass. You've treated me horribly tonight."

He ran his hands through his hair.

After a long agonizing minute, he had said nothing.

Fine. I could find my own way back home. I huffed and stalked out. My feet dug into the carpet when he scooped me into his arms.

"You're not going anywhere," he whispered in my ear.

"Webb, put me down. If you're not going to talk to me, then take me home."

He wasn't going to kiss his way to an apology, although his lips did feel wonderful.

"I told you that I'm not letting you go." He carried me to the couch.

"Well, I'm not giving into your..."

He raised an eyebrow. "What? This?" His lips smashed onto mine.

I pushed him.

"Jo." Pain coated my name. "I know I was an ass. I'm sorry." He dropped down on the couch with me on his lap. "I need you."

Huh? I knitted my brows. "You have a funny way of showing it."

He untied his bow tie. Then he traced the outline of my sweetheart neckline, his fingers dipping inside. "You scared the crap out of me."

Was he talking about before or after the fundraiser? "When?"

"When you ran out. I just knew what was going to happen."

"What?" I tried to straighten, but he grasped my hip, keeping me on his lap.

"Hear me out. Kate was never going to show up. Nicki lied to make sure you would be there. She was supposed to slip into the event and lure you away to Ben."

"What the—"

"Wait." He pressed a finger to my lips. "Remember when we were at my house in Maine, your father told me that things around here were a little hectic, and we had intruders on base? Well, she was one of them. She was trying to get to me."

"And let me guess, she ran into Ben?"

He nodded, removing his finger from my mouth.

"Why didn't she just go to the gate and ask for you?" I placed my hands on his chest.

"She's not allowed anywhere near the base. We had her banned from here."

I wasn't going to ask why. After her little stint in Maine, I had an inkling, anyway. "So how did she know we would be there tonight?"

"She'd been lurking outside my house." He fingered the ruby on my neck. "Pretty."

I looked down at it. The jewel was pretty, but that wasn't the topic. "And how was she supposed to lure me out to Ben?" I lifted my gaze to his.

"After your run-in with her in Maine, she knew you would come to her without any reservations."

I couldn't argue with that. Only I probably would've killed her.

"And she told you all this?"

He let go of the ruby and gently wrapped his fingers around my wrists.

"Not at first. When I asked her where Kate was, she blackmailed me into dancing with her. Said she would make a scene if I didn't. So we danced. She seemed to let her guard down. She told me she hadn't heard from Kate since before the night at the mansion. I knew then she was up to something. But I assumed she wanted me. Then she brought up Ben, and I put two and two together. One of the sentinels had seen a female lurking around the base shortly after we left for Maine, and Ben had been at the base, too. When you ran out, she laughed and said Ben was going to eat you alive."

He didn't seem to want to eat me alive. When

he let me go, I thought I could reason with him and get him to talk.

"What happens now?" I laced my fingers through his.

"I don't know. I have no idea where your father took Ben. I don't know what happened to Nicki, either. When I saw you take off, everything became a blur. I gathered the sentinels and your father, and we went in search of you."

"Webb, are you mad at me? Did I say something wrong in the car on the way over there?"

"No." He placed his hand on my cheek. "You take my breath away, and... I was having a hard time controlling myself in the car. All I wanted to do..." Black wove through his blue eyes as they began to change.

"What is it?" I prodded.

His lips grazed mine. "When I first saw you in that dress, I thought my heart stopped. Then in the car when I was able to kiss you, it stopped again. But what sent me over the edge was hearing you say that you're crazy for me. At that moment, I wanted nothing more than to bring you back here and..."

I think my heart stopped. Or was it beating so fast I couldn't feel it anymore?

"I'm here now, baby," I whispered.

He groaned.

My chest rose and fell as he trailed his fingers over my jaw and down my neck.

His fingers stopped in my cleavage again. I sucked in a breath.

"Stunning," he said.

In this moment in his arms, I knew, without a doubt, I was in love with him.

10

In the morning, Dad had left a note taped to the fridge for me to meet him and Sam in the control room. After Webb brought me home last night, I'd checked on my brother. He'd been tucked in, sleeping in his bed, so I'd curled up in mine and passed out. I'd had no trouble getting my mind to relax, thanks to Webb, who'd agreed to not hold in his feelings during our long talk.

Unsurprisingly, when I entered the control room, the place buzzed with activity. Vampires typed on keyboards and chatted on phones. Dad's note said he and Sam would be in the office next to Sawyer's workstation. I knew exactly where that was. I sauntered down the few steps to the lower level, careful to stay inside the yellow lines marked on the floor. Only people with special clearance were allowed to step outside the boundaries, since Dad had implemented the stricter security measures.

Sawyer rolled back his chair as I approached him. He'd been one of the sentinels who worked with Sam the night I went missing, showing my brother the ropes on how to operate a computer program.

"Hey, Jo?" Sawyer, like the majority of the sentinels who worked for my dad, stood over six feet tall, was in great physical shape, and had shoulder-length hair. The cool thing about Sawyer was the color of his eyes. His were a mixture of blue, brown, green, and gold. Every time he blinked, a different color dominated.

"Hey, there," I answered.

He pointed to the office. "Sam and your father are waiting."

"Thanks." I turned and glided in. "What's going on?"

"Pumpkin, good morning." Dad lifted his gaze from his computer screen.

"It's about time." Sam dropped his feet from the desk. "Pops wouldn't tell me what happened until you got here."

"You don't remember?" I slid into the chair next to Sam.

"Not after some storm came in."

"Ha. You were the storm, Sam," I said.

Dad tapped on the keyboard then gave us his full attention. "I wanted to wait until I had both of you here."

"Why are we in the control room?" We usually found Dad in his office upstairs.

"Maintenance is fixing a leak in my bathroom. Anyway, we have several things to discuss." Dad had a slight grin on his face, as though he were proud. "Son, your anger last night brought out your ability to manipulate earth and air."

"I did?" Sam's eyes widened. "How come I don't remember?"

"You were enraged. As a new vampire, your powers will usually surface when your emotions change," Dad said.

"Like my telekinesis did?"

"Yes, Jo. Both of you will learn to harness your abilities and use them when necessary, not only in fits of anger."

A tickle skated across my nape.

Good morning. See? You need to practice. Webb's voice ignited my limbs.

I jerked around to face the door. He handed a sheet of paper to Sawyer before sauntering in.

"Ah, Lieutenant," Dad said. "Please close the door."

Webb did as Dad ordered. Black cargo pants hugged his hips, and a black T-shirt stretched across his toned chest, with the SEAL emblem in the upper left corner. The word *Jupiter* arced over the top of the emblem, and the word *sentinel* was underneath. His blue eyes gleamed as he settled next to Dad's desk.

"Do you want to get a chair, Lieutenant?" Dad asked.

"No sir. I can't stay long. We're tracking some chatter."

"Fair enough." Dad nodded. "Back to the topic at hand. Both of you need to practice."

"Commander, I've been working with Jo on hers."

"You're becoming quite the magic doer," Sam said.

"You are too, Son."

"Seriously?" Sam studied Dad. "How are we able to manipulate the elements?"

Dad shifted in his chair. "Alchemy." He went on to explain how vampires absorb energy from nature, which Webb had told me.

Sam's mouth hung open through the entire explanation. When Dad finished, Sam shook his head as though he still couldn't wrap his mind around the concept. *Welcome to the club.*

"Ms. Costner called this morning. You both begin your tutoring sessions later in the week."

I smiled, happy she agreed. I wanted to learn more about her and how she cast spells.

"Dad? What about Ben? Is he okay?"

"What happened to him?" Sam asked.

"Wow. That must've been some rage you were in, Sam. You don't even remember?" I asked.

"All I know is that I wanted to beat the crap out of him."

Webb muttered something I couldn't make out.

"From what I could tell, Son, your Empath abilities are stronger than I suspected. Not only can you feel emotions, but you can suck someone's energy right out of them."

"What the heck are you talking about, Pops?"

"Wait," I said. "I read about this in the library. An Empath is also referred to as an Energy Vampire. They can drain the life from anyone, including humans, and use it to their advantage."

"That's right, pumpkin. It depends on the strength of the Empath. For example, Tripp is a weak Empath and can only feel emotions. He could never pull energy from another person."

Sam's mouth fell open again. "So, what could I do with someone's energy?"

"It's different for all Empaths," Webb chimed in. "If what I'm hearing is correct, then you took more than Ben's anger. You took all the energy he needed to stay conscious. Since you're inexperienced, I'm not surprised he passed out, but with practice, you could take just enough to make them too weak to retaliate."

"So I used his anger to fuel my own?"

"That's correct," Webb said.

"Did I kill him?" Sam's forest-green eyes flashed vampire black.

"No, he's alive." Dad rubbed his jaw.

"Is he here? Is he all right?" I sat up straighter.

Dad looked over at Webb then back to Sam and me. "Ben got away. He woke up when Sloan and Olivia were stopped at a red light."

"What?" I popped to attention. This wasn't good. Ben definitely wasn't one hundred percent human, not with the way his eyes changed from brandy-colored to red. "Are we going to help him?"

"If we can find him, then we'll try," Dad said. "His father told one of my men that Ben was at a baseball camp for a few weeks. He said he watched

Ben go through security at the airport yesterday morning. We know he didn't. We checked his flight, and he wasn't on it. We have men searching now."

Sam and I exchanged a look. Baseball camp had always been a dream of Sam's. He and Ben had talked about going together this summer.

"Does Mr. Jackson know you're looking for Ben, Pops?" Sam asked.

"No. And we didn't say anything about what happened last night. We were there to see how Ben was feeling after his hospital stay here last week," Dad said.

"And what will you do when you find him?" I swung my gaze from Webb to Dad.

"We'll need to get him under Dr. Vieira's care and run tests." Dad pushed to his feet. "I can't stress enough that both of you should not talk if he happens to call you." Dad pinned his gaze on Sam.

My brother raised his hands. "Don't worry, Pops. I have no intention of talking to him."

Dad circled around Webb and planted himself in front of Sam and me. I didn't want to see him. His thoughts were...

My eyes grew wide when I remembered his voice in my head.

"What is it?" Webb asked, coming to my side.

"Pumpkin, are you okay?"

Was I ready to ask Dad about mind-reading? I reached over and grabbed my brother's wrist. He looked at me as if I were some kind of lunatic. I held on and closed my eyes. Nothing.

"What are you doing, Jo?" Concern tinged Webb's voice.

Opening my eyes, I let go of Sam. "When Ben was holding me, I could've sworn I heard his thoughts. I mean...um... He was saying things, but his lips weren't moving."

Dad looked horrified, as did Webb.

"Were you able to read Sam's thoughts?" Dad asked.

I laughed nervously. "No. I got nothing."

"Can you read anyone's thoughts in this room without touching them?" Webb squatted, peering up at me.

"No. But wouldn't it be the weirdest thing if I could read your mind, Dad?"

His eyes narrowed as he chewed on the inside of his cheek.

"Well?" Dad's silence rattled me.

He combed his hair with his hand and rounded the desk, going back to his chair. He eased down and sighed as though he had lost the battle of the century.

"Was Ben the only one whose mind you could read?" he asked, finally.

"I think I read Matthew's mind when he escorted me to the main house."

"That's how your mind-reading abilities start." Dad continued to chew on the inside of his cheek.

"You're not making any sense," I said.

"Yeah, Pops." Sam fidgeted in his seat.

Webb rose and went to stand against the wall.

"I'd just walked out of an office building when I bumped into a human lady." Dad was focusing on something behind me. "Instantly my head filled with words and gibberish. I'd been working hard at the time, and I thought I needed to rest. But as I bent down to pick up the package, our hands touched, and my mind was awash with words—her words. When we broke the connection, my mind cleared.

"I had to make certain I wasn't crazy, so I found another human and compelled him into shaking my hand. Same thing. After several random experiments with humans and vampires, I'd found I could only read humans' minds."

"But I don't think Ben is human." I bounced my knee.

"We don't know that for sure," Webb said.

I'd put money on the fact Ben wasn't.

"As my powers grew," Dad continued. "So did my mind-reading abilities."

"Will I be able to read vampire minds?" I asked.

"As your powers grow, I'm certain you will. The question is, will you be able to only by touching them, or will that not be necessary?" Dad shook his head.

"Have you ever figured out why I'm the only one you can read without touching?"

"Your telekinesis gives off strong electromagnetic waves. My telepathy means I'm sensitive to this radiant energy, which, I suspect, allows me to read your mind at a distance."

His theory made sense, if we were talking about anything other than humans.

Oh, yeah. I wasn't human anymore.

"Man, this is too much to take in for me," Sam muttered.

"Why do you look distraught over this, Dad?" I should've been the one panicking. I didn't want voices in my head.

"Your powers are growing, Jo," Webb said. "And that makes you more of a threat to Edmund or any of our enemies."

Sawyer poked his head in. "We have a situation."

"What?" Webb pushed off the wall.

"The main gate is swarming with media."

"Why?" Dad jumped out of his seat.

"They want to talk to the girl with the violet eyes." Sawyer pinned his gaze on me.

"Huh?" I, too, flew out of my chair.

"It's best if you see the footage," Sawyer said.

Sam and I exchanged a look before following Dad and Webb out of the office and over to Sawyer's desk. He tapped a few buttons on the keyboard, and the scene out at the gate emerged on the widescreen monitor on the far wall. Media trucks, newscasters, cameramen, and nosy neighbors crowded the street.

"I don't understand." Dad pinched his eyebrows together.

"Apparently, Jo's face is on the front page of the people section in the *Herald*," Sawyer said.

"Why me?"

"Those cameras last night," Sam murmured.

"Oh, no. Does the picture show my fangs?" I prayed it didn't.

Dad whirled on me. "Please tell me you didn't have your fangs showing, young lady." Smoke billowed from his ears. Okay, imaginary smoke.

"I covered my mouth with my hand."

"Find me a paper," Dad barked to no one in particular.

Chairs scraped along the floor, doors opened and closed, and vampires scurried to find Dad a newspaper. Before anyone could produce a copy, Sawyer had the *Herald*'s website on screen with my mug staring back at us. The headline read, *Beautiful Creature Changes Her Appearance in the Blink of an Eye.*

I gasped. Sam choked. Webb uttered a few words not for children under the age of ten. Dad... well, his skin darkened to a deep red.

Two pictures of me sat side by side—one of me with my silver eyes and the other with purple eyes and fangs hanging over my lips. I thought about running. I thought about stabbing myself with a cobalt sword. Either would be a better punishment than what Dad had in store for me.

A brave soul ran up, handed the newspaper to Webb, then beat feet back to his desk. Phones rang. Dad ignored his as he glared at me. Webb pulled his phone from his pocket as he walked away.

"How did they know Jo lived here?" Sam asked. "Is it even legal for them to print pictures without permission?"

Did it even matter now? My photo was plastered on the computer screen.

"No, Son, it's not. Both of you go up to the apartment." Dad's tone deepened. "I need to sort this out."

I headed toward the exit, not waiting for Sam. I wasn't hanging around Dad right now. Not when he looked as though he wanted to kill me. The way Sam could feel Dad's fury, I was surprised he wasn't running out, as well. As I climbed the stairs to the small landing area above the control room, I had a horrible thought. Would the Council add this to my record? Humans weren't supposed to know vampires existed.

Humans. I halted in my tracks. What if Mr. Jackson saw me in the paper? Would my mugshot be the evidence he needed to confirm that something weird was taking place under my dad's authority?

11

The next morning, I jumped out of bed, praying today would be better than yesterday. I held out hope Dad would go easy on me. I still hadn't seen him since he went red after seeing me on the front page of the newspaper. Webb had called around midnight to tell Sam and me that Dad would not be home because he had a meeting with his superiors. Yeah, I was in deep trouble.

I slinked out of my room and into the bathroom. Voices trickled down the hall. The hushed whispers were too low for even my vampire hearing. The only thing I could make out was Dad's deep baritone.

I took my time in the shower, washing every part of me three times. I was in no hurry to venture out into the family room. But I did want to ask Dad about my best friend, Darcy Rose. After Sam returned to the apartment shortly after me, he'd informed me that Darcy would be here sometime today. Apparently, Dad had approved her to stay on base until her father could work out his debt issues. Mr. Rose was a big-time lawyer out of Boston who had defended a vampire or two in the past. According to Edmund, Mr. Rose owed a great deal of money to a colleague of Edmund's, which was why Darcy had been kidnapped by Edmund. He'd planned on holding her hostage until her father could pay his debt. Fortunately for Darcy, we'd been able to rescue her when we invaded Edmund's mansion in Newport, RI, last week.

After a few silent pep talks, I got out of the shower, toweled off, and dressed. The longer I took, the longer I put off Dad's wrath.

I steeled my shoulders and padded into the kitchen. I had no choice, really. My throat burned with hunger.

Sun spilled in from the wall of windows as I walked toward the light or maybe my own death. I reached the family room and stopped, saying a quick prayer.

"No amount of prayers will get you out of this

one, young lady," Dad said. "Have a seat at the bar." He tapped a button on his cell phone.

I followed his order, climbing onto the barstool and interlaced my fingers. Dad poured blood into a mug, and my fangs dropped.

"Drink," he said, sliding the mug toward me.

I promptly downed the thick red liquid. The burn in my throat immediately cooled. I set down the mug.

"Now, let's talk about the photo."

"I'm sorry. I didn't know my fangs—"

"Jo, it's too late for excuses." Dad's voice was surprisingly even. "I know incidents like this will happen. As a new vampire, sometimes it's hard to control your senses. I get it. I also knew the risk involved when Alia invited you and Sam. Thankfully, she came to our rescue. Her father, however, is furious."

I didn't doubt Mr. Costner was outraged by my display of weakness, especially since he hadn't been keen on Sam and me attending his soiree.

"How did she cover for me?"

"She explained to the reporter that you were trying out a few costumes with her permission." He grabbed my empty mug.

I tilted my head. "I don't understand. Why would the reporter believe her?"

"Her father compelled the man into believing Alia's story. A follow-up article is in the paper this morning."

I glanced around the counter for the newspaper.

"I don't have a copy yet. Regardless, we got lucky on this one." He pinned me with a hard expression. "If humans find out—"

"I know, Dad. I'll do my best not to let it happen again." I wanted to promise, but I couldn't. Not with me still growing into my powers. I didn't want to dwell on the subject any longer, though I did want to read the article. "Is Darcy staying on base for the summer?"

"I'd planned to tell you yesterday. I've set her up with her own room in the human barracks, and she'll work alongside Ms. Simpson in the library." He walked over to the sink behind him and washed out the mug.

I was glad Darcy would be living on base. She would be protected not only from Edmund, but also from Ben. If he were turning into a vampire, then his thirst for human blood could get her killed.

"By the way." Dad's voice drew me away from thinking about Darcy. "Tomorrow, you and Sam have a physical set up with Dr. Vieira." He turned to face me as he snatched a dish towel off the counter next to him then dried the mug.

"What's with the physical?" I asked.

Dr. Vieira had been analyzing some of our blood samples, and as part of the Eternal Protection Law, we still had a few more weeks to donate blood.

"Standard procedure for any new vampire." He finished drying the mug and set it down in front of me as he wiped his hands.

"Will Dr. Vieira be able to use the chip inside me to get his information, or is he going to pull more blood?"

Vampire law stated at the end of the bloodlust stage, all new vampires were required to have a computer chip inserted under their skin. It was a way for the vampire government to keep track of their people. The tiny device housed all our personal information and even stored stats like our heart rate data and blood type.

"The chip is not sophisticated enough to analyze your DNA. Besides, he wants to compare the new results to the old ones he'd taken from you when you were a day-old vampire."

"Why? Is there something wrong?" I tapped my foot on the bottom rail of the barstool.

"Your DNA shows some anomalies."

"Like what?" I wiped my clammy hands on my jeans, still moving my foot.

"Let's wait until Dr. Vieira has all the results."

I laughed nervously. What else could I possibly have in my DNA?

"It's funny?" Dad asked.

"Well, kind of. I would've never thought in a gazillion years that I carried a vampire gene. Now you're telling me Dr. Vieira thinks there's more to my DNA. Again, what does that mean? Are you going to tell me I'm part lion or wolf?" I laughed again. Saying it out loud was even more absurd.

"Jo, try not worry about what Dr. Vieira speculates. He's a great doctor and very interested in our genetics."

I admired the vampire. I'd never thought about my future before, but hanging around Dr. Vieira was proving to me that maybe I'd want to learn more about medicine and genetics.

"Really," Dad answered my thought.

"Yeah. Maybe. I'm curious about how natural-born vampires can switch from human to vampire. And as you said, we're still evolving. I want to know everything about our species, especially if Uncle Patrick can fabricate a serum to force pure humans to become vampires. I want to learn how to stop him. You didn't see how evil Blake Turner was. I don't want to live among a creature like him."

Wow! Where did all that come from? I knew I'd been curious. Even Dr. Vieira caught on to my curiosity.

Dad circled the bar and hugged me. "I've seen vast changes in you in such a short time. You sound like a woman who knows what she wants. Are you sure you're still my teenage daughter? Where's the one who argues with me or throws temper tantrums?"

I smiled as he backed away. "Don't worry, Dad. That part of me is still there."

"Darn. And I was hoping I didn't have to deal with any more outbursts."

We both laughed, a new sound from Dad. I rarely heard any type of happiness from my father.

After our conversation, Dad retreated to his office. I hung out in the apartment, listening to music since neither Webb nor Sam was around. Webb and the sentinels had training at an offsite location and wouldn't return until tomorrow. Sam tagged along with Dad's permission. Every chance my brother had, he trained. Olivia had been bugging me to train, and I needed to continue my physical exercises. My powers would only go so far in a fight. Although if I could master my abilities, I wasn't sure I would need to exert myself physically.

The apartment was quiet except for my music. It was great to spend time by myself after all that had happened over the past week with Edmund trying to kill me, Nicki making an appearance, and Ben. Well, I hoped Dad would find him soon. As I lay on my bed, "The Crow and the Butterfly" by Shinedown began. The song made me think of Webb, mainly because he'd said how my skin was as soft as a butterfly's wing. How I wished I was back sitting in Webb's living room, watching the waves crash along the shore. I'd probably not get a chance to go back for a long time. I wasn't certain of that, but my intuition didn't give me a warm and fuzzy feeling, especially with my upcoming trial.

I traded my fleeting thought of my trial for thoughts of Darcy. Dad had said he would let me know when she arrived. I was dying to ask her how she'd been doing since we rescued her. If she talked with Ben, how did the exchange go? Did she notice anything unusual about him? How did he treat her?

At least now that she knew vampires existed, I could talk more freely about my life. Well, to a certain extent. I didn't think Dad would want me to share my special abilities.

My phone rang. I turned down the music. "Hello."

"Pumpkin, Darcy is here. Come down to the lobby. We're meeting her at the library," Dad said.

I hung up, turned off the small stereo I had in my room, and slipped on my shoes. I pocketed my phone in my jeans then headed out to meet Dad.

He was talking to Ruth, the receptionist, when I exited the elevator. I smiled at Ruth, who looked up at me from her seat behind the circular desk. Her blond hair was up in a pretty bun, and her lips were painted a peach color. Dad stood in front of the chest-high counter, signing a piece of paper.

"Please make sure this gets out today, Ruth," Dad said, handing the paper back to her, then he turned to me and extended his arm.

I walked into him as he draped his arm over my shoulder. Then we walked out in the bright sunshine and humid air. I welcomed the warmth. A silly part of me thanked the vampire gods for allowing my species to walk in the sun.

"How's your bloodlust?" Dad asked.

A vampire rode by us on his bike.

"It's getting better. I didn't have any cravings when the human lady, Lauren, drove us into town the other night." I'd been surprised at myself. It had been hours since I had blood that day.

"In another month or so, your blood cravings should diminish considerably. The magic number, I've found, is three months."

"So I could be around humans more?"

Another bike rider sped past us as we stopped at the entrance to the library.

"I wouldn't go that far just yet," Dad said. "In fact, I want to prepare you. Today is Ms. Simpson's reading circle with a group of military children who live on base. They're all human, Jo. There's no spell to mask their scent. If I get any signs you're losing control, we'll leave."

"Dad, I'm fine." I didn't know how I would react to a room full of humans. "Does Ms. Simpson know we're vampires?" I'd only met her once.

"She does. She's one of a few humans on this base who does," he said as we climbed the stairs.

Several scents accosted me when we entered the library—old books, lemon, humans, and Darcy's cotton-candy fragrance. Dad held me back from stepping farther into the room.

"Oh, my God," Darcy squealed, skipping toward me, her blond ponytail bouncing.

"Darcy," Dad said. "We talked about this. Let Jo get used to your scent for a minute."

"Sorry, Mr. Mason."

"I'm good, Dad." My throat didn't burn, my fangs didn't drop, and my body didn't crave any human blood—at least, not at the moment. I chalked up my lack of craving to the fact that I'd just had my morning ration, and to my maturity as a vampire, which Dad and I had just spoken about.

"Girls." Ms. Simpson rose from her chair, pushing her bangs to the side. "Why don't you sit over there and catch up before the children arrive?" She pointed a crimson nail to a table behind her desk.

"Come on, Jo. We have a lot to talk about." Darcy tugged on my wrist.

"Ms. Simpson, how is your mother?" Dad asked.

"The doctor is running more tests. He tells us not to worry."

Darcy and I slid into the chairs, sitting across from one another.

"Jo, focus, girl." She lightly kicked my shin.

"Ow. I was listening to... Never mind." I was here to catch up with my best friend, although I was curious what was wrong with Ms. Simpson's mother.

"How are you?" Darcy gushed. "I can't even believe I'm here because my father made a deal with the devil. And"—she sucked in air—"I can't believe your picture was in the newspaper. Have you seen it? What happened?"

She finally took another breath. I had to take in oxygen, just listening to her.

"Um...I'm not sure where to start, after all that." I chuckled as I rested my elbows on the table.

"Sorry. I've been dying to talk to you. I don't have your number. I tried to call Ben to see if he had it, but I got his voice mail. Have you've seen Ben?"

Dad's voice entered my head. *Change the subject. She doesn't need to know about Ben.*

Without looking at Dad, I shook my head. "No, but Sam told me he went to baseball camp," I lied.

"Where is your sexy brother?" She smiled.

I narrowed my eyes.

"What? He's hot."

"Darcy," I warned. "Sam's off-limits."

"He's a big boy. He can make up his own mind," she argued.

Not that I had any authority over who my brother dated, but I didn't think Sam had the patience for Darcy, let alone for a human.

"Are you forgetting he's a vampire? Wait. You like Ben. I saw how he kissed you on the boat."

The kiss was passionate, and I got the impression Ben and Darcy were in love.

"Oh, yeah..." She touched her lips. "There's nothing between us, not anymore. He took me to the school dance." She sat back in her chair. "Afterwards we went to the movies a few times. Now, I don't know." She shrugged a delicate shoulder.

Excited voices pierced the air. We both glanced at the toddlers who were running in as though they had been given a cup of sugar before reading time.

"Children," Ms. Simpson said in a raised voice.

A little girl bounced up to my dad. "'Mander, 'Mander," she cooed.

Dad opened his arms, and she leapt into them.

"How is my little wolf?" he asked, twirling her.

Wow! I had a hard time digesting my father and kids. Maybe since I'd never seen him with small children.

"Come on," Darcy urged. "We should help Ms. Simpson. We'll talk more later."

She bounced off to wrangle a couple of boys, and I had to find out who'd snagged my dad's attention.

"Who is this pretty little one?" I asked Dad.

"Jo, this is Abbey Quade." He settled the little

girl on his hip while she rested a tiny arm on his shoulder.

"Hi, Abbey." I raised my hand. "I'm Jo."

"Why do you have thilver eyes?" Abbey's cute little lisp sprayed saliva my way.

"Do you like my eyes?"

She straightened in Dad's arms. "They're not as pretty as Webb's." Freckles dotted her rosy cheeks as her dark lashes shuttered bright blue eyes. "Or my daddy's."

"Oh? Who's your daddy?" I looked at my own father.

He wiped something from her nose.

Without warning, she leaned forward and touched my face with her tiny hand.

A tingle spread through my body before the room around me disappeared, and I was running through the woods. Why was I running? I glanced over my shoulder, but I didn't see anyone. As I turned back, I tripped over a fallen branch. Footsteps trailed behind me. I pushed myself to my feet and looked over my shoulder again—and found a pair of red eyes glowing in the darkness. I couldn't move.

In a snap, the vision was gone.

"Abbey, we talked about touching people," Dad said, taking a few steps away from me.

What in the world just happened? I'd had a similar experience with Kraft, but I was the one touching him. Actually, I was drinking his blood.

Dad set Abbey down. "Go find a spot. Ms. Simpson is about to read."

She ran across the carpeted floor, black hair sweeping from side to side.

"Care to explain, Dad?" I asked in a whisper. "She's human, but her touch definitely wasn't."

He grasped my arm and walked me over to the base of the stairs. I glanced upward. I loved the mathematical design of the room. The number pi bordered the edge of the ceiling. The bannister had three-dimensional geometric shapes, while celestial planets hung from the wood beams throughout the library.

"Abbey and her mother live on base. Her father is a sentinel and has been missing in action for over a year. She's a special little girl. More than likely, her powers will develop before she decides if she wants to change."

I remembered Sloan, one of the sentinels, explaining something about two of their teammates missing, which was why the military flew the POW-MIA flag. "Will her father ever return?"

"We've been searching for Quade and Crowe for a while." Dad scratched his neck.

The children—a split of four boys and four girls —had settled down on the beanbag chairs. As Ms. Simpson read to them, all were enthralled, including Darcy, who lounged on the floor next to Abbey.

"What happens if Abbey touches a human? Will they experience a vision like I did?"

"Anyone can."

"Is the vision I had of my future?" *Please say no.* Red eyes were an omen.

"Possibly, or she might've been showing you hers."

Sawyer breezed in. "Commander, we have a situation." His eyes fluctuated between gold and brown. "A fire broke out at the training facility. Two sentinels are down. And we have one of the Plutariums in custody."

I gasped in shock as my heart crawled into my throat. Was Webb one of the sentinels? *Oh, please let him be okay.* Sawyer said two sentinels were down. Did that mean Sam wasn't hurt?

Darcy jerked her head in my direction.

"Let's go." Flecks of red speckled Dad's eyes.

Darcy ran up and grasped Dad's hand. "What's wrong?" Her brown eyes held fear.

"Go back to the group," Dad ordered. "It's not your father."

I guessed he'd read her mind.

"Oh." She let go and sighed.

"I'll see you later," I said to Darcy. I had no intentions of staying here, knowing my brother and Webb could be the ones hurt.

"Full report, Sawyer." Dad took long strides as he left the library.

"We don't know which two are down, and we're not sure who they have in custody. Communication was cut off when Sloan radioed in." Sawyer jogged alongside Dad.

Like Sawyer, I jogged to keep up with Dad. I prayed that not only Sam and Webb but all the sentinels were all right.

We had just crossed a street near the main building when Sawyer said, "Sir, one van is offloading the injured, and the other is headed to the prison."

I sprinted for the medical facility, bursting through the lobby doors.

"Ms. Mason, slow down," the sentinel on duty ordered.

I nervously stabbed the elevator button. *Come on.* I bounced up and down before banging on it again. As the ding sounded, Sam stormed into the lobby. A cut marred his right cheek.

"Are you all right?" I asked in a shaky voice as my heart was pounding to get out of my chest.

"Where's Pops?" he demanded.

"Is Webb hurt? What happened?"

"Calm down, Sis. Olivia and Tripp had minor injuries." He stalked past the circular desk. "Pops. Where is he?"

Fear wound through his tone. Why was he afraid?

"Tell me where Webb is." My freaking heart was a beat from stopping.

"Sam," called Ruth, our receptionist. "Your father just phoned. Meet him at the prison wing."

"Where's Webb?" I asked again.

"He's not hurt. He was escorting Jonah in." Sam rushed out.

Jonah worked for Edmund Rain as his right-hand man. I shook off the willies, and at the same time let out a sigh of relief that Webb was fine.

I ran out to catch up to Sam. The prison sat behind the main headquarters. The easiest way to get to it was to walk outside from the lobby and around to the back.

"How did you capture Jonah?" I asked as we made a right at the end of the building and down a side street.

The first time I'd seen Jonah, he'd been

choking a cop, who he'd beaten into a coma. Then, when I was still human, he tried to capture me. The sentinels caught him and locked him in the base prison, but he'd escaped. He reminded me of a bad dream that kept returning night after night.

"I don't know. It's all a blur. One minute we were listening to an instructor, the next the alarms were blaring."

"How did you get that cut on your face?"

"I fought one of the Plutariums. Edmund has some new minions."

We'd killed a few of his team members at the mansion last week. I guessed we had more Plutariums to kill now. Not something I was looking forward to.

We turned right onto the courtyard that separated the prison building from headquarters. A chill came over me as I looked up at the brick structure. I hadn't been in this place since Edmund staked me with cobalt swords.

Sam and I crossed the carpet of grass where we met Sentinel Kraft, who guarded the entrance. He wore his usual garb—black cargo uniform with fingerless gloves. His blond wavy hair touched his broad shoulders, and colorful tattoos painted his arms.

"Are they up or down?" Sam asked, as though he were in charge.

"Third floor. End of the hall," Kraft said with his arms crossed over his chest.

"Wait here, Sis," Sam said over his shoulder as he stepped in.

No way. I wasn't waiting out here. I had to make sure Webb was okay. I ignored my brother and walked up to the door.

Kraft raised his hand. "Sorry, Jo. I have orders not to let you in."

"What!"

Sam vanished inside.

I was about to argue when Webb appeared in the doorway. Red slashed his arms, blood covered his left earlobe, and his right eye was swollen shut.

I ran to him. "Are you—?"

He held up his hand to stop me. "Fine." His voice was hoarse. "Kraft, the commander may be a while. I'll be in the medical facility." He squinted his good eye as he stepped out into the sunlight. "Let's go." He grasped my arm as though he were carting me off to my own prison cell.

A stray dandelion brushed my leg as we crossed the courtyard. Once we were in the entryway of the main building, Webb shoved me against the wall, sweeping his gaze over me. His fangs descended. Blood sped through my veins. I automatically twisted my hair up off my neck as though he compelled me to expose my skin. He growled his approval before he lowered his head, his fangs inching closer. My pulse quickened.

He sucked my skin. I moaned. His tongue swirled once, twice, as if prepping the spot. He licked his way around my ear and neck, his fangs scraping, teasing. My tummy knotted, a warm feeling slithering down. My fangs descended.

"Webb, you need blood," I said weakly. "Take mine."

His spine stiffened as he jerked away. "Come on. Let's go see Dr. Vieira."

I slumped against the wall. "Why won't you drink from me?"

"I told you why." His swollen eye twitched.

"I don't want to wait another month." I sounded like a two-year-old.

"Jo, this isn't up for discussion."

Stubborn vampire.

I wanted to protest and demand he take my blood, but I'd only be wasting my time. So I pushed off the wall. "Webb, what happened?"

"We were ambushed. Somehow Edmund found out where we were."

We climbed the steps up to the fourth floor.

"The other mole?"

"More than likely," he said, touching his bad eye.

"What's my dad going to do to Jonah?"

When we reached the fourth-floor landing, he opened the door. "Don't worry about Jonah."

"You don't want to tell me, do you?" I asked, walking into the hall.

He kept silent as he stepped alongside me.

I tried another angle. "Was Kate there?"

"No," he barked.

Silence stretched between us as we made our way to the medical facility. By the way he snapped, part of me got the impression she had been there. Then again, he could just be in a bad mood from the raid. I wanted to push for answers, but an argument wouldn't help him or me.

12

The medical facility was divided into two areas. Against the left wall was a gray metal box with a slatted roller door. Above it was a hooded vent. A stainless-steel bench lined both sides of the metal box. In front of it, a black lab bench spanned the length of the room, with small openings on each end for access to the area between the two structures. A refrigerator and a sink were along the back wall, with wood cabinets to the right.

A familiar face greeted us when Webb and I entered the medical facility. I hadn't seen Dr. Case since he'd locked me in a coffin to die. His wavy brown hair had grown out, curling around his ears. His brown eyes seemed to shudder with regret as he looked at me.

"What's Dr. Case doing here?" I asked Webb.

"Penance," Webb said as he strode down the center, passing four desks on his right. "Case. You're behaving, I hope."

I stayed and leaned against the first metal desk, eyeing Dr. Case, who was behind the lab bench next to Dr. Vieira.

"Funny, London. Why wouldn't I? You guys have a babysitter glued to my ass," he replied scornfully. "Jo, nice to see you."

"Is it?" His sarcasm rubbed off on me, bringing out my lingering anger at what he'd done to me.

Dr. Vieira lifted his head from a microscope. "Interesting reaction." Then he glanced in the microscope again.

"Where's Tripp and Olivia?" Webb asked as he unlocked the refrigerator on the back wall.

"I'm right here." Tripp stalked out of the room in the back right corner, clipping his sentinel sword to his belt. "Olivia is still out. What did you find, Doc?" He smoothed back his sandy blond hair.

"The bullet was filled with a sedative," Dr. Vieira said. "The same substance given to the sentinels who were guarding the prison the night Edmund escaped."

"You mean the night I almost got beaten to death," Dr. Case said.

My uncle, Patrick, had tried to kill him after Dad had interrogated them.

"Do you know what's in this?" Dr. Vieira arched a brow at Dr. Case.

"Look, I agreed to help, but—"

"But nothing, Case. We made a deal—your help in exchange for the person who killed your sister," Webb reminded him as he scarfed down blood.

I remembered Dad telling me a sentinel had killed Dr. Case's sister. Was Webb ready to hand one of his brethren over to him? He'd worked for Edmund.

"You can't trust him," I said.

"We know, Jo," Dr. Vieira said. "And we don't. But we need his help. The thumb drive we recovered from the mansion has a slew of medical data we can't decipher. We're hoping Dr. Case can give us some insight."

"Make no mistake," Webb said, glaring at Dr. Case. "One misstep—"

"What's so interesting, Doc?" Tripp piped up, slicing the tension in half.

"Something in the sedative seems to be attacking the white blood cells."

"Are you saying Olivia could die?" There were only a few ways for us vamps to leave this earth.

"Not likely." Dr. Vieira rubbed his jaw. "Whatever was in the bullet isn't as strong as the endotoxin."

"Why has Tripp recovered so fast?" He and I made eye contact as he walked up and leaned against the desk next to me.

"Luckily for Tripp"—Dr. Vieira removed the slide from the microscope—"his immune system is like granite because of his bloodline."

"What're you talking about?" I glanced at Dr. Vieira then back at Tripp.

Tripp's mouth curled upward at the edges.

"Jo." Webb set the blood container on the lab bench across from me.

"It's okay, Lieutenant," Tripp said. "She'll find out, sooner or later. And it's not a secret in our world. Some of my ancestors are wolf shifters," he said casually.

"Come again?" I angled my ear closer to him, unsure I'd heard him correctly.

"My great-great-great-grandmother married a wolf shifter."

"You mean you're part vampire and part wolf?"

My voice hitched as I fought to process the information.

"Tripp is ninety-five percent vampire. Only a small part of his DNA has the wolf gene. Because of this, his immune system is harder to penetrate," Webb explained.

I'd only been kidding when I asked Dad if my DNA was part wolf. Nausea suddenly churned in my stomach. "Are you telling me there are people who turn into wolves?"

"Why is that so hard to believe, Jo?" Dr. Case asked. "You're a vampire."

I growled my annoyance at his cocksureness. Then I swung my gaze to Dr. Vieira. "My dad said my DNA had some anomalies. What does that mean?"

"What is she talking about?" Webb moved closer to me.

"Now, both of you. Don't get ahead of me." Dr. Vieira wiped the lens of the scope with a cloth. "I'll know more after your physical tomorrow, Jo."

The double doors whooshed open.

"Lieutenant." Kodiak Snow, a sentinel, strode in, dressed in black cargo pants, black T-shirt, and black boots. His once shoulder-length blond hair was now cut short. "Ms. Simpson just called. Abbey Quade is missing."

"How?" Webb asked.

"Ms. Simpson took them out to the park after the reading session. That's all I know."

"Has anyone called her mother?" Webb plucked his phone from his cargo pants.

"Sawyer left a message on her phone, sir," Kodiak replied.

"Tripp, get a team together and scout the area around the ball field," Webb ordered. "Snow, get down to the park and make sure Ms. Simpson and the other kids get home safely."

Both Tripp and Snow promptly left.

"I want to help." My heart clenched. What if someone had kidnapped her? Intruders had been common, of late.

"You can come with me." Webb turned to Dr. Vieira. "Call me when Olivia's awake."

Webb tapped the screen of his phone as he walked to the back door of the lab.

I pushed off the desk and trailed behind him.

"Did you get hold of her mom?" Webb asked the person on the line.

I imagined he was talking to Sawyer, since Kodiak mentioned he'd been trying to contact Abbey's mom. We climbed down the four flights of stairs as Webb continued to listen to the caller then gave a few orders before he hung up. Once outside, Webb called Dad to fill him in.

The sun cast long shadows along the sidewalk as we made our way to the human side of the base. After he ended his call with Dad, I glanced up at Webb. His swollen eye had opened.

The park came into view when we passed the women's barracks on our right. Houses dotted the street in the distance to our left. Salt from Mt. Hope Bay lingered in the air.

"Abbey couldn't have gone far," I said, more to myself than anything. Or at least I prayed she hadn't.

Webb didn't say anything as we crossed the street to the park. Ms. Simpson was talking to Kodiak when we arrived. Darcy had the other children corralled near the merry-go-round.

"Lieutenant." Kodiak nodded to Webb. "We have a sentinel with Mrs. Quade now. Tripp and his team are checking the surrounding area. I'm going to take the children home. Their parents have been notified, too."

"Ms. Simpson, can you accompany Kodiak?" Webb asked.

"Yes," she said. "Also, I'm so sorry about all this. I should've been paying more attention, but I got a phone call from my mother." Her eyes were filled with tears.

I ran over to Darcy as Webb asked Ms. Simpson some more questions.

"What happened?" I asked.

A colorful jungle gym sat behind the merry-go-round, and two of the boys climbed up the ladder, chasing each other as though nothing happened.

"Not sure. One minute Abbey was here..." She stared off into the distance.

"What is it, Darcy?" I followed her gaze to the trees. "Did Abbey go into the woods?"

She blinked and shrugged at the same time. "Maybe. What if she did? What if Edmund—"

"Hey." I grabbed her shoulders. "Look at me. There's no reason for Edmund to take Abbey."

Lurking wasn't Edmund's style. He had known all the secret passages in and out of the base, since he'd been a sentinel, but Dad had barricaded all the tunnels and every entrance and exit Edmund knew about.

"What if he's here to kidnap me again?" She dropped her gaze.

For as long as I'd known Darcy, she'd always been happy, and nothing bothered her. That was until Edmund ruined her bubbly personality. I hated to see my best friend in fear for her life.

"Darcy." A blond-haired boy tugged on her hand. "I want to go home."

"And who are you?" I asked.

"Jeffrey," he said.

"Well, Jeffrey. Do you know where Abbey is?"

He shook his head. "I want my mom."

"You see that tall blond-haired man with the ponytail, with Ms. Simpson and Webb?"

He nodded, looking at Kodiak.

"He's going to take all of you home."

At that moment, Kodiak walked up. "You kids ready to ride in a truck?"

All of them shouted or squealed their delight —well, all the boys, not the girls. I wouldn't be excited about a big black truck, either, unless Webb was in it.

"Follow me," Kodiak said to the children.

They all followed the tall sentinel across the park. As their voices faded, I focused my attention back to Darcy. "Let's go for a walk. Maybe we can help in the search." I had to do something to get her mind off Edmund.

Don't go far.

I glanced over my shoulder at Webb and answered, *We won't.*

"Jo, I'm scared."

I wrapped an arm around her. "I know, but don't be. This place is tighter than Alcatraz."

It wasn't. At least, I didn't think so, but I had to comfort my friend.

Tennis courts, a baseball field, and basketball court lay behind the playground. The scent of lilacs mixed with the salt air as we strolled out to the bleachers.

"Do we have to sit here?" Darcy scanned the dense trees, their branches swaying in the breeze.

"Come on. It will be like we're at one of Sam's games in high school. Remember how we used to make fun of the girls who drooled over Sam and Ben?"

A tentative smile played across her lips. "Yeah, that was a blast."

We slid into the second row.

"Look out there." I motioned to Tripp. He was walking the edge of the wooded area that lay beyond the outfield. "The sentinels will not let anyone in," I assured her.

"Why aren't you afraid?" she asked.

"I know my dad wouldn't let anything happen to you or anyone," I said, hoping to put her at ease. Dad had sentinels everywhere, and security was tight, but that didn't mean someone couldn't get past security, especially since he still suspected a mole among the sentinels.

The wind picked up, carrying a faint scent of baby powder. Seeking a better whiff, I hopped off the bench.

"What?" Darcy's voice shook.

"Stay here." I jogged into the outfield, letting my vampire nose drag me toward the scent.

By the time I reached the scoring booth, Tripp and Webb flanked me. They must've smelled it too.

"I think she's in there," I whispered.

Webb plowed through the door, ripping it off its hinges. Tripp and I entered behind him. An electrical panel hung on the wall to the left of the door. Tripp flicked a switch, and the room came to life. Boxes and plastic bins stacked one on top of the other banked the left wall. Pristine white bases lay on the floor along the staircase.

Sniffling echoed.

"Abbey." Webb's gentle tone contrasted with his alpha actions as he hurried to the back left corner and squatted. "Hey, what's all the crying for?" He reached out then stood up with Abbey in his arms.

Her tiny hands locked around his neck. "Daddy. I saw my daddy."

"Where?" He hoisted her up.

Tripp and I shared a look. I'd bet the shock on his face mirrored my own. Her father was missing in action. How could he be on this base?

"In the woods." Tears streamed down her freckled cheeks.

Again Tripp and I exchanged glances. Webb walked over to where Tripp and I were standing, which was just inside the door.

"Hey, Abbey." I tilted my head to the side. "How do you know it was your daddy?"

"He's got red eyes." Her tone held conviction that the words she spoke were true.

Fear lodged in my throat. "Is it true, Webb?"

"Tripp, I'll take her home. Make sure we scrub every inch of this base."

Why was he avoiding the question? "Well, are you going to answer me?"

"Later, Jo," Webb said as he carried Abbey out of the scoring booth.

I stood frozen for a second. Then I glanced at Tripp.

"I have no idea." He raised his hands. Then he pulled his cell phone from the clip on his belt, punched in a number, and brought the phone to his ear. "Lane, I need you to get a lock and secure the scoring booth."

As he talked, I headed back to Darcy, who was standing near the bleachers. I scanned the area, the woods in particular. Was there someone with red eyes in the woods? Was it Edmund? Or Ben? He had escaped from Olivia and Sloan the other night. Maybe it was Ben. After all, he'd been here at the main gate trying to see me when I was in Maine.

"Thank God she's okay," Darcy said as I strode up to her.

"Come on. Let's go back to my apartment until my dad is done with whatever he's doing." I didn't want her to be alone. I didn't want to be alone, either.

Besides, she was new to the base, and with Ms. Simpson helping Kodiak, I wasn't sure where to take her. Dad would probably get mad since I was still new as a vampire and he didn't trust me completely around humans. Her scent wasn't bothering me right now. Plus I didn't feel any type of hunger at the moment.

We walked in silence. When we approached the main entrance to my building, Dad and Sam sauntered up. I wanted to ask them about Jonah, but Darcy was with me. Dad wouldn't like it at all if I brought up Jonah in front of her, and I didn't want to scare Darcy any more than she already was.

"Darcy and I are going to hang out in the apartment, and my hunger is fine," I said to Dad, hoping he wouldn't say no to the idea.

Dad arched a brow.

"Please, Dad? I don't want Darcy sitting in the women's barracks all by herself."

"I'll get a sentinel up to the apartment. I need to finish a few things. Son, meet me in the control room while I walk Jo and Darcy up to the apartment."

I rolled my eyes at Dad. "You're going to have to trust me sooner or later."

"It's okay," Darcy said to me. "No offense, but I would feel comfortable with a sentinel."

Dad nodded at Darcy—as a thank-you, I imagined.

I didn't take offense. I'd been in her shoes when I was alone in Webb's office with him as a human. I did get scared, thinking he was going to sink his fangs into me.

Sam went to the control room while Dad, Darcy, and I rode the elevator up to the apartment. Dad called Kodiak to see if he was almost finished dropping off the children. Then he called Webb and told him to meet him in the control room, too.

Darcy and I talked about how her mom wanted her to go and stay with her grandmother for the summer. Apparently, her grandmother lived up in Canada.

"Does your mom know what happened to you?" I asked as we entered the apartment.

"Yes and no. My dad explained to her that I was being held for ransom because of one of his cases. But she doesn't know about vampires. She'd have my dad and me committed if she did."

We both laughed.

Dad disappeared into his room. Darcy and I relaxed on the couch. No sooner had I turned on the TV than did Kodiak show up. Then Dad came into the family room.

"The parents okay?" Dad asked Kodiak.

Kodiak made himself comfortable on a barstool at the island separating the family room from the kitchen. "A little shaken, but overall, okay. They also know Abbey is safe with her mom now."

"Good," Dad said. "Jo, I'll be back in about an hour." He grabbed his keys from the table next to the door, then he was gone.

Daylight waned as we flipped through channels. Sam had begged Dad for a TV so he could watch sports, mostly. Dad had broken down recently and bought one.

Watching TV seemed to calm my mind, and right now, I wanted nothing more than not to think about my DNA, Abbey, Edmund, Darcy's safety, and all the other vampire drama in my life.

"There's an episode of *The Vampire Diaries* on. Do you want to watch it?" she asked, a little too excitedly.

So much for escaping paranormal drama. I broke out in a fit of giggles. "You want to watch a vampire show with your best friend who is a vampire?"

Kodiak even laughed. "You girls watch that crap?"

"I do," Darcy said, rather proudly. "Well, I just started. After I found out Jo was a vampire, I had to see what the show was all about."

I rolled my eyes as we both settled in, and the show opened. Kodiak mumbled something under his breath. I harrumphed several times through the next hour as I compared my own life to the make-believe vampire series. Even Kodiak spewed noises along with me. In TV land, vampires were created by being bitten by another vampire. In my world, humans became vampires only if they carried a gene, and even then, they had to choose to activate that gene. Though if Edmund succeeded in his quest to build an army of vampires, maybe the TV show wouldn't be too far off the mark.

With the credits rolling, I stood up to stretch my sleeping limbs then darted to the fridge. All the vampire biting on TV spurred my hunger.

"Stay tuned for breaking news," a lady's voice said from the TV.

I tossed Darcy a bottle of water then warmed my mug of blood. The microwave dinged as Dad, Sam, and Webb trudged into the apartment. Kodiak stood at attention.

"At ease, Snow." Dad threw his keys on the hall table.

"Is ESPN on?" Sam snatched the remote from Darcy, plopping down on the lone chair.

"We were just watching—"

"The news," Kodiak interrupted, cutting off Darcy.

I snickered. I guessed the manly sentinel didn't want his superiors to know he'd been watching a vampire soap opera.

"Authorities are concerned we might have a widespread problem on our hands. In the last two months, several teenagers have been reported missing in the tri-state area."

The room fell silent as we all directed our attention to the pretty lady on the screen.

"We have reporters standing by in Providence and Portland. We'll start with Portland. Dale, what have you found?"

The screen changed to a short, squat man who was wearing a white golf shirt. "Well, Dee, the authorities here in Maine are not sharing much information. What we do know is the missing teens are all boys."

The mug slipped out of my hands, shattering on the floor. Did Edmund have anything to do with the missing teens? He had kidnapped several from Durfee High School, but when we raided the mansion, we'd only rescued two.

"What is it?" Webb appeared at my side.

"What happened to the two boys we rescued?"

"They didn't make it, Jo." He bent down to pick up the broken pieces.

My heart went out to them and their family... but if they had lived, they could've turned into monsters like Blake Turner. I grabbed some paper towels off the counter near the stove. Webb deposited the broken mug into the trash under the sink while I wiped up the blood.

Dad turned off the TV and sprang into commander mode.

"Darcy, Kodiak will take you back to your room."

I stood up with the dirty paper towels in my hand. "Dad, can she stay?" I didn't want to be alone, and something told me she didn't, either. She'd been thinking too much about Edmund today, and this was her first night here.

"*No,*" he said.

Darcy frowned. I contemplated arguing, but I wasn't sure I could trust myself. What if I woke up in the middle of the night and snacked on her? Or what if Sam did that? We said our goodbyes and made plans for me to see her tomorrow.

Once Kodiak and Darcy had left, I resumed cleaning the rest of the floor then threw away the towels and washed my hands.

Sam asked, "Are the reporters right?"

"I don't know. I'll contact my superiors," Dad said.

"I'll check in with Stan and George," Webb stated. "Also, I did get more info on that lady, Lauren.

I wiped my hands on my jeans as I made my way over to the couch and sat down. I tucked my legs underneath me as I grabbed a pillow, making myself comfortable.

"My sources tell me, she's a lawyer out of Boston. In fact, she works in Mr. Rose's office." Webb leaned on his knees as he eased down into a chair, keeping his eye on Dad.

"Seriously?" How odd. "Did you know that when you read her card?"

"No." Webb swung his gaze to me.

"Lauren is the least of our worries." Dad scrubbed a hand over his face. "It's late. Let's get some rest. Jo and Sam, remember you have your physical in the morning."

I disagreed with Dad. Lauren played a role in our lives somehow. I just didn't know how yet.

13

—————

Darkness squeezed me as fog swirled, clinging to my body. I adjusted my vision to see better, only to find myself imprisoned by tall redwoods. A musty, decaying odor hung in the air. It had to be from the decomposing detritus seeping between my toes. A light shone from somewhere in the distance.

A familiar voice cut through the fog-laden night. "Follow the light, my child."

My eerie feeling melted into downright fear. That old man had graced my dreams several times before.

"You must hurry," the old man said calmly.

The hairs on the back of my neck stiffened. Stepping toward the thin ray of light, I prayed with all my might I could wedge my body through the opening.

A twig snapped under my foot. The sound ricocheted like cannon fire. Creatures started howling.

I ignored my sixth sense that told me to turn around and run. I pushed on, but my shirt caught on a piece of bark. I unhooked it and kept going.

"Very good. Now, follow the paved path."

What path? All I saw through the fog was broken branches and leaves.

"Go around the large rock," the old man instructed. "There you'll find the path. I urge you to make haste, child."

Panic set in, along with the desire to strangle the old man. I stepped cautiously, ensuring I didn't step into a hole or off a cliff. After ten agonizing steps, I zigzagged around another cluster of trees before the rock the old man spoke of shone like a lighthouse through the fog. Inscribed in the jagged stone was *He who enters must not linger.* What did that mean?

As the fog lifted, so did my gaze. Instead of the tall trees, headstones and coffins dotted the landscape in every direction beyond the rock. I thought to run, but a faint memory reminded me to listen to the old man.

"Time is of the essence," he warned.

I scanned the landscape once again and found the old man kneeling at an altar in front of an open coffin in the distance. A halo of light beamed down over him as he looked directly at me.

"Serapis, guide the child," he ordered.

I walked around the rock to find the panther sauntering up the narrow path toward me, amber eyes glowing. I automatically turned, searching for refuge. But the trees behind me had vanished. In their place, a large brick wall rose high into the midnight sky.

"You can only move forward from here, my child. Wait for Serapis."

The panther bowed his head, as if to say, "Hi. Nice to see you again."

I slowly nodded in return, going up to the amazing animal. He wiped his nose against my thigh, and I unthinkingly petted his head.

The area came to life. Men, women, and children roamed aimlessly, as though they were searching for life or loved ones. I quickly removed my hand, and the people became coffins. I stilled when I spied a body in the coffin the old man knelt in front of. My throat became dry, my legs weak.

"You must join me, child. I need to prepare you."

I shook my head. Something in me told me I shouldn't go anywhere near him or the coffin.

A bang sounded from somewhere behind me, jarring me out of my stupor.

The old man's voice lowered to a growl. "Serapis, bring her."

Backing away from the panther's narrowed gaze, I screamed, and so did the creatures and maybe even the dead. Howls and hoots competed with me until something soft and soothing rose above everything and everyone else.

"Wake up, Jo," the voice said, low and soft. "Pumpkin."

Another scream tore from my lungs as I opened my eyes. "Let me go. I don't want to go over there. I can't." Tears streamed down my cheeks.

"Shhh. You were dreaming," Dad crooned, holding me.

I shook violently as the dream burned in my brain. I wiped away tears.

"A bad dream?" Dad asked.

"The old man. He's back. He was kneeling in front of a...coffin. He sent his panther to guide me to him. He wanted me to join him. I didn't want to see who was in there."

"Panther?" Sam staggered in, hair sticking in every direction. He crawled up the bed on the other side of me.

"Tell me more of your dream," Dad said. He made himself comfortable as he sat back against the headboard.

"I want to hear about the panther." Sam yawned.

As the three of us lounged on my bed, shadows playing on the ceiling, I pitched into a play-by-play of my dream. I even recounted my first one, when I'd met the old man.

"So you don't know who was in the coffin?" Sam asked.

"No. And I don't want to know." I sniffled.

"As vampires, our dreams can give insight into our futures." Dad had mentioned that to me before.

"Does that mean I'm the one in the coffin?" I might not be enamored with my vampire status, but I didn't want to die. I still had things I wanted to accomplish in my life.

"There's a reason the old man wanted you to see who was in the coffin. From what you've told me, he seems to be helping you."

"He may be, but he's also confusing." In my first dream, a few weeks back, he'd rattled off some wisdom about me protecting humanity.

"Most dreams are, pumpkin." He draped an arm over my shoulder.

I leaned against him with my head on his chest as Sam fell asleep.

"Dad, tell me more about Abbey," I said.

"The vision she showed you. Was it your dream?" He crossed one ankle over the other.

"I don't know. When she touched me, I was in a forest, but my dream didn't have someone behind me with red eyes. Does her father have red vampire eyes like Edmund?"

His hold on me tightened. "Edmund is her father," he whispered.

The world spun, or maybe my head twirled with shock. I wasn't sure I was even breathing. "I thought her father..."

"Quade is essentially her father. He met her mom, Rachel, not long after Edmund was out of her life and out of the sentinels."

"Are you sure then that Abbey is Edmund's child?" I straightened and looked at Dad.

"Yeah, she is." He pulled me to him. "Rachel found out she was two months pregnant when she and Quade met. And Dr. Vieira tested Abbey's DNA against Edmund's medical records."

"So does Edmund know?" I didn't think he did, for some reason.

"He must never know." He kissed my head. "He and my brother would use her as a lab specimen to fund their mission of building the perfect army."

"But she's his flesh and blood." Edmund was an evil vampire, at least to me, but that didn't mean he shouldn't know he had a daughter. Maybe if he knew he had a child he would change his ways.

"Yes, and she's human right now—a perfect age to study genetics. Aside from her mom and Quade, only Webb, me, and now you have this information. And I'm telling you this because I know you'll keep asking. And I don't want you to bring up this subject in front of any of the sentinels again. It is not to be discussed, whispered, or questioned from here on out. Do you understand, Jo?"

Inwardly, I smiled. For Dad to trust me with this information said a lot about how far our relationship had come. A month ago he would've told me it was none of my business.

"I get it, Dad. So how does she know her father has red eyes?"

"I suspect her visions."

"Oh! She was trying to show me today when she touched me."

"Maybe," he said.

We sat quietly. The only sound in the room was Sam's breathing, which I hadn't noticed until now.

"Do you think she saw him earlier today?" I murmured.

"No. We found Ben's car not far from the base. We think he was trying to sneak in again." He rose. "We have a few hours until daylight. Get some rest."

"What about Sam?"

We both looked at my brother. He had one arm underneath the pillow while the other one was tucked in close to him.

"Leave him. He'll be fine."

Wow, I hadn't slept in the same bed with my brother since we were toddlers. Most of our foster homes hadn't had enough beds, so we would share. Now we were adults, and even though I loved him to death, it seemed awkward.

Dad retired to his room. I tried to sleep over Sam's heavy breathing and occasional snorts. A few times I punched him then laughed. My efforts didn't work at all. He was dead to the world.

So I lay lost in thought about Abbey and Edmund. Aside from both having black hair, I didn't see any resemblance between the two.

"You can't sleep?" Sam asked as he stretched.

"How can I, with you snoring?" I turned on my side to face Sam and tucked my arm underneath my pillow.

"You want to tell me what's bothering you? Is it your dream?" He rubbed his left eye.

I wasn't allowed to tell him what Dad had shared about Abbey. "What do you think the future holds for us, Sam?"

"Sis, I'm not a fortune teller. I'm an Empath." His tone was soft.

"I know. But what do you think?" Neither he nor I could foresee the future, but I wanted his thoughts.

He sat up, adjusting the pillow behind him. "I think we have a very challenging road ahead, Sis. If the story on the news is correct, and Edmund is responsible, we have a battle to stop his operation. Then there's Ben. We don't know what he is now or what he's going to do. And let's not forget the death of the Secretary of the Navy. Dad's innocence is still up for discussion."

I'd forgotten all about Dad's grand jury hearing, although he hadn't yet mentioned when it would be.

"The most important topic"—Sam raised his eyebrows—"is your court hearing for Blake's death. When is it?"

"No idea. I guess I should ask Dad." Not that I wanted to even bring up the subject.

A tiny ray of light sneaked in through a slit in the curtains.

"Was Kate or Edmund at the training facility yesterday?" The less I thought about the Council and what they might do to me, the better.

"Kate was, but not Edmund. At least, I didn't see him."

"I figured as much."

"Didn't Webb tell you?" He looked down at me.

"He told me she wasn't there." I should be upset that he lied, but all I felt right now was worry about our future, about why Kate wanted to kill Webb and what Edmund had in store for us. Plus the dream kind of freaked me out. Was it a snapshot of what the future held? If so, who was in that coffin? "So she's still trying to kill him?" I sat up.

"It looks that way. Jo." Sam grabbed my hand. "You know I would never betray you. Never. You're my family, my life."

I wasn't even thinking about that. Deep in my heart, I knew Sam would never betray me or I, him. Still, his reassurance was exactly what I needed to hear.

***

Dr. Case greeted Sam and me as we entered the medical facility. He had his hands in the pockets of his blue lab coat.

"What's he doing here?" Sam asked.

"Helping." Dr. Case waved his hand out to his right. "You'll be in the room in the far back corner."

I shrugged. I'd fill Sam in later. The three of us walked down the center aisle of the medical facility with Dr. Case in the lead.

"A special room just for you two," Dr. Case said, standing off to the side of the doorway. "Go on in."

Sam and I walked in. Wow, he was right. Our names were taped to the monitors mounted on the wall—two for Sam and two for me. Two exam tables and two carts with needles, charts, cotton swabs, and specimen slides sat in front of the monitors.

Dr. Case flipped a switch, and the monitors on the wall powered on.

"Glad to see you wore your workout gear," Dr.

Vieira said, gliding into the room. "Up on the tables, both of you." He punched his password on the keyboard. "Okay, Dr. Case. I'll take it from here."

Without a word, Dr. Case left and closed the door behind him.

"You don't trust him?" I hopped up onto the paper-covered table in front of the monitor with my name on it.

"As you learned yesterday, Jo, he's here to help decipher any data we have from the thumb drive. Nothing more."

"Is Olivia okay?" Sam asked as he made himself comfortable on his bench.

"She's stable. Her immune system has been compromised, so she'll need time to recover."

"Have you found out what was in the bullet?" I asked.

"We're working on it. Now, let's get started."

Dr. Vieira slipped his hands into a pair of latex gloves. Then he began drawing blood, swabbing our mouths, checking our hearts, and measuring our height and weight. Once he completed those tasks, Brian, his curly-haired lab assistant, came in and collected our DNA and blood samples then left the room.

Dr. Vieira picked up a wand-like device,

pressed a button on the handle, and scanned my computer chip, which was embedded in my lower back on the right. The wand beeped once before my information scrolled across the screen.

Josephine Juno Mason, born December twenty-first. Father: Steven Mars Mason. Brother: Samuel Jove Mason. Blood type: AF negative. Heart rate: twenty bpm. Eye color: silver and violet. Hair: black with purple streaks. Notes: A diamond-shaped birthmark behind the left ear. A seven-pointed star tattoo located on the back, upper right shoulder.

I read through each line at least five times. I'd forgotten about my birthmark. No one could see it unless I had my hair up, away from my ears.

Dr. Vieira repeated the routine on Sam. I gleaned one new thing about my brother. His heart rate was fifteen beats per minute.

"Why is Sam's heart rate lower than mine?"

We'd learned early that, as we grew, our pulse would decrease to five beats per minute.

"Everyone is different, Jo, and male vampires advance faster than females in some respects. Females, on the other hand, gain their powers before males."

Dr. Vieira examined us thoroughly, recording every stat in the computer as he progressed from one area to the other.

After two hours, he pulled off his gloves. "Let's discuss my findings so far." He sat down on a rolling stool adjacent to the exam tables, putting the keyboard in his lap, and tapped a few keys. "Here's your basic data, vitals, height, weight, et cetera."

Wow, I had grown two inches since turning vampire—five feet, eight inches. Sam had grown four, to six feet, four inches.

"You both have the same blood type." Dr. Vieira hit a key, and the screen advanced. "Heart rates are dropping nicely to the normal vampire level. I would say another few months, and you should be right in line with five beats per minute or thereabouts."

The exam room door opened, and Dad strolled in. "Are these two healthy, Damon?" Dad clipped his phone to his belt.

"Better than healthy. I won't know the results of the blood work and DNA samples for at least two weeks. It depends on how backed up the lab is."

"What about the anomaly you spoke of?" Dad settled between the exam tables, stance wide.

"I'd rather wait until the lab results come back before I say for certain." Dr. Vieira looked at Dad then me.

"Humor me, Damon. What do you think is going on with Jo?" Dad crossed his arms over his chest.

Dr. Vieira rose then set the keyboard on top of Sam's cart. Then he cleared his throat. "The tests I ran on Jo after she turned vampire a few months ago revealed that her DNA has a quadruple helix structure. Normal natural-born vampires have a triple helix. I hadn't said anything to you, Steven, because I wasn't certain of this, and I'm still not."

Dad chewed on his cheek as if he was thinking. Or was he mad?

So I had a different DNA makeup than normal vampires. What was the big deal?

Tripp and his wolf bloodline popped in my head. "Dad, did Mom have any wolves in her lineage?"

Sam snorted. "Are you crazy?"

"Um...dead serious. Talk to Tripp?"

"What?" Sam gaped. "Tripp is a wolf?"

"Let's not get off track," Dad said. "To answer your question, Jo, not that I know of. Our lineage has always been—"

"Odd," Sam supplied.

"What does this mean, Damon?" Dad asked, his gaze on Dr. Vieira.

Dr. Vieira ran a hand through his short brown

hair. "For as long as I've been studying genetics, especially ours, I haven't come across a natural-born vampire with a quadruple helix." He pinned his brown eyes on me.

"I take it I'm normal?" Sam asked.

"Your earlier tests are normal." Dr. Vieira's hand went over his face.

"You seem a little concerned for some reason," Dad said as he uncrossed his arms. "Is there something else you're not telling?"

He let out a heavy sigh. "If I were in Patrick's shoes, and I was trying to genetically change humans into vampires, I would want to study Jo. Look, we know he's developed something that works. Only there are flaws. If he finds out Jo is different, he'll want her. You know he will, Steven. I'm not trying to scare anyone, but we have to think like him."

"Shit!" Dad barked.

Electricity charged the air. My mouth hung open as horror settled in my veins. I'd rather be dead than in the hands of my uncle, Patrick. I remembered when we'd found Sam. He was lying on a table in a glass-enclosed room with his arms hanging off the sides. His skin was pale, and he had a weak pulse.

Sam swore.

"Are you sending their samples to our lab in Boston?" Dad began pacing.

"Yes. And I've already spoken to Fred Lambert, who's in charge of the lab. I've asked if Grace can run the samples. She's discreet and trustworthy," Dr. Vieira said.

"Put a rush on them if you can, and make sure it is discreet. If Edmund gets wind of this info, Jo's life will be in jeopardy." Dad blew out a breath, his fangs extended.

What else was new? He wanted me dead anyway. At least, he'd told me so. Regardless, I had to live my life. Even as a human in foster care, I had to protect myself from other kids or even foster dads, although I didn't do a very good job. Sam had always been my protector.

"He's already planned my death. So what's the difference? I'll never be able to live a normal life, will I?" It was more of a question to myself than anything.

"Not unless Edmund is dead," Sam said, matter of fact.

Dad looked as though a zillion questions were running through his mind.

Suffocating silence hung over us.

Dad bit the inside of his cheek. Dr. Vieira started to power down the monitors.

"Can I go?" What was the point of worrying or watching Dad have a meltdown?

He glanced down at me through silver eyes. "We do need to take extra precautions with you."

"Now, Dad," I said. "You're protective enough. I don't need for you to put a noose around my neck."

Since I started living with Dad, he'd kept a close eye on me, to the point that I had a body-guard on me at all times. But that was mainly due to my bloodlust, given the humans who lived on base. Over the past week, he'd loosened the restrictions. I liked not having someone watch me all the time.

He arched a brow as though I'd given him a great idea.

"By the way, Doc. Are we free to drink any type of blood now?" Sam asked as his fangs slid out.

"Not until the final results are back."

"Then I need to run to the apartment." Sam jumped down. "Are you coming, Sis?"

Sam and I practically ran out before Dad protested. We wandered through the long hall-ways and stairwells of the building—Sam in his world, me in mine. I agreed with Dr. Vieira. Uncle Patrick would want to study my DNA. But I couldn't worry about my uncle or what he might do. Besides, as long as I stayed on base, I was protected. Or at least I hoped I was.

"I don't like any of this," Sam finally said as we approached a bank of elevators.

"I don't, either. But whether Edmund finds out about my unique DNA or not, he isn't stopping his plan. He'll attack us no matter what. We just have to be ready. Sam, promise me one thing."

"What?" The tips of his fangs glinted in the bright hall lights.

"If anything happens to me, please make sure Webb doesn't do anything stupid, or...you or Dad."

He scowled, showing more of his fangs. "Huh? Are you insane? Are you giving up already, Sis?"

"No way. But I don't have nine lives." I pictured myself lying on that table in the glass room.

"Where is this coming from? You're a fighter, Jo." Sam stopped just short of the elevator.

"Ha! I've never been one to fight. You know that." I glanced up and into his angry eyes.

"Oh no. Weren't you the one who ditched the vampires to go to the funeral home to find me? Weren't you the one who fought in the basement of the hospital and again in the mansion?"

I shrugged.

"Yeah. That's right. You were the one who saved me both times. You were the one who saved

Webb. This should make you angry. This shouldn't make you crawl in a hole and die." He pulled me into the tightest hug ever.

"My dreams don't show me good things, Sam."

"Your dreams are wrong." He let go of me.

The elevator dinged, and surprise, surprise, my tall and sexy vampire sauntered out.

"What's wrong? What's going on?" Webb asked as his eyes shifted into vampire mode.

"My sister thinks because she had one dream that her future is doomed. I'm out of here." He shook his head in disgust then jogged down the hall.

Whatever. I wasn't going to argue with him. Sam had anger problems. When we lived with Mr. Jackson, he'd set up Sam to attend an anger management class. But he never had the chance to attend since he was kidnapped. His temper had actually gotten better over the last few months. He seemed to have fewer anger outbursts since starting to feel others' emotions.

"Are you going to tell me what's going on?" Webb blinked.

My fangs slid out. "Can I get blood first?" Like Sam, I needed sustenance. I wasn't purposefully holding the great news from him, although I wouldn't be surprised if Dad hadn't already called him.

He nodded as we began to walk. When I entered the apartment, Sam was leaning against the bar, drinking from a glass.

I ignored the grimace on my brother's face as I reached into the fridge.

"Well, did you tell him?"

"No," I snapped. My fangs dug into my lip. I closed the fridge and narrowed my eyes at Sam. He was itching for a fight. At first, I chalked up his anger to him worrying about me. Now, though, he was getting on my nerves.

Webb hung back. "I already know."

Why did he ask, then?

It wasn't worth the aggravation to even ask.

"Why are you so upset, Sam? All I asked was for you to make sure you guys didn't do anything stupid if I died. That doesn't mean I'm giving up. And I have no control over my DNA or what Edmund is going to do." I placed my hands on my hips.

Sam dumped his glass in the sink. "I'll be in my room."

"What? No response?" I asked. *Let your brother go*, my inner voice told me.

He stalked out.

Without warning, Webb's strong arms were around me. "I'll just have to tie you up and not let you go anywhere." He grinned as he lifted me onto the counter.

Please do.

He arched a brow.

Did I say that out loud?

"No. Your telepathic connection must be open," he informed me with a wicked grin.

Heat pinched my cheeks.

He leaned in, his gaze dropping to my lips. "Would you like me to?" he asked with a seductive growl.

As long as you're on top of me. "Um..."

"I'd prefer you on top," he whispered in my ear.

Holy cow! There was something wrong with my powers today.

"Webb? How come you're not freaking out like my dad?"

"Do you really want to talk about this now?" He nibbled on my chin.

"Yes and no." I wanted to be naked... I quickly concentrated on closing off my mind.

He regarded me. After a heartbeat, he said, "I am worried. Make no mistake about it. But I've been in 'fight and protect' mode since Edmund left the sentinels. The news of your DNA just means we need to keep our senses sharpened and make sure he doesn't get ahold of this information. Now, you interrupted me."

My body turned liquid as his lips drew closer to mine. My brain, though, was focused on every-thing *but* Webb.

I'd meant what I said to Sam, about taking care of Webb and Dad. My life balanced on the edge of something. I just couldn't put my finger on what.

14

After my physical, life moved on without incident. Three weeks passed, and everyone dove into routine. Darcy worked in the library, helping Ms. Simpson catalog new books she'd received from donors. She was stuck here until her father paid his debt. She didn't mind, though. Her time on base gave her the opportunity to learn more about my paranormal world. She figured, if her father continued to defend and enter into deals with vampires, then she should know as much about my species as possible.

Sam and I spent our days in the secret vampire library with Ms. Costner, learning and testing on all school subjects. I'd welcomed the lessons and homework. The activity kept my mind from wandering and dwelling on my life and all the unanswered questions. Who cut the brakes on the limo? Webb had said we'd probably never know. How would my hearing go? Would the council find me guilty? Was my DNA different from normal vampires? My DNA results weren't back from the lab. After several phone calls, Dr. V. had been told the lab in Boston had a large backlog, and the lab tech he'd requested had been out on medical leave.

Aside from our school lessons, Ms. Costner taught us how to unleash our powers without being angry. The key was visualization and breathing. Sam and I were now at the point where we could use any of our abilities, angry or not, which quelled Dad's uneasiness somewhat. I didn't think my dad would ever be comfortable with Sam and me as vampires. Maybe years from now when we were older.

Speaking of Dad, he'd received word from the council that my hearing had been scheduled. In one week, the direction of my life would be decided. In the meantime, after our sessions with Ms. Costner, I'd been ordered to train with Olivia, who'd recovered from the drug-filled bullet. Webb and Dad wanted to ensure my fighting skills were in tip-top shape. I'd argued my powers were better suited to protecting me than punching and kicking were, but I lost the battle.

"There will be times when your fighting skills will come in handy over your powers," Dad had said.

Whatever.

I actually enjoyed spending time with Olivia. When she had time, she would hang out with Darcy and me in the evenings. On the nights Webb had free, which weren't many, I'd spend time with him. The sentinels met almost every night, planning some mission. I tried to tease the information out of him, but my kisses and touches didn't hold a candle to the sentinel oath of silence. No matter. I had fun playing.

"You're not concentrating, Jo," Webb said.

How could I? Didn't he know he was my distraction?

We had ventured out to the sentinel's training area located south of the base. He wanted to teach me how to throw a dagger. We'd been out here for over an hour, and I'd thrown several daggers at a target he had set up on a tree in the distance. All of them fell short of the target.

"Sorry. Why am I learning how to throw one of these?" Olivia had taught me a dagger was a weapon used for powerful thrusts.

He grunted. "You want to be able to distract your opponent, especially at a moment's notice." He handed me another dagger as he shifted his body behind me. "Now, wrap your hand around the pommel and breathe in. When you throw, extend your arm, snap your wrist, and breathe out in one fluid motion."

I snorted. As long as his body touched mine, there was no way I could function.

"You have to tune me out," he whispered, inhaling.

"Stop, Webb. You're not making this easy."

"It's not supposed to be. In a fight, you'll have all kinds of distractions."

I moved away.

He caught my arm. "A few more throws before the sun sets."

I snarled. "Get away, then."

As he laughed, I gripped the pommel, took in a breath, cocked my wrist, and flung the dagger. A thud sounded as the blade punctured the target in the distance.

"Nice. Why didn't you do that earlier?"

I snubbed him and concentrated. That throw had to be luck. So I threw another one, and this one hit the target again. Not dead center, but still...

Now I wanted to see if I could hit the center.

Webb stood off to my right with his arms crossed over his chest. He stared at me with one eyebrow raised. I picked up a dagger that was on the ground near my feet, positioned it in my hand, then threw. This time, the blade hit to the left of the center.

"See? That wasn't so bad." He grinned as though he were proud of me.

Okay, that wasn't perfect, but I'd take it for now. I just needed to practice more. He collected the daggers around the target, and I picked up two that were on the ground near me. After I handed them to him, he inserted them into the sheaths strapped to his legs. The others he wrapped in a brown cloth that had pockets for the daggers, then rolled it and tied it together. Then he slipped it into one of the pockets on his cargo pants.

"Come on. We'll take the long way around. Your father isn't expecting us for another hour."

I'd forgotten about my meeting with Dad and Mr. Rose, Darcy's father, who Dad had hired to be my lawyer. I'd questioned his choice of a human to defend me. He responded, "There's more to Mr. Rose and his connections to our world than you know." My concern wasn't his connections. Was he a good lawyer? Could I trust him to defend my life when I hardly knew him?

We set off for home through the dense wooded forest. The farther in we walked, the darker it seemed to get.

I kept my senses open, making sure I didn't fall into one of those debris-ridden traps. I'd fallen into one once before, when I'd chased a coyote to sate my hunger. "Webb, what do you think the Council will do with me?"

"It's hard to say." He glanced around like the perfect soldier, keeping watch.

"Do you think Mr. Rose is a good lawyer?"

"Your dad wouldn't have hired him if he didn't think so."

"I know, but what do you think?" As the court date drew closer, I needed more reassurance. I had tried not to dwell on my plight during the past few weeks. Now, amidst nature, my mind spiraled into worry. "Well?"

I slid a sidelong glance his way, but he wasn't there.

I turned back to find the vampire frozen under a low-hanging branch, pain or confusion on his face. His heartbeat roared in my ears. I scanned the trees up, down, far and wide. Then I opened my senses, trying to detect a scent, a sound. Nothing.

"What's wrong?" I asked as I refocused on the handsome vampire.

His shoulders tensed. His biceps bunched. "I think I love you, Jo."

The words hit me square in the chest like a grenade.

My heart stopped for a brief second before it sputtered to a start again. The wind calmed, the leaves froze, and the animals held their breath. Or maybe I was imagining him, what he'd said. I opened my mouth, but... I couldn't form any words.

He stalked toward me. Raw dominating power radiated off his sculpted body.

My brain's circuit breaker seemed to be stuck in the off position. The closer he got, the harder my heart knocked on my ribs.

"Did you hear what I said?" He peered down at me through his ridiculously long lashes.

I craned my neck, my mouth still parted.

Grabbing my nape with one hand and my lower back with the other, he yanked me to him. "I've been wanting to tell you for so long. I love you, Jo Mason. I love every part of you, mind, body, and soul."

The soft tenor of his voice, the feel of him

against me, the words he just spoke sent my pulse into overdrive.

I was afraid to even speak, still didn't know if I could. So I rose up on my toes and brushed my lips over his. He growled, low and deep, sending a warm prickle down my spine.

Happiness, elation, shock, love, lust, desire coursed through me.

I opened a telepathic connection as our tongues twisted in a slow, deliberate kiss. *I love you.*

His kiss turned frantic.

Everything around me felt so new and different, even in the darkened forest. Whatever life had to throw my way, I could deal with it. At least for the moment.

A trilling sound rent the world I was lost in. Webb's lips broke from mine as he growled. It took me a minute to regain my senses.

He pulled out his phone. "What is it, George?"

"I talked to Robert Pride today. You know, the guy who Lauren Dryer said was her father?"

"Go on."

My vampire hearing perked up.

"He doesn't have a daughter, niece, or granddaughter," George said. "The only family he has is a son, who lives in Idaho. So Stan did some checking on his own. It appears Lauren Dryer's real name is Diane Wallace. She's a private investigator."

My eyes grew wide, and so did Webb's.

"Anything else, George?"

"No, sir. If I find anything else out, I'll let you know."

The phone went dead, and so did Webb's arm. He held the phone to his ear as he stared off into the trees.

Well, our beautiful moment was definitely gone now. While I wanted to resume where we left off, I was curious. Who was this woman? Who was she investigating? Was she investigating *us*?

His phone chirped, breaking us from our zombie mode.

"Yes, Commander. We'll be there in five." He pocketed his phone and started back toward Dad. "Mr. Rose is here."

"What are you thinking?" At the moment, I wished I could read vampire minds.

We walked a ways before he answered, "Someone has hired this woman to watch us."

My thoughts exactly.

"Why, do you think?" I didn't think Edmund would hire a PI, much less a human. He would have one of his vampires watch us. Vampires could be stealthy creatures.

"Let's ask Mr. Rose," Webb suggested.

Ah. Webb had mentioned she did work in Mr. Rose's office.

We walked a little faster, and my pulse increased even more as we walked into Dad's office. Beside Mr. Rose, Lauren Dryer—or Diane Wallace or whoever she was—sat like a lady out of the Victorian era, her posture straight yet loose. Her hands were cupped together in her lap, her chin jutted out, and her legs crossed at the ankles. The term "proper lady" came to mind, confident and delicate.

"There you two are. How did training go, pumpkin?" Dad asked.

"Good. I'm an expert in dagger throwing now," I said as I looked at Mr. Rose then Diane.

She smiled coyly, seemingly unruffled by my comment. Mr. Rose, on the other hand, fidgeted in his seat. I'd met him a couple of times while at Darcy's house. Both times, he seemed relaxed and happy. Today, however, shadows colored the area beneath his brown eyes, and his pallor gave me the impression he was afraid.

"This is Mr. Rose and Lauren Dryer." Dad waved his hand to the humans.

"That is not her name," I blurted out. "Who

exactly are you?" I took one step before Webb stopped me.

"Commander, Lauren Dryer is not her name," Webb reported.

Dad pinched his eyebrows then glanced at the lady, who still hadn't moved. She didn't even seem surprised.

Mr. Rose held up a hand. "Before you get all upset, Steven, Webb is right. But we can explain."

"Gary," Dad's voice strained. "Either start talking, or I'll have you removed from here, along with your daughter. There won't be any protection for your family." Dad pressed his knuckles into the desk as he leaned forward and relaxed ever so slightly.

I didn't think Dad would put Darcy in danger. Maybe it was just his way of getting Mr. Rose to talk. I prayed so, anyway.

Mr. Rose let out a sigh. Webb and I went over to stand near Dad.

"Lauren—"

"No, Gary. Let me," she interrupted. "I'm a private investigator, working for Gary's law firm. My real name is Diane Wallace. Because of the nature of some of our cases, I don't use my real name."

"Do you know what we are?" I asked.

Dad whipped his head around toward me, expression horrified. Webb didn't move.

It was a valid question. Mr. Rose knew, and she worked with him.

"She does," Mr. Rose murmured.

"Come again?" Webb said.

"I do," Diane announced clearly, glancing at Dad, Webb, then me.

Dad ran a hand through his hair. "Let's all move to the couch," Dad said, nodding toward the small sitting area he had in one corner of his office.

After we were all seated around the coffee table, Dad cleared his throat. "I warned you, Gary." Dad narrowed his gaze. "Start talking. Or I'll have your memories wiped clean."

Diane gaped, her eyes wide.

I smiled smugly. What did she think she was messing with?

"I could...have you...reported," she said hesitantly.

"Ma'am, you could do a lot of things. But I warn you," Dad said easily, as though he'd given this speech a thousand times, "you'll walk around this earth forever, not knowing who you are or where you came from."

"Why not just erase their memories now?"

What was the point of all this? We didn't want humans to know we existed. So why not erase their memory of us?

Because, Jo. We can't erase one memory. We'd have to clear her mind completely, and we don't like doing that. It can draw attention to us. Plus the Council doesn't approve of it, either. Webb squeezed my hand before nodding to Dad.

"Okay. First, how does she know about us?" Dad set his angered gaze on Mr. Rose.

"As you know, Steven, I've been working and defending your kind for a few years. However, while my firm knows of the cases, they don't know my clients are vampires. Well, Diane found out one day when she walked into my office and one of my clients had his fangs out. I tried to play it off, but he almost attacked her in a rage. At that point, I had no choice. She hasn't broadcasted this news to anyone."

"And you know that how?" Webb asked.

"The vampire who almost bit her threatened her life and those of her family."

"So, why walk in here and threaten us now, Ms. Wallace?" Dad asked.

"I'm tired of your kind thinking you can rule humans with a drop of your fangs." Her voice was more confident now.

"What were you doing up in Maine near my house?" Webb asked before she could answer Dad's question.

"What?" Mr. Rose turned to her.

She clasped her hands together. "I'm not allowed to say. Client confidentiality."

"What client?" Mr. Rose prodded.

"Ms. Wallace, I can easily find out," Dad said. "So please share with us why you were watching my daughter and my lieutenant. And tell us why you cut the brakes on their car."

"Diane? Cut the brakes? What is he talking about?" A bead of sweat trickled down Mr. Rose's temple. "Steven Mason is not like the other vampires. He won't harm you. But he is the most powerful of his kind. He…"

Without thinking, I went to sit next to Diane. Dad and Webb made a move to stop me, but I held up my hand.

"A test, Dad." I took hold of her delicate hand and closed my eyes.

"What is she doing?" Diane tried to jerk her hand away.

I clamped down harder on her cold, sweaty palm and concentrated. The voices and sounds around me disappeared as I entered her world. She was frightened, angry, and hungry. A warm jolt slid through me into her. She twitched. Her heart rate sped up.

Her thoughts started flowing. *She's crazy. I didn't try to kill them. These people are crazy. Mr. Jackson was right. I hate my mother, sometimes.*

My eyes flew open. "Why are you working for Mr. Jackson?" I released her hand.

Dad and Webb both swore.

"You can read minds like your father." Mr. Rose seemed horrified.

"I can now." I might've imagined it with Ben and Matthew.

"So Mr. Jackson hired you to do what, exactly?" Webb's voice held steady.

My throat grew scratchy from Diane's sweet strawberry scent, so I returned to my seat next to Webb.

Diane looked to Mr. Rose for help.

"Unless you want Steven or Jo to resume reading your mind, I suggest you explain," Mr. Rose warned her.

"Mr. Jackson," she said, "is worried about his son. He hired me to investigate Steven Mason. He explained to me how Sam Mason went missing from school grounds, then the military came in and removed Sam's sister, Jo. He didn't see the twins after that, and about the same time, Ben became angry, lost. Then one day he went missing. He'd said he showed up here to see if you would help." She glanced at Dad. "A few days later, he gets a call from you, telling him Ben was here in the medical facility. He suspects the change in his son has something to do with the Mason family. Those are his words. He's tried to go to the authorities, but he feels someone high on the government chain keeps sweeping his concerns under the rug." She wound her fingers together.

I couldn't argue with her, and neither could Dad or Webb.

"At first I declined," she continued. "I knew how difficult it would be for me to work with the government. But then I had the incident in Gary's office, and something clicked. I started to believe Mr. Jackson had a viable concern. So I took the case. I'd followed Gary the day he came here to pick up Darcy. When I did, I spotted the limo leaving. On a whim, I tailed you." She glanced at Webb. "I didn't cut the brakes on the car. I swear I didn't. You can read my mind if you have to."

"Her thoughts didn't show she did, Dad."

Diane's shoulders slumped, and Mr. Rose let out a small breath of air.

"What have you reported to Mr. Jackson?" Webb asked.

"Minimal. I wasn't certain of anything even after I followed you to Maine. Sure, I had my suspicions. But even I wasn't comfortable sharing them with Mr. Jackson. He wouldn't believe me. So I told him you had a house in Maine and everything seemed normal."

"And when did you speak with him?" Dad asked.

She had spoken to someone when she was at the diner, after she'd dropped us off.

"When I dropped both of you at the diner. Why?"

"And you were alone the whole time?" Dad ran his questioning as if he were the lawyer in the room.

"Oh, I see. You think Mr. Jackson had time to drive up during the day. Do you really believe he is capable of killing?" Her voice hitched.

"Anything is possible," Webb said.

She nodded her agreement.

"Webb, please escort Mr. Rose and Ms. Wallace off base." Dad went over to his desk.

"I thought we were going to discuss Jo's hearing?" Mr. Rose pushed to his feet.

"Not today." Anger still hung in Dad's voice.

"Then I would like to see my daughter, at least."

"You can call her later."

"Steven, please." Mr. Rose collected his briefcase.

Dad's head shot up as he slammed a hand down on his desk. Diane flinched. I almost crawled up on Webb's lap.

"I suggest you follow my orders, Mr. Rose! My patience has run thin with you. I specifically told you to come here alone, but you insisted on bringing a colleague, one who could help the case. I don't see how she can. You weren't even up front with her true identity. You lied to me. How am I supposed to trust you to defend my daughter? I need time to mull this over."

"You can't keep my daughter from me." The human seemed to have grown some *chutzpah*.

I considered applauding Mr. Rose for his fatherly concerns then threw out the idea. Dad would only send his rage my way.

"If you would like to take Darcy, I can't stop you. I'll call down and have her things brought to the lobby." Dad lifted the receiver.

"Wait." Mr. Rose grabbed the back of his own head. "We'll leave. I'll call Darcy tonight."

Dad lowered the phone.

Diane, Mr. Rose, and Webb left quietly. Dad stayed silent.

I couldn't have imagined that Mr. Jackson would've been the one who severed the brakes. I refused to believe he would do such a thing. He might've been angry at how his efforts seem to fall on deaf ears but killing someone wasn't in his nature. I was sure of it.

15

That night after we'd met with Mr. Rose, I jolted awake and ran from my bedroom, out of the apartment, and into the balmy summer night toward the base gate. My sweat-soaked tank top clung to me as my bare feet slapped against the rough pavement. I brushed my hair from my forehead as I jogged until I found the dirt road into the woods. I wasn't sure I could find the cinderblock building that Webb called home, but I had to. I had to find him. I had to stop him from going on his mission.

Tears poured out as I continued to run. Sticks, rocks, and other sharp natural debris poked my feet. The moon lit the ground every time I cleared a cluster of trees. My breathing was heavy as I stopped at the end of the dirt road, searching for the small safe house. I wrapped my hand around the ruby on my necklace as though it were a crystal ball. I hadn't taken the gem off since Dad had given it to me the night of the fundraiser.

Leaves kicked up at the slight wind, the chafing sound soothing to my ears. A porcupine scurried around a tree.

A fishy scent lingered. The bay wasn't far— which meant I had miscalculated. I didn't think the safe houses were close to the water. Not sure, I backtracked anyway, walking this time. Off to my right, a light shone. I picked up my pace, skirting brush and thicket. I blew out a breath when I saw Stan's truck. Webb still hadn't returned the vehicle to his friend.

I used the railing to pull myself up, hopping onto the porch. A familiar female voice spoke in a soft tone. Was that Nicki, inside Webb's house? What was she doing here in the middle of the night?

My muscles vibrated, or maybe it was the porch. The light above flickered violently. The alarm on the truck shrieked. I balled my fists and pressed my lips together as I held back a scream. The greater my rage, the more my powers in-tensified.

My heart slammed against my ribs, the sound hollow in my ears. The voices in my head warned me to keep it together. I let out a strangled laugh.

As I wrestled with my yin and yang, the door opened. Webb stood in the doorway with low-slung jeans and no shirt. My gaze swept over him, and I was certain my heart would've fluttered endlessly at how handsome he was if it weren't for Nicki standing behind him. I desperately tried to hold back the tears filling my eyes. I thought he didn't want anything to do with her?

"What's wrong, Jo? Did something happen?" Webb asked as if I shouldn't be surprised Nicki was in his house.

I hesitated before I turned and bolted off the porch. If I stayed I'd unleash my powers causing someone to get hurt, and I didn't want Webb injured. I'd almost taken the life out of him once. So I ran, tears streaming down my face. How could he? He hated her. Why? Why was she even here? He said she wasn't allowed on base. Tears continued to pour from my eyes, sticking to my sweaty face. I ran faster, deeper into the night, seeking a way out. I leapt over a stump and dodged a trap before dropping to my knees, hiccupping.

I knew in my heart he loved me and that nothing was going on between him and Nicki. Or did I? Doubt wiggled its way into my brain. Regardless, it hurt to see her in his house, close to him.

"Jo?" Webb shouted. "Jo? I'll find you. You can't evade me." His voice scraped every nerve ending, even though I loved the huskiness and silkiness of his tone.

And while I wanted him to catch me, wrap his strong arms around me, I didn't want him to see me as a blubbering mess.

I planted my hands into the wet earth and propelled myself forward like a sprinter at the snap of the gun. I had no idea where I was going.

"You can't run forever," he said, his voice drawing closer.

Water lapped the shore as I cleared the trees and stepped onto the beach. *Great.* Now where? The base stood far off to the north, the lights twinkling. To the south, more trees. I had two choices. Either run for the base or swim to the other side of Mt. Hope Bay. If I darted for home, I wouldn't get in unless I scaled the barbwire fence. Maybe electrocution would pale in comparison to the way my heart hurt at the moment. Or maybe the sensation would kick my heart back into gear. I shook off the thought.

Crossing Mt. Hope Bay was definitely not going to happen. I didn't know how to swim.

"Hesitating and thinking about your options will get you killed," Webb said, standing feet away, looking like an Adonis beneath the moonlight.

I wanted to run away and run to him at the same time.

"It's not what you think, angel." He inched closer, his tone licking my senses.

I dug my feet in the cool sand and shuffled backward. "Why was she in your house?" I checked behind me to make sure of where I was going. I stopped before I stepped on a rock. In fact, there were a few rocks sticking out of the sand.

"What were you doing out this time of night?" His gaze slid over me like butter, his lids dropping to half-mast.

I wrapped my arms over my chest. I was only wearing a pair of boxer shorts and a tank top, and the top stuck to me. "You didn't answer my question."

"Why do you run every time, angel?" He now stood a foot away from me.

So, I won't kill anyone. Oh, and my feelings are hurt.

I glanced around again, hoping I could find a way past him.

"You're not going anywhere until we talk."

I darted for the tree line. I didn't want to talk until my heart stopped hurting.

The vampire was quick on his feet. His arms encircled me, pulling my face into his bare chest. I inhaled his delicious scent, a mixture of sweat and soap.

"Let me go." I kicked and wiggled to no avail. "Webb, I'll hurt you." My words were muffled as the fight in me slowly died.

He grinned against my ear. "You couldn't possibly."

"I can't breathe." I thought about licking his chest. *Shut up*, I screamed in my head. *You're supposed to be mad at him, not wanting to make out.*

His arms loosened a little. "Why were you walking around in the middle of the night?"

"You're going to die." The words fell from my mouth, cold and hard.

His heart rate increased. "What are you talking about?"

My palms stuck to his heated chest as I eased back a fraction. "You can't go on the mission. You just can't. Please don't go. Please. Promise me you won't."

"Whoa! Slow down." His hands flattened on my cheeks.

Tears surfaced again as I thought about my dream with the old man and all the coffins again. This time, I'd seen who rested in it. A salty tear found its way into my mouth, and Webb mopped the rest with his thumbs.

"Tell me slowly why you think I'm going to die." A loose hair fell out of the leather strap he had holding his ponytail in place.

I recounted my dream, play by play, word for word, coffin after coffin, sharing with him how I'd seen him dead, lying in the coffin, and what Dad had told me about dreams.

When I finished, I shivered, and I could've sworn he did, too.

"I don't discount what your Dad told you. I don't take your abilities lightly, either, but we've never proven our dreams were a window into our future or anyone's future."

"Then what about Abbey? She has visions." No one was certain if the little girl could see into the future.

"Jo, I can't live my life based on a dream or a vision. This mission is important, and I have to go. If we're successful, then Abbey might see her dad."

"You know where he is?" Excitement stirred to life, then I quickly squashed it. "Quade..." I sucked in air. I wasn't supposed to talk about it.

"I promise I'll be back in one piece."

"And walk into Nicki's arms when you do," I chided. I probably shouldn't have said that. I was being a brat. But my feelings were hurt.

He growled and let go of me. "Nicki got past the guards tonight. She showed up at my house. I called to have someone remove her from the property. When I opened the door, I was expecting to see a sentinel. Not you, shaking the house on its edges."

"I'm sorry," I said, then I turned and walked down to the shore. Why couldn't I get mad without all the drama of vampire powers? Why couldn't I be human again? I dipped my toes in the surf. A cloud blocked out the bright moon for a split second as the fluffy clouds skated by.

"I need you," he whispered as his hands came around to settle on my stomach. "I need your trust as much as I need your love."

"Why did you lie to me? When I asked you if you saw Kate at the training facility, you said no?" I needed his trust just as much as he needed mine.

He sighed in my ear. "I know I shouldn't have lied to you. I knew Sam would tell you. But I didn't want to talk about it. I'm sorry." He kissed my ear. "It won't happen again."

I leaned back against him. The trust between

us was important, but his life was in danger. "You can't go."

"Let's talk about this after we've had some sleep."

Sleep would be impossible now.

THE NEXT FEW days passed by in a blur. I couldn't sleep. If I did, it wasn't restful. One thousand four hundred and forty minutes per day, my nerves ramped up and down like a sine curve. One minute, I briefly forgot about my dream and Webb, and then the next, I couldn't shake the image of how peaceful Webb looked in the coffin. He wore a white button-down shirt, open at the collar, with red spots dotting the area over his heart. At the waist of his black slacks, his left hand rested over the right, and a small smile painted his features.

I had no idea what the old man was trying to tell me. Then again, in my last dream, I hadn't given him a chance to speak. Somehow I forced myself to wake up.

"Pumpkin, are you with us?" Dad asked.

"Huh?" I lifted my head.

I'd been sitting with Dad and Mr. Rose as they

discussed the specifics of my case. Yes, they had worked out their issues. Mr. Rose didn't bring Ms. Wallace with him, and she wouldn't be in the courtroom during my hearing, either. Dad didn't like the woman, and he made that clear to Mr. Rose before they began deliberating about my life.

"Jo, you need to be alert for this," Mr. Rose said.

"Why did you think Ms. Wallace could help my case?" If he'd told us why, I hadn't heard it.

"Diane Wallace is a great investigator. She can get information out of anyone. So, I had her look into Grayson Manor and also St. Anne's Academy. Blake Turner was admitted to your vampire hospital then accepted into the school too easily. The process involves an extreme amount of paperwork, and my gut told me something was amiss. Not to mention, Blake wasn't a natural-born vampire, and you have to be in order to have access to any vampire facility. If I can show the Council of Eternal Affairs he didn't carry the proper DNA and find out who within the vampire government helped him, I can then prove he shouldn't have been in that school in the first place."

"How does all this support my innocence?" I picked at a nail.

"Let's get something straight, Jo." Mr. Rose

scratched his head. "Regardless of who Blake was or how he was changed into a vampire, you still played a role in his death. The Council in your world, similar to the human world, does not take that lightly."

"But I was defending myself."

"That may be. Remember, even in self-defense, there are laws," Mr. Rose said.

I raised my eyebrows at Dad. "What is he saying?"

"Let's not get ahead of ourselves. We'll do everything to prove Blake was set up to kill you." Dad leaned forward in his chair, resting his elbows on his desk.

"There's a 'but' coming. Isn't there?" I gave up picking at my nails and instead began tapping my foot on the floor.

"You weren't supposed to use your powers on school property." Dad scrubbed a hand over his jaw.

"What? They never told us that." My voice squeaked.

"Regardless, Jo. Someone died. So the school has to involve the Council," Mr. Rose supplied.

"Does that mean I go to jail even though I was defending myself?" I tensed. I remembered when Sam spent a couple of nights in jail for getting into fights at school. One of the boys he fought—his dad had pressed charges. Anyway, Sam had told me how creepy and lonely his experience had been.

"Again, don't jump to conclusions," Dad said softly.

The gentleness of his tone didn't help calm my nerves.

"Why don't you tell me what happened?" The attorney clicked his pen, ready to write.

I looked to Dad. I didn't want to go through the specifics of that day.

Dad nodded. "He needs to know, pumpkin."

I let out a breath. "I'd gone to the ladies' room to freshen up between classes." I paused, thinking back for a second. "Just before I walked out, my uncle Patrick's daughter, Jewel, walked in." I didn't know we were related at the time. Not that it would have made any difference. The human was trying to kill me. "She threatened me with a dagger. Then Blake Turner barged in, bloody and ready for a fight. A second later my friend Zea came in. Jewel held a dagger to her throat while Blake and I fought. At some point I looked over to check on Zea, and she had her fangs in Jewel. Then Blake and I continued to fight. Before I knew what was happening, Jewel drove the blade into my leg. Zea was gone, and both Jewel and Blake fell to the floor." My stomach churned as I recounted the event.

"Did you know Blake was dead?" Mr. Rose wrote furiously, underlining the last sentence.

I shook my head.

"Anything else?" Mr. Rose asked.

"Gary, I mentioned the incident that happened the day before where Blake attacked a friend of Jo's and had also pushed Jo down the steps at school," Dad added.

Mr. Rose jotted more notes down.

I didn't have anything else to add. "May I be excused? Ms. Costner will be here shortly, and I would like to prepare."

"We're through here anyway. Gary, why don't we walk with Jo to the library, and you can visit with your daughter. She should be working." Dad pushed to his feet.

Darcy had been living in the library. My feisty little friend had become quite the bookworm. She enjoyed helping Ms. Simpson and reading to the kids.

Mr. Rose packed his notepad into his briefcase, and the three of us walked out of Dad's office.

The library was quiet when we entered except for Webb's voice. Off to the right in the children's reading area, six small children with wide-eyed expressions listened intently as Webb read to them. The breath halted in my lungs. Webb was reading to the kids? Why was I surprised? I'd seen how gentle he'd been with Abbey when we found her.

Dad and Mr. Rose walked ahead of me, quietly slipping into some empty chairs behind the group. I shuffled closer, hanging outside the circle. I didn't want to disturb the magical aura Webb had over everyone.

Darcy nodded at me from her spot on the floor. Like Abbey, Darcy lay on her stomach, with her elbows propped up and her face cradled in her hands. Ms. Simpson leaned against a bookcase, flicking her gaze to me and Dad.

I lowered myself to my knees and settled in to listen to the vampire I was in love with read from a children's book.

"He ran as fast as he could so the bear wouldn't see him. But his instincts told him to lie down and play dead." Webb's inflection elicited a collective gasp from his captive audience.

"What's *insinck* mean?" Jeffery asked.

"The word is *in-stinct*," Webb said. "Two syllables. Sound it out with me."

The children repeated the word *instinct*, or

tried. I smiled at how cute they were in their efforts. Abbey's lisp caught my attention. Her blue eyes sparkled as she repeatedly practiced.

"Just think of the word *stink*. When you smell something bad," Webb said.

"Like poop." A curly-haired boy snorted.

The kids erupted into hysterics.

"Okay, I'm sure Webb has to get back to work," Ms. Simpson said, breaking up the fun.

All of them protested.

Abbey jumped up and leapt into Webb's lap. "Don't go." Little hands found their way around his neck.

"I'm sorry, Abbey-doll. I have work to do."

She touched his face. "Don't be sad," she said to him.

"I'm not sad," he replied. "Papa bear is over there." He pointed to my dad. "Why don't you go and say hi?"

She hopped down, and instead of running to my dad, Abbey ran to me. I braced myself as I held my arms out and picked her up.

"Jo, you came back." Her nose touched mine.

"I came to see you before my teacher arrives. I have school." I tucked a strand of her hair behind her ear.

"What thool? This is a library."

"I know. My school is upstairs." I turned and pointed up to the second level. "You see that door in the far corner? That's where my classroom is."

"In the thecret library?" Spit sprayed my face.

I glanced over at Dad, who was walking toward me.

"She's well beyond her years." He smiled proudly.

I wasn't going to ask how she knew about the vampire library. For all I knew the little girl was reading my mind. At least I didn't have any visions when she touched me.

Abbey abandoned me, and Dad lifted her into his arms. Darcy and her father ventured over to a quiet spot away from everyone. Ms. Simpson handed out coloring books and crayons to the kids.

"So, I'm sorry we haven't seen each other, Jo," Webb said, sauntering over to me. "The last-minute details of the mission have taken up all my time."

I was sad but glad that we didn't get to see each other. Every time I saw Webb, I was reminded of my dream. Like now, standing here, with him... All I could see was him in that coffin.

"What did Abbey mean when she told you not

to be sad?" Did she know about Webb's fate, too? "Did you have a vision when she touched you?"

"We don't have visions every time she touches us."

She was lying on the floor now, coloring in a book. Dad was talking to Ms. Simpson.

"I don't know what she meant. But I am sad I haven't been able to have you in my arms. Spend time with me tonight."

He had on his black cargo uniform. His T-shirt stretched across his broad chest, and his hair hung loose today.

"I can't." I hated to say those two words.

"Can't or won't?" His raised voice drew Dad's attention.

I walked away and climbed the steps to the vampire library. When Dad was present, my privacy was non-existent. Regardless, I didn't leave Webb standing alone because of Dad or my privacy. I still held some animosity over Nicki being in his house in the middle of the night.

Plus, he refused to take my dream seriously. Dad even sided with Webb. Both agreed the mission was extremely important to rescuing two of the missing soldiers. I didn't doubt it. Saving anyone's life had to be important. But wasn't Webb's life just as important? Why was I the only one who saw that?

I tucked myself on the corner bench outside the secret library, waiting for Ms. Costner and Sam. I had only seen my brother in the mornings lately, unless we had our tutoring sessions. Our training sent us in opposite directions during the day.

A human scent drifted my way, and I lifted my head. Darcy strolled down the carpeted runway, the tips of her fingers sliding along top of the wooden railing.

"A quarter for your thoughts," she said as her gold-speckled mascara glinted under the skylight.

"I think the saying is 'a penny.'" I gave her a weak smile.

"I know. But that's so cliché." She lowered her tiny frame to sit crisscross, facing me. Her hair was perfectly coiffed. Her makeup was painted on to perfection. The crisp, rich fabric of her clothing spoke of money.

"Is your dad any closer to settling with his client?" I raised my knees to my chest then wrapped my arms around my legs.

"He says it depends on your case. I guess your dad is paying him a decent sum of money. The amount should take care of his debt with this other vampire he supposedly defended. So, why the brooding nature?" she asked.

"I'm not sure you would understand." I didn't doubt she would understand about brooding over a boy. She had a few boyfriends since I'd become friends with her. But there was no way she would grasp the nature of vampire powers or dreams.

"Jo, come on. First, I know it's about Webb. And I also know you're in love with him."

"And how did you get so psychic on me?" I rested my face on my knees while looking at her.

She giggled. "It's not about being psychic. I can see it when you're around him. Look, not that you're asking, but I'll share it with you anyway. My mom always tells me the universe is in constant motion, and so too is our fate, our destiny."

What in the world did that mean? I shifted my position and tucked my legs under me as I faced her. "How does all that pertain to Webb and me?"

"Jo. You told me about your dream. You have these abilities that defy humanity. What's to say your dream will come true? You said yourself you didn't give the old man a chance to speak. What if you did? What would he say?" She leaned forward, elbows on her thighs.

I shook my head. "I can't dream again. I just

can't. What if I do, and I see Webb's death while he's on this mission?"

"And what if you dream and don't?"

Sure, I had a fifty-fifty chance. But did I want to gamble?

"Don't what?" Sam's voice interrupted my thought.

Darcy and both turned our heads. Sam stalked toward us with a sense of purpose.

Darcy's heart beat faster as she swept her gaze over my brother before swallowing hard.

I slapped her on the arm. "Hey, he's my brother."

"So. He's also a guy, and eye candy, and—"

"Ewwww." I scrunched my nose.

"Darcy, you and me are not happening." Sam shook his head, his black hair brushing over his shoulders.

"Remember our superb hearing," I reminded her.

A smile curled her pink lips. "I know. I should go."

"Thanks for the girl talk," I said.

She giggled as the freshman girls did in high school as she jumped off the bench and brushed by Sam.

"Not happening, Sis." Sam sat down.

"Oh, chill. You should be flattered." Darcy was pretty. She never had a problem getting boys.

"Whatever." He rolled his green eyes.

"Don't you think she's pretty?" I had yet to see my brother with a girlfriend.

He was about to answer when he suddenly jumped off the bench to help Ms. Costner. She was walking with a stack of books in her arms.

"Oh, thank you, Sam," she said as she adjusted the bag over her shoulder then smoothed down the blue silk blouse she was wearing. Then she removed a keycard from her tan capris and held it up to the panel on the wall next to the door. Two beeps and the door to the library opened.

I hopped up and followed Sam and Ms. Costner inside. Large bookcases stretched along every wall, with ladders placed on each one for ease of reaching the shelves close to the ceiling. I settled into one of the plush oversized chairs while Ms. Costner rummaged through her bag. Sam set the books on the table in front of the sitting area. As Sam sat down in the chair next to me, Ms. Costner spread out her own papers and books.

For the next three hours, we studied math, science, and English. Once we had the core subjects out of the way for the day, Ms. Costner dove into a few topics on magic. My ears perked up, and I straightened in my chair.

"For the final hour, I want to explain the basis of magic. I won't get into everything today, as this topic has many facets and should be studied over the course of a year or two." She leaned against the table as she did against her desk at the human high school.

"We're vampires," Sam said. "Not magicians."

"And you're an astute vampire, Sam," Ms. Costner said teasingly.

I rolled my eyes at my brother.

"What?" he protested. "It's not like we're going to use this. We're learning the elements, not how to cast spells."

"That's where you'll find in our world, Sam, alchemy, elements, and magic intertwine," Ms. Costner said as a matter of fact. "With alchemy or magic, for example, there are three functions—produce, protect, and destroy. Whether you're manipulating elements or you're casting a spell, the basis is the same. You must learn how to use your powers to protect, and you must understand how they can destroy. I might be able to teach one magical spell that could protect anyone or anything when all else fails."

Sam sat up straighter.

"What do you mean?" I asked.

"Elements can be harsh on your opponent. Encasing them in a block of ice—like you did, Jo—can hurt a person. A human, definitely." She placed a strand of her blond hair behind her ear.

"Isn't that the point of using our powers?" Sam asked.

"Not always. Sometimes you'll want to contain or distract your enemy for one reason or another," she explained. "So, a spell to shield or to mask will ensure one's safety."

"Like you did when you masked the scent of humans at the fundraiser," Sam and I said at the same time.

"That's one way." Ms. Costner dragged her chair from behind the table and positioned it in front of us. Then she sat down. "Enough about me. I'll begin with numbers."

Sam and I exchanged looks.

"The ruling forces of magic are numbers. Pythagoras reasoned how the entire universe could be expressed with numbers."

"The power of three," I mumbled.

When I was in her math class at the human high school, she had lectured on Pythagoras, and he believed the universe was divided into three worlds.

"Correct. In fact, he's quoted, 'The world is built upon the power of numbers.'"

"Is that how you cast spells?" Sam asked, angling his head.

"Numbers create a chain reaction." She rose, circled her chair, and stood behind it then lightly gripped the back of it. "For example, there are certain characteristics of the number one through the number ten. And in any combination, these numbers spark magic."

She went on to explain number theory. I guessed I shouldn't have been surprised that our math teacher was fascinated with numbers or that she developed spells on sequences of numbers and not words. Always emphasizing the power of three, she expounded on the combination of 888, which represented the higher mind, or 666, which spoke to the mortal mind.

The hour flew by as Sam and I asked questions and took notes. At the end of the hour, my brain hurt.

"We'll dive into how numbers correspond to vibrations in our next session." She returned her chair to its original spot behind the table.

Sam and I were gathering our notes when the door opened. Webb breezed in, hunky body and delicious scent. I guessed Webb was back to finish our conversation.

"Your chariot is here, Sis." Sam tucked his notebook under his arm. "Ms. Costner, see you next week."

"I'll be at the hearing," she said, slipping folders into her black leather bag.

"Wait, you're coming to my hearing?" My jaw hung slightly open. "Why?"

"Your father asked me, and I want to observe. Will you be there, Webb?" She flicked her gaze toward him.

"No, ma'am. Duty calls." He gave her a weak smile.

My hands began to shake at the thought of him leaving on a mission that might claim his life.

Webb and the team of sentinels were scheduled to leave the base at dawn on the day of my court case. I had no idea where they were headed or what lay ahead, but somehow, my dreams did.

16

The fridge sang behind my bedroom wall. A clock ticked loudly in the family room. My heartbeat even rang in my ears as I tried to close my eyes. Hours of tossing and turning ended when I kicked off the blankets and plopped into my clothes-infested chair. I refused to sleep. I didn't have the courage to dream.

Even if I did, would it matter? Webb and Dad weren't canceling the mission.

I pulled my legs to my chest, rested my chin on my knees, and gazed out at the night. The dark grey building across the way looked ominous beneath the moonlight.

A branch scraped at the edge of my window. I cleared my mind—or at least tried to, concentrating on the tattering of the branch kissing the glass pane.

In one hour, the sentinels were scheduled to depart for their mission. I had no idea where. The details were secret to everyone outside the SEAL team.

A light tap sounded before the door opened and closed softly. Boots scuffed along the wood floor.

"You shouldn't be in here," I whispered, rocking in my seat, not looking behind me.

Webb had never been in my room, and I was surprised Dad let him come in.

The bed creaked, and I glanced to my right. Webb was dressed in his black cargo uniform. Knives and daggers were strapped to his legs. His sentinel sword was clipped to his belt, and a gun was tucked in a holster on the other side of his waist.

"You plan on killing someone today?" I asked, swiveling my attention back to the moonlit night.

"Normal gear," he said, low and silky. "Are you still avoiding me?"

He'd begged me to spend time with him last night and the night before. I refused. I was a brooding, crying, emotional wreck. I figured the more I distanced myself from him, the easier the toll would be on my psyche if he didn't return. How idiotic was that? Regardless, it was my warped way of protecting myself.

"Would you at least sit with me?" His sad tone sliced at my heart. "I want to hold you. I don't want to leave with you—"

"A basket case?" I stifled a nervous laugh.

"Nothing is going to happen to me. How many times do I have to tell you?"

I growled and glared at him.

He grinned.

I jumped out of the chair and knocked him backward onto the bed, punching him. "If you die, I'll hunt you down and kill you myself."

He cocooned me in his arms as he peppered kisses along my cheek and neck. "I would like for you to kill me." He rolled me over so he was on top. He pressed his hands into the mattress on each side of my head. "We should return within a week, if everything goes well."

"And if it doesn't?" I raised an eyebrow.

"Then we'll be home sooner." He pinned me with a soft look.

I licked my lips. "Does my father know you're in here?"

His fangs dropped. "He's downstairs, imparting his last words of wisdom to the rest of the sentinels." He lowered his head, and his fangs grazed my pouty bottom lip. "Tripp will stay behind on this mission and accompany you to the hearing today."

"Why? Dad and Sam will be here." Wasn't Tripp essential to helping him on this mission? After all, Tripp was Webb's right-hand man.

"We need him to work with Viking II in the event we have any problems. And your dad wants him as your bodyguard."

Viking II was the other vampire SEAL team. Normally, Dad had one vampire SEAL team on base while the other one was deployed. After our raid at Edmund's mansion, Dad had both vampire teams on base.

I could protect myself. I didn't need Tripp to babysit me. Besides, Sam was more than capable of protecting me. After all, he'd been by my side my entire life.

None of that mattered at the moment. I closed the tiny space between us and kissed Webb. A rumble crawled up his chest.

When our lips met, my heart raced in two different directions—excitement to feel his warmth, his love... and sadness and fear at the unknown and what lay ahead.

He continued his soft, gentle kisses, staring

into my eyes. The love in his eyes mesmerized me. With each kiss, each peck, each touch—our souls fused together, one stitch at a time. Tears surfaced, and I closed my eyes. I wanted to at least show him I could be strong for him, even though inside I was a mess.

"Open those pretty eyes, Jo." He smoothed back my hair while the other hand was still on the mattress beside my head. "I don't want to leave you. Please understand I have to do my job."

"I know. I'm sorry for being a brat. I'm afraid for you, though." I traced the outline of his lips. "I love you."

A corner of his mouth curled. "That's the first time you said it out loud. Say it again."

"I love you." The three meaningful words rolled off my tongue with ease and poured out of my heart with pain.

"You have my soul, angel. Completely." He drew a heart over mine.

He rolled off me and lay on his side. He propped up on his elbow and traced circles around my belly button. We enjoyed the quietness of my room and each other. I wanted to stay like this forever. Time passed.

Fate knocked.

"Jo?" Dad called from the other side of my door.

We both sat up.

"I'll be right out," I replied.

"Your dad will know where we are at all times." Webb assured me as he kissed me one last time.

I held on to him for dear life, my pulse beating wildly out of control. I prayed for him, the sentinels, and anyone else on the SEAL team who was headed into harm's way.

He let go of me and walked to the door. "Jo?"

I lifted my head, tears on the verge of dropping.

"Your love will keep me alive."

After he walked out, I collapsed on my bed in a heap of tears. I cried until sleep claimed me.

A bright orange sky glowed in the distance. I slowly shuffled forward, following a group of people. A man and woman in front of me had phones to their ears. The other people surrounding me whispered and tittered.

Suddenly, an explosion rocked the earth. I flew backward into a dark hole as the bright orange glow faded. Screams rang out.

I hit something hard and sucked in air.

"Sis? Jo? Wake up."

I opened my eyes and looked around, disoriented. I shook my head slightly, trying to dislodge the fuzziness.

"You were dreaming again," Sam said, eyes wide. "Did you dream of the panther?" He sat on the edge of my bed.

"No." I couldn't make hide or hair of my dream. So I shoved it aside.

He pushed off the bed. "Dad is getting ready. I guess I need to wear a suit," he said, sounding disgusted.

"You don't own one." I smiled at my brother. He hated anything other than jeans and a T-shirt.

"I do now. Dad gave me one of his. It was either that or my school uniform. And I'm not wearing that clown suit." He rolled his eyes as he ambled out of my room.

I guessed I had to wear something dressy. But what?

Then again, would my attire matter to the Council of Eternal Affairs?

Within an hour, Sam, Dad, Tripp, and I were in a black SUV that glided along the highway. We weren't far from Boston; the tall buildings graced the skyline in the distance. Rain pelted the windshield. Dad and Tripp talked about some new military weapon. Tripp nodded every now and then, keeping his hands on the wheel at ten and two.

Sam had ear buds in his ears—listening to music, I imagined. As for me, I passed the time daydreaming about Webb, mostly. I'd wanted to ask Dad tons of questions, but I couldn't. If I did, I'd cry.

"Pumpkin," Dad said. "What was your dream about this morning?" Concern colored his tone.

"Nothing really. Why? Did something happen to Webb and the sentinels?" I held my breath.

"Relax. They're fine. They left on a plane out of the base in Newport two hours ago."

I expelled the air in my lungs. The Boston city skyline made me remember... "Dad, are my DNA results back yet?"

"Dr. Vieira said the lab is working on it now."

Traffic grew heavier as we got closer to Boston. Before long, the car slowed as we inched through the Boston tunnel. When we emerged on the other side, Tripp flicked on the blinker. We eased off the freeway onto the side streets. Red light, green light, red light was the pattern until we turned down a long driveway of a very tall building. Tripp braked at a black wrought iron gate and pressed a button on a box just outside the driver's window.

"State your name and who you're here to see," a baritone voice blared through the box.

"Commander Mason and company. We're here for the Turner hearing," Tripp said.

"Park in the visitor's spot near the elevators," the male voice instructed.

The gate slid to the right. When it opened wide enough, Tripp drove underneath and into a visitor spot. He killed the engine. Sam pulled out his ear buds.

"Before we go in," Dad said, "I want you, Jo, to follow Mr. Rose's instructions. Don't blurt out anything. And please don't use your powers in this building. It is forbidden to use any of our abilities in any vampire government facility. The only one allowed is telepathy. Are we clear?"

"Yes, sir," I said. I prayed I didn't get angry. While I'd learned how to control my powers, I wasn't perfect.

"Son, same goes for you."

"I get it, Pops. I'm not as talented as my sister, anyway."

I stuck out my tongue at my brother.

"Still, any use of powers will get you jailed and fined," Dad said as he opened the door.

Once Dad said his peace, we piled into the elevator. Sam fidgeted with his black tie. Dad had given him a gray suit. The dullness of his attire made his green eyes stand out like a lighthouse cutting through the dense fog. Dad, on the other hand, was outfitted in his blue dress uniform, with all his medals on display. Unsurprisingly, Tripp wore his black cargo uniform, although he didn't have all the weapons strapped to him like Webb had. The only one visible, anyway, was his sentinel sword.

"Do they allow weapons in here?" Sam asked, seemingly admiring Tripp.

"Only the sentinel sword," Tripp responded, arms folded across his chest.

"Why?" We weren't allowed to use our powers. A weapon wasn't that different.

"It only responds to my touch. It would be of no use to anyone else. And the sentinels have special permission to enter with weapons."

I'd thought of a host of other questions and comments, but the whoosh of the elevator door washed all of it away. I wiped my clammy palms on my black pants. Then rubbed my ruby necklace between my fingers for good luck.

Dad and Tripp exited before Sam and me.

"We have a few minutes before we need to be in the courtroom. Mr. Rose is waiting for us in a private room," Dad announced. "We'll go over any last-minute details."

Sam and Tripp stood guard in the hall while

Dad and I slipped into what looked like a board-room. A large rectangular wood table sat in the middle, with tall back leather chairs positioned around it. Mr. Rose stood in front of a bank of windows, overlooking the city of Boston. The rain continued to fall, and drops skated down the glass.

"Ah, you're here," Mr. Rose said, removing his hands from his pants pockets. He wore a navy suit with a crisp white shirt and royal blue tie. His sand-colored hair was slicked back—with gel, I assumed. "Let's have a seat." He pulled out a chair.

Dad and I did the same, rolling our chairs closer to the enormous conference table.

"I was able to find out two of the judges on the case." Mr. Rose kept his gaze on Dad. "Dyson and Radisson."

"You don't know the third?" Dad asked.

"No. I heard through the grapevine the elders were appointing a new judge to their ranks."

"So, is there a jury?" I had no clue how the vampire government ruled their nation.

"No," Mr. Rose supplied. "The decision will be decided among the three judges—or elders, as they're called in your world. Now, the solicitor representing St. Anne's Academy will be Maddox Tinsley."

Maddox had been one of the solicitors on the

panel when Dad had to make a case for Sam and me to stay on base during our bloodlust quarantine instead of being admitted to Grayson Manor.

"She seemed nice when I met her," I commented, for no apparent reason.

Dad harrumphed, and Mr. Rose's face twisted into an are-we-talking-about-the-same-person look.

"So she's not nice?" I asked.

"You let me worry about all this, Jo." Mr. Rose glanced at me with confidence and control. "I've been handling cases for vampires for a couple of years. I know these people, how they tick, and what they're going to do."

I shrugged. "Okay." I still was unsure as to why Dad hired a human to represent me.

Tripp stuck in his head. "Commander, a word, please?"

Dad disappeared with Tripp.

I pushed back my chair and walked over to the window. "I've never spent any time in Boston. Is that the Charles River?"

Mr. Rose spun around his chair. "Yes, it is. On the other side is Cambridge, home to some of the best colleges in the country. I'm hoping Darcy will get accepted to Harvard, but Mrs. Rose is set on her going to Boston College."

I almost laughed. Darcy didn't have the grades to get into Harvard. At least, I didn't think so. She had gotten a few bad grades in English and math. Plus, Darcy had expressed her lack of interest in college in general. She wanted to go to beauty school and become a hairdresser.

Silence swirled as we both enjoyed the view. Three rowing teams were racing each other, looking majestic against the dreary backdrop of the city.

"What if they find me guilty? What happens then?" I wrapped my arms around my waist, a shiver crawling up my spine. Dad and Mr. Rose had avoided the questions when I asked them a few days ago.

"They have special places for the criminals. But, Jo, you're not going to jail." He rose from his chair and walked over to stand near me.

"How do you know?" I looked up at him.

"I'm the best." He put his hands in his pockets.

"You're also overconfident." The words slipped.

"I am. And if you were in my shoes, you would be, too."

"Do you know something I don't?" I asked, still looking at him.

"Dr. Vieira has evidence that speaks to your innocence."

My jaw dropped. Before I could get the words out of my mouth, Dad stepped back in, running his hand through his hair.

"What's wrong?" I asked. Was Webb in trouble?

"It's not Webb," he said as he looked at his watch. "We found Ben."

"Where is he?" God, I hoped he was okay.

"Let's worry about the trial," Dad said, glancing at his watch again. "It's time. Tripp will be outside. Sam and I will go in and take our seats. Pumpkin, listen to Mr. Rose."

I nodded as Dad exited.

I pushed thoughts of Webb, Ben, and my DNA aside for now. I took in a deep breath and prayed that I would walk out of this building a free vampire.

17

When I crossed the threshold into the courtroom, my nerves sprang to life, my hands shook, and my breathing ramped up.

Mr. Rose strolled in ahead of me, confident and professional. Tripp lagged by my side as though we were walking down to the altar to get married.

"Clasp your hands in front of you and breathe," Tripp whispered. "Don't look at anyone."

Of course, as soon as he said that my reflexes took control, and I glanced around. A few familiar faces sat among the crowd. Mr. Banks, head of security at St. Anne's Academy, sat next to Ms. Lawrence, the headmistress. Ms. Weston, a teacher at the school who actually didn't like me for punching her accidentally, was seated beside Ms. Lawrence; and Ms. Chapman, head of the admin department, took up the first row behind Maddox Tinsley. Directly behind them, my friend Zea Yangstrom sat next to a man who resembled her. Both had curly brown hair, although Zea's draped her shoulders. She waved and smiled. Wow, I hadn't seen her since the day she ran out of the bathroom at school. She'd been my only witness to the fight I had with Blake Turner.

I gave Zea a slight nod before leaning into Tripp. "Where's my dad?" As soon as I asked, I spotted him and Sam in the first row behind Mr. Rose, along with Dr. Vieira. Next to Dr. Vieira was Ms. Costner. Others who I didn't know filled the remaining chairs. Heads bobbed, whispers buzzed, and stares shot my way.

Suddenly, I had a desire to flee. I glanced around for the exits. What would happen if I did run?

"Don't worry about anyone. Keep your sights on Mr. Rose," Tripp said as he opened a small gate.

Reluctantly, I shuffled over to my human attorney. Why did I get the feeling I was walking into hell?

The base of my skull stung as it always did before Dad's voice entered my head. It felt like a brain freeze from eating ice cream too fast.

Keep your thoughts positive.

I tossed a look over my shoulder, meeting Dad's green eyes. *Have you ever been in my shoes?*

A few times.

Don't want to know. I turned and grabbed hold of the arms of the chair as I slowly lowered my butt into it. Tripp saddled into the leather chair on my left and placed a hand on my knee.

My head jerked up. "What are you doing?"

A warm feeling coursed through me, and my body relaxed. I'd forgotten Tripp's healing abilities were like a drug.

"Thank you." I sat back and sighed.

Silk black curtains draped the wall behind the high wooden bench in front of me. At a lower height on the right was a raised platform with a chair.

To the left of the judge's bench, a door creaked open. A tall black-haired guardian walked in from a side entrance. In my world, guardians were equivalent to the human police. Like the sentinels, he was dressed in all black. Instead of the cargo uniform, though, he wore a short-sleeved T-shirt, a simple pair of black pants, and shiny loafers.

"All rise," the guardian said.

Chairs scraped along the floor, sighs echoed, and a few spectators coughed. Then silence crawled through the cold room as we waited for the judges—or I should say elders. Minutes passed before a familiar face entered. Gregory Hollings, a solicitor who had been lead council in charge of our quarantine case, strode up, taking a seat behind the bench.

Dad grunted.

Something wrong? I peeked over my shoulder at Dad.

He had a scowl etched into his face. *Nothing. Turn around.*

I'd bet he wasn't too pleased with Hollings being the newly appointed elder. The other two vamps took their seats. All three of them appeared to be the same age, with variations of dark hair and dark eyes. However, I'd given up on ages when I became a vampire. I couldn't tell how old any vamp was, since the majority of them were fairly young.

Once the elders slid into their chairs, the guardian said, "Please be seated."

More whispers ensued as we followed the guardian's orders.

Mr. Rose retrieved a pen from his jacket pocket. Tripp scooted closer to me, and I scanned the nameplates on the bench. Hollings filled the perch on the left, Dyson in the middle, and Radisson on the right.

"Any news from Webb?" I asked Tripp in a low tone, trying to keep my mind from wandering. My stomach was in knots as I waited for the trial to begin.

"No." His bronze eyes flickered to vampire black for a split second.

"Shouldn't he have checked in?" I'd thought Webb would've at least called by now. I had my phone glued to me. Then again, Dad said in the car before we got to Boston that Webb's plane had taken off two hours ago, or now three hours. I guessed it depended on where the team was headed.

"Jo, stay focused on the trial," Tripp said.

I knew I should, but I didn't want to. I just wanted Webb to call and for me to walk out of here today.

"You didn't answer my question." I shielded my mouth with my hand, hoping my voice didn't make it to the other vampire ears.

One of the judges cleared his throat. "We're here today to weigh in on the facts of the case between Josephine Mason and St. Anne's Academy."

Hearing my name, I turned my attention to the elders' bench.

"In particular, Ms. Mason's behavior, and if she is responsible for the death of a newly turned vampire, Blake Turner, on school property. We'll hear the prosecution's case first then take a short break. When we return, we'll hear from the defense. Ms. Tinsley and Mr. Rose, you know the protocol." Dyson articulated his words clearly and decisively. "Once we've heard both sides, Elder Radisson, Elder Hollings, and I will discuss the case and render a decision based on the facts. Lastly, let me remind everyone. Powers are prohibited in this courtroom. Let's begin. Ms. Tinsley, you have the floor."

Rising, the prosecuting solicitor smoothed out her fuchsia skirt. "Thank you, Elder Dyson. My client, St. Anne's Academy, has filed formal charges against Ms. Mason for not only destruction of property, but for the death of a student on school grounds. With that I will call my first witness, Ms. Lawrence."

Ms. Lawrence rose and stepped around Mr. Banks before gliding to the witness stand like an Olympic skater, graceful and elegant, draped in a black business suit with a pink collared shirt. She unbuttoned her jacket as she took her seat.

Then the guardian approached her and swore her in. His speech wasn't any different than that of the human court system.

"Ms. Lawrence, how long have you been headmistress of St. Anne's Academy?" Maddox asked as she walked to stand near Ms. Lawrence.

"Twenty years," she replied, keeping her eyes on Maddox.

"And during those years, have you seen as much chaos in your school as you had in the two days Jo Mason had been there?" Maddox glanced my way for a brief second.

"We certainly have had our share of outbursts, but no, nothing like her powers or the destruction of school property. And more importantly, we hadn't had any deaths on school grounds."

I didn't know what she was referring to. Was the fight between Blake and me that destructive? I hadn't taken inventory of my surroundings after he collapsed.

"Please share with the court the estimate for the damage." Maddox's voice sounded too excited, as though Ms. Lawrence's answer was the key to my demise.

"The costs total a half-million dollars." The headmistress glared my way.

Letting the answer set in, Maddox twirled a

pen expertly in her long fingers. The elders eyed her, probably speaking to her telepathically to keep moving.

"And please describe the damage." The pen rolled over her forefinger then under her middle one.

"The first day, several panes of glass had shattered, auditorium chairs were ripped from their bolts, and blood stained the new carpeting in front of the stage. The second day, the girls' bathroom was completely demolished from broken tiles, water damage, and stalls completely torn apart," Ms. Lawrence explained.

"Wow," someone in the crowd said.

"So in two days, one girl cost you a half million dollars in damage." Her inflection emphasized every word.

"Objection," Mr. Rose argued. "We've already established the cost."

"Nothing further." Maddox puffed up her perky breasts on her way to the table where she sat down.

Mr. Rose stood, buttoning his jacket. "Ms. Lawrence, have you ever had students who've used their powers in the school?"

"Yes."

He inched closer to the witness. "In fact,

you always have one or two students who are destructive in nature, whether they hurt another student or damage school property. Correct?"

"Sure. Teenagers will act out." She angled her head at Mr. Rose.

"Would you agree then new vampires have a hard time controlling their new powers?" He tucked one hand in his left pant pocket.

"Mr. Rose, Jo Mason's powers are not normal." Ms. Lawrence pursed her lips together.

"Answer the question, Ms. Lawrence. A yes or a no will suffice."

"Yes," she sighed. Again her brown eyes sent a laser beam toward me as though she were trying to drill a hole in me.

"Explain to the court your procedures for admitting new students," Mr. Rose said as he was now standing next to Ms. Lawrence, facing the spectators.

All three elders listened intently as though they were watching a good movie.

"Objection," Maddox blurted out. "This question doesn't speak to the matter at hand."

"A little leeway?" Mr. Rose asked the elders.

The three elders whispered, then Hollings spoke up. "We'll allow it."

On a nod, Mr. Rose repeated the question. Maddox huffed.

"Once the application is completed, we request the student's file from the office of registry. We verify they've been approved by the solicitor's office, and they're legal vampires."

"And what do you mean by legal?" Mr. Rose asked.

"For one, we confirm they've had the chip implanted. Then we verify they've gone through their quarantine. Every student should have their discharge papers from Grayson Manor and a certificate of their chip implant." Ms. Lawrence fidgeted in her seat.

"Did Blake Turner's file have both of these documents?" Mr. Rose asked.

"Of course he did," she said, sounding shocked, as though Mr. Rose was accusing her of not doing her job properly.

"You're certain of this?"

Maddox stood. "Again, Elders. This question has nothing to do—"

Hollings held up a hand and pinned her with a glare. She eased down onto her chair.

"Mr. Rose, my staff is relentless when it comes to following our laws," Ms. Lawrence assured him.

"Someone in your government signed the documents. So, can you share with the court whose name is on Blake's documents?" Mr. Rose continued his questioning.

"Objection." Maddox's tone hardened. "How is she supposed to remember names on any of our documents?"

Ms. Lawrence swung her gaze from Maddox to the elders. I did too. Where was Mr. Rose leading her? He'd said he thought someone within our government had to have helped Blake or, even scarier, Edmund. The hairs on my nape stiffened. Was someone in the vampire government working with Edmund? I would've turned around to see Dad's expression, but his voice was in my head.

I'll kill the bastard rang loud and clear.

"Ms. Lawrence, answer the question," Hollings urged, ignoring Maddox's objection.

All three elders tilted their heads in anticipation.

"I wish I could, but his records have disappeared." Ms. Lawrence dropped her gaze to her lap.

Maddox sagged in her chair. The elders exchanged surprised glances. Hushed whispers circled the room.

The case started to unravel. I didn't know if that was good or bad for me.

"How?" Mr. Rose asked, not missing a beat.

"Right after he was declared dead, we went to pull his file. But it was gone. We searched everywhere. And we haven't been able to locate it since."

"Someone went to great lengths to make sure you didn't examine the file closer." Mr. Rose added evenly.

"Opinion," Maddox countered. "Not relevant."

"I'm done." Mr. Rose sauntered back to the table with a noble air about him.

"Ms. Lawrence you may step down," Dyson said. "Your next witness, Maddox."

She called Mr. Banks as the headmistress took her seat back behind Maddox, and Mr. Banks slid into the witness chair. Before Maddox questioned him, the guardian swore him in.

"Mr. Banks, as head of security for St. Anne's Academy, how many fights have you and your team had to break up?" Maddox started.

"In my ten years at the school, at least one or two a year. None of them worth discussing." Mr. Banks watched Maddox as she wrote on a piece of paper.

"Then would you say in your time at the school, you've never seen anything quite like the mess Ms. Mason inflicted?"

"Objection. Leading the witness," Mr. Rose piped in.

"Sorry, I'll rephrase," she said with a smile in her voice. "Describe the scene on the first day of school, when you and your team entered the auditorium."

"We found Ms. Weston, one of the teachers"— he waved to where she was sitting—"flat on her back, with the Turner boy pinned underneath her. There was blood everywhere. Chairs had splintered in two. More were piled on top of one another. We found Zea Yangstrom out cold on the floor."

My only memories of that incident were of Blake's red eyes and how I wanted to kill him. Okay, I probably shouldn't reveal that thought to anyone.

"And what did you find when you walked into the girls' bathroom?" She clasped her hands together on the table.

"We had two people down. The girl, Jewel, was still breathing but pale. The boy, Blake, had several holes on his face with blood-soaked clothes. He, too, was pale. The bathroom looked like a war zone. The stall doors had been torn off their hinges. The mirrors were shattered. The tile on the floors and walls were smashed as though someone had taken a sledgehammer to it."

Dad grunted behind me. I glanced at Tripp. His lips were curled at the edges as though he was enjoying hearing all this. Either that or he was proud of me.

"And what about Ms. Mason?" Maddox asked.

Mr. Banks ran his hand through his military crew cut. The first time I'd met him, he had been bald.

"She seemed to be in a trance. That's all I can tell you," he said, his deep voice resonating.

"And where do you think Blake Turner got the holes on his face?" Maddox asked.

That day with my anger hyped, I'd turned water into ice balls, which hit Blake like bullets.

"I'm not sure," he responded. "But what I am sure of is the boy was dead."

A round of gasps filled the room, and with it, more whispers.

"In your opinion, Mr. Banks, did Jo Mason kill Blake Turner?" Maddox picked up a pen.

"Objection. Speculation," Mr. Rose intervened.

The elders gave her a pointed look, then Radisson said, "Maddox, stay on topic."

"Mr. Banks, isn't it true that Ms. Mason not

only attacked Blake Turner the day before, but also attacked Ms. Weston?"

"Yes. She punched her."

I couldn't argue with his answer, at least, not entirely. Blake had attacked Zea and was draining the blood out of her. I tried to stop him, but Ms. Weston had gotten in the way. I did apologize to her, although she hadn't accepted my apology. Actually, if I remembered correctly, she politely dismissed me with a comment about penance.

"He's all yours, Gary." Maddox tucked a few strands of her blond hair behind her ear, seemingly proud of herself.

"I only have one," Mr. Rose said, not moving from his chair. "On the first day, did Blake sink his fangs into Ms. Yangstrom, my client's friend? Which was why Ms. Mason was trying to stop him?"

Mr. Banks addressed Mr. Rose. "Yes, according to the students I questioned, Blake did attack Ms. Yangstrom. But Ms. Mason wasn't the one to stop him. Her brother subdued Blake."

Sam had been holding Blake back when I let loose with my fists.

"Nothing further." Mr. Rose scribbled a question on his pad before sliding it over to me. It read, "Is it true?"

I wrote, "Yes." I wasn't sure why he was asking for confirmation.

Mr. Banks stepped down and then out through the door the guardian had entered from earlier.

"Ms. Tinsley, continue with your next witness," Dyson said.

"Zea Yangstrom," Maddox announced.

The pen fell out of my hand as I almost lost my breakfast. I leaned into Mr. Rose. "Why is she testifying for them? Shouldn't she be on our side? She's my only witness."

She was the only one who could save me. At least, in my mind she was. After all, she too had been attacked.

"Calm down," Mr. Rose whispered. "Normal procedure."

Normal for whom? Nothing about this trial seemed normal. I'd been defending myself and trying to help a friend. Why was I worried? She was my *friend*. Wasn't she? Certainly she would tell the truth.

Dressed in a black-and-white polka dot sundress, Zea slowly made her way to the stand, clenching her fists at her sides. My nerves jumped as she eased down into the witness box. She glanced my way, giving me a sad I'm-sorry smile before the guardian stalked to her and swore her in before resuming his position at the side door.

I bounced my knee.

"Zea." Maddox's black high heels clicked against the floor as she made her way to Zea. "Take the court through your recollection of the events the day you were attacked in the girls' bathroom."

Zea adjusted her white headband. "Jo had gone to the bathroom between classes. And when the bell rang at the start of class, she didn't return. So I'd gone to check on her. When I entered, a woman came out of nowhere with a dagger. After that, the only thing I remember was Jo strangling Blake."

I choked on air. If the audience had said anything, I couldn't hear it. The only thing I could hear was the obscenities Dad screamed in my head.

I jumped out of my chair. Tripp latched onto my arm.

"You're lying!" I snarled at Zea.

My body shook with rage, along with the table.

"I have an enormous amount of healing power, Jo," Tripp whispered. "But I'm not sure I can tame the wild side of your telekinesis. Remember you can't use your powers in this building. I want you to breathe."

Laws and rules didn't enter into my psyche. Frankly, I didn't care.

"Okay, everyone. Quiet down," one of the elders said.

Zea looked down at her hands or something in her lap.

"She's lying," I insisted.

Tripp pulled me down into my chair. The nameplates on the elder's bench slid back and forth, one dropping to the floor.

"Mr. Rose, may I remind you that powers are restricted in this building. If you don't want your client removed, I suggest you make her understand our laws," Hollings stated.

"Jo," Tripp whispered. "You don't want to be taken away. They'll inject you with a sedative if you continue to use your powers."

Pumpkin, you need to listen to Tripp. Dad's voice was calm.

"Why aren't you objecting?" I glared daggers at Mr. Rose.

He was supposed to be the best of the best. Right?

The crowd tittered. Some of them said, "I knew she was guilty."

"Order," Dyson commanded.

A high-pitched noise punctured my eardrums. Wincing, I covered my ears. "What is that?"

The only one who seemed to be unaffected was my human attorney.

"The elders have a button underneath their bench that sends out a very high-pitched alarm that only vampires can hear. That's their way of quieting vampires," Mr. Rose said.

"What are we, dogs?" I asked sarcastically.

"It worked, didn't it?" he pointed out.

The room had fallen silent, and so did my telekinesis.

"Now, Ms. Tinsley, please continue." Dyson jotted on a pad.

"Nothing further." Maddox strutted to her seat as if she were the queen of the courtroom.

If I had liked her when I first met her, that emotion was history now.

"Mr. Rose, your witness," Radisson said.

He stood, buttoning his suit jacket. "Ms. Yangstrom, isn't it true you ran out of the girls' bathroom?"

"I did." She nodded slightly.

"Isn't it also true Blake was still alive when you ran out?" Mr. Rose walked over to her.

"I don't remember." Her voice wavered.

"Why did you run out, Ms. Yangstrom?" Mr. Rose asked.

She glanced out into the crowd. "I ran for help."

At the time, I'd assumed that was why she'd run out, but...

"Then why did the guardians find you curled up in the boys' bathroom?"

That.

"I don't remember." Her cheeks flushed pink, as though she were embarrassed.

I grasped the arms of the chair tightly, trying to restrain myself from strangling Zea. I didn't understand why she wasn't telling the truth. Did the school coerce her into lying? She was under oath!

"Do you hate the taste of blood?" Mr. Rose's tone was gentle.

She searched the crowd again, and the man who resembled her nodded. My guess was he was her father.

"Answer the question," Radisson said.

"Yes," she responded softly.

"Please tell the court what happens when you drink blood," Mr. Rose urged.

"I get dizzy." Zea glanced down at her lap.

"Isn't it also true you lose track of your surroundings? And they become distorted?"

What? I knew she hated the taste of blood. But how could blood have that effect on a vampire? We needed the sticky red stuff to survive.

"It depends on how much I drink," she responded.

"You took a lot from Jewel, the human you bit that day, didn't you?" Mr. Rose prodded.

"I don't remember," she said.

I cocked my head to one side as I stared at her. Didn't she remember the dagger at her throat?

"Zea, may I remind you, you're under oath," Mr. Rose said.

Maddox came to her rescue. "If she doesn't remember, she doesn't."

Hollings held up his hand at Maddox before turning to Zea. "Ms. Yangstrom, we're not here to judge you and your dislike for the taste of blood. I want you to think hard about your answer. Did you take a lot of blood from Jewel?"

Zea's eyes watered as she stared at the man in the audience. "I did. I got sick and ran out."

The elders wrote in their notepads.

"Nothing further." Mr. Rose returned to the table.

"That's it? You're not going to ask her why she's lying?" I tried to keep my voice low.

He wrote something down, ignoring me. At

any moment, I was debating whether to strangle my attorney instead of Zea.

"Ms. Tinsley, call your next witness," Dyson ordered.

Zea strolled past with her eyes downcast.

Who throws a friend in front of an oncoming train? Oh, wait. She does.

"Elders, no more witnesses. The prosecution rests."

In my mind she didn't need anyone else. Zea was her key to finding me guilty.

THE TIME ALLOTTED for a break was short. Dad, Sam, and Tripp scurried off to check on the sentinels. Mr. Rose and I returned to the private room we were in before the hearing started. I wasn't supposed to mingle with anyone other than family and my attorney, since the trial wasn't over yet. My muscles twitched. I wanted to seek out Zea and ask her what the hell she had been smoking.

"Why did she lie?" I was still shocked as I dropped into one of the leather chairs.

Across the table, Mr. Rose read through a file, preparing for his first witness.

He peered over the piece of paper in his hand.

"She probably was told to say some of those things."

"But isn't that perjury?"

"Sure, if we could prove it. I'm not sure how well you know your friend, Jo. But she has an intolerance to blood. She gets disoriented for a period of time after she drinks. My goal in questioning her was to prove to the elders she's not a credible witness."

I would never grasp the concept of Zea—or any vampire, for that matter—not liking blood, much less being intolerant of it.

I had to move past Zea—for now, anyway. I also had to trust that Mr. Rose did show her testimony wasn't credible. "Are you putting me up on the stand?"

"More than likely," he mumbled as he continued to peruse through his file.

My phone chirped. Looking at it, I smiled, and the events of the past few hours faded. After tapping the message icon, I read through the text.

We're getting ready to hop on our second leg of the trip. I wanted to say hi and check on the trial.

My fingers flew over the letters on the screen. *It's going okay. We're on a break.*

I know. Your dad just called. I might not be able to

message you once we land. Be strong and listen to Tripp. I love you.

Those three meaningful words seemed foreign to me. I never imagined in all my life I would find someone, vampire or human, who loved me. Still, my heart expanded, and I got goose bumps along my arms.

I love you, too. Be safe.

I was about to pocket my phone when it buzzed again. I looked at the screen. I had another text from an unknown number. It read, *I'll see you soon*, followed by a heart-shaped emoticon and the name *Ben*.

I read it again. Was the text really from Ben? I glanced at Mr. Rose, who was still buried in his file. I looked past him and out the window. Rain still fell, and the city skyline wasn't as visible as it was earlier.

As I tapped my foot, I debated whether to respond. Dad had said no contact with Ben, but my curiosity was killing me. Where was he?

Before my decision was made, another text came through. *You looked pretty that night I held you on the street near the fundraiser. I can't wait to see you.*

"Jo, it's time," Mr. Rose said.

I lifted my gaze. Mr. Rose was standing with his briefcase in hand.

"Is there something wrong?" he asked.

I shook my head. I probably should tell Dad. But what could he do about the text? Besides, I had a trial to focus on. Ben couldn't get to me. I had Dad, Sam, and Tripp with me. Pocketing my phone, I bit my lip as I pushed to my feet and met Mr. Rose at the door. I'd tell Dad after the trial was over.

Everyone filed back into the courtroom. We went through the same protocol as we did earlier, rising and sitting when the elders entered.

"Mr. Rose, please call your first witness," Radisson said.

"The defense calls Dr. Damon Vieira."

Dr. Vieira took the stand and was sworn in.

"Dr. Vieira, please take us through this autopsy report," Mr. Rose instructed as he walked over to the bench and handed a copy of the report to the elders.

"First, Blake Turner did not carry any vampire DNA. He was a pure human. Second, as the report outlines, Blake had the beginning of a third helix structure, but nothing that matched our DNA patterns." His gaze held steady at Mr. Rose. "Third, when a natural-born vampire changes from human to vampire, our heart muscle shrinks in size. Not Blake's. His grew even larger than a human's."

Whispers created a hum. Even the elders spoke low to one another. Whatever Blake had been injected with, I prayed it wasn't the same solution as the one Ben had been given. Otherwise, Ben might turn into a carbon copy of Blake.

"In addition, I found other oddities," Dr. Vieira said. "In our species, we have a lot of internal changes. But the one organ that doesn't grow, shrink, or change within us is our brain. It will stay the same as any human's." He rubbed his chin. "Blake's brain was shrinking."

More whispers ensued.

"Based on your results, what have you concluded?" Mr. Rose asked.

"One, Blake's system couldn't get enough blood to keep his organs functioning. Also, I would guess he couldn't keep his hunger for blood sated, which might be why he attacked Ms. Yangstrom. Therefore, it is my conclusion he died because of all the changes to his body."

Mr. Rose ambled back to the table. A feather dropping to the floor could have probably been heard at the moment.

Talk about drama to the nth degree. Wow! Way to keep the room on the edge of their seat.

"Anything else you would like to add?" Mr. Rose queried.

"Yes. The two teenagers we rescued from Edmund Rain's mansion have the same autopsy results as Blake Turner."

"Dear Lord," a woman blurted out. Hollings flipped through the report. Dyson was writing.

"Why haven't we heard about these other two boys?" Elder Radisson arched his bushy eyebrows at Dr. Vieira.

"I apologize," he said, glancing up at Radisson. "I was preparing for this trial and haven't had time to submit it."

Radisson jotted something down on his notepad.

"Are you finished with your questioning?" Dyson asked.

"Yes, sir." Mr. Rose lowered his body into his chair.

Without waiting for the elder's cue, Maddox sprang to life. "Dr. Vieira, is it true that Jo Mason used her power of manipulating air to kill Blake Turner?"

"Objection," Mr. Rose sang.

"Nothing further," she said as she sat down with a satisfied grin on her face.

How did she know about my powers? Aside

from my telekinesis, most of my other abilities weren't common knowledge—at least, not that I knew of.

Hollings checked his phone then whispered to the other two elders. They both nodded. "We need to take a break," Hollings announced. "Court will resume in thirty minutes."

I didn't know why we were taking another breather, but I wasn't complaining. The trial was getting intense.

18

D ad, Mr. Rose, and I settled into the client-attorney room. Tripp and Sam stood outside the room, guarding the door. I wasn't sure why since we were in a secure government building.

Mr. Rose pulled what looked like a protein bar out from his briefcase. I wasn't hungry at all. Not even for blood. Dad had packed blood in case we needed it. As I relaxed in one of the comfy leather chairs, I checked my phone. I didn't think Webb would have sent me a message yet, since he was jumping on another flight not that long ago. But I did want to see if Ben had.

Nope. No messages. "Dad, I didn't have time to tell you earlier, but Ben sent me a text on our last break. You said you found him. Did you have him picked up?"

Dad glanced up from his phone. His green eyes flashed to vampire silver as he pinched his eyebrows together. "Let me see your phone." His voice was calm.

Dad was sitting three chairs down from me, along the same side of the conference table. I slid my phone down to him. He picked it up and tapped the screen. After he read the text, he reached inside his jacket and pulled out a pen. Mr. Rose handed him a piece of paper without prompting.

Dad jotted something down on it before he stood, walked to the door, and opened it. "Tripp, have this number traced."

Tripp took the paper.

"Tell Sawyer to ping me on my phone when he gets the location," Dad said. "I'll step out of the courtroom if I have to."

I thought Dad had found Ben. Did his order mean he hadn't?

Dad closed the door and returned to his seat.

"Did you not find Ben?" I asked. I spotted a paperclip sitting on the table. I picked it up.

"He wasn't in the location we tracked him to," he said as he slid my phone back to me.

"Was that location in Boston?" I asked. Ben's text did say he would see me soon. Did that mean today? If so, how? Were he and Nicki devising another plan to corner me as they did at the fundraiser that night?

At that moment, Dr. Vieira came in.

Dad turned in his chair. "What is it?"

Dr. Vieira ran a hand through his hair. "Grace from the lab just called. She informed me that their computer system has been compromised. Whoever hacked into it also erased their entire system. They're trying to restore the data. She's not sure if the backup was completed after she entered the twins' results. I thought you should know."

The air thickened.

"Son of..." Dad scrubbed a hand over his face as he got out of his chair.

Mr. Rose busied himself by reading through a thick packet of stapled paper.

Why would someone want to steal lab data? Unless somehow Edmund found out about my unique DNA?

Dad chewed on the inside of his cheek as he got out of his chair then walked over to the window.

Silence blanketed the room as Dr. Vieira and I watched Dad. Mr. Rose kept reading.

"Are you thinking that Edmund might be the one who stole the data?" I asked Dad.

"That thought has crossed my mind. If that's the case, then we definitely have someone on the inside of our organization who's helping him." Dad rubbed the back of his neck as he mumbled a few obscenities under his breath.

The only people who knew about my DNA were Dr. Vieira, Dad, Sam, Webb, and me. I wasn't certain if Brian, the lab assistant, knew, or even Dr. Case.

"Damon," Dad said. "Head over to the lab and see what else you can find out."

Nodding, Dr. Vieira pivoted on his heel and exited.

"Has Ms. Wallace reported in yet on what she found out about Grayson Manor?" Dad asked as he looked out over the city.

The dark clouds rolled over the skyline.

"She assured me she would call or text as soon as she knew." Mr. Rose joined Dad at the window.

"What's going on?" I bent the paperclip into odd shapes to pass the time.

"I may have found the person who helped Edmund get Blake into Grayson Manor and the school," Mr. Rose said, tucking a hand in his pocket. "This information will help your case."

"Who?" The paperclip fell from my fingers.

"I'd rather not say until I have confirmation."

"What if you don't get the info before the trial ends?" I was curious why he didn't have it already. The way the trial was going, I didn't feel confident about my chances of walking out of this building today.

"Jo, let me worry about that," Mr. Rose said. "Right now, let's go through some pointers on how to handle yourself on the stand."

For the remaining time we had, Mr. Rose and Dad coached me not to get angry, not to use my powers, to answer the questions with surety, to tell the truth, and to think about my answer before I spoke. I could do all those things. After all, my freedom was at stake.

By the time they finished giving me pointers, it was time to get back into the courtroom. Dad had a few things to check on. He wanted to see if Sawyer had traced the number that Ben had texted me from. He also wanted to check with the control room on Webb's ETA to their location.

Dad went right out of the conference, and Mr. Rose and I went left. Sam and Tripp followed. The audience in the courtroom had dwindled down to half. Aside from the people I didn't know, Ms.

Lawrence talked with Ms. Weston. Ms. Costner sat next to Sam. Zea and the man she had been with were not present, and Mr. Banks had departed long ago.

As soon as we were seated, Mr. Rose pulled out his phone, tapped the screen, and scrolled through a text. I was about to ask him if the message was from Ms. Wallace when the elders settled in.

"Call your first witness, Mr. Rose," Hollings said.

Mr. Rose set his phone on the table. "I call Maddox Tinsley to the stand." He looked at Maddox then back at the elders.

A collective gasp sounded throughout the courtroom.

"What!" Maddox blurted out as she jumped out of her seat.

I was just as shocked as she was. Did that mean she was working for Edmund?

"I have reason to believe that Ms. Tinsley knew that Blake Turner was not a natural-born vampire but a victim of Edmund Rain's experiment to turn humans into vampires. I also have proof that Ms. Tinsley was the solicitor who signed off on Blake's documents." Mr. Rose fixated on the elders.

"And where is this proof?" Dyson asked, leaning forward on the bench.

The door to the courtroom opened, and everyone turned, including me. Ms. Wallace walked with a confident air about her, holding a folder in her hand. Dad was right behind her.

"Who is this human?" Maddox asked, looking worried.

Ms. Wallace handed the folder to Mr. Rose before taking a seat next to Sam. Then Dad sat down beside her. I angled my head toward Dad, and he smiled.

I faced forward, hoping that whatever Mr. Rose had in that folder would end this case. I wanted my name cleared and my innocence proven so I wouldn't be the topic of conversation when I returned to school, and I didn't want other kids to be afraid of me.

"If it pleases the court, I would like to enter the contents of this folder as exhibit A." Mr. Rose got out of his chair, walked over to the bench, then handed the folder to the elders. "I also request that, with this new evidence, my client be dismissed of all charges."

Maddox dropped into her chair, looking defeated.

"Please explain yourself, Ms. Tinsley," Hollings ordered as Dyson read through the folder.

"And may I remind you that as an officer of this court, you are under oath," Radisson said, clasping his hands together and resting them on the bench.

Mr. Rose took his seat as everyone waited for her to speak.

Maddox sat, staring at something directly in front of her.

"Your signature is on these documents." Dyson's voice hitched. "This is the missing file from St. Anne's Academy." The surprise turned to anger. "I'll give you two seconds to start talking, or I'll have you removed from this court and thrown into a cell."

At least a minute passed before Maddox let out a sigh, turned her gaze to the elders, and said, "I'm sorry. Edmund Rain threatened me and my family. He told me that if I didn't help him get Blake Turner into the school, he would start killing those close to me. Then when I followed through on his request, he told me to make sure I got this case and that I proved Jo Mason was guilty of killing Blake. If I didn't, he would kill my mother and father then me." A tear slid down her cheek.

I wasn't surprised Edmund was at the root of

all this, continually making my life hell. I knew he somehow had enrolled Blake into St. Anne's Academy. He'd told me himself when he kidnapped me. But he never told me how or who was responsible.

I felt a pang of sympathy for Maddox. I didn't want to see any harm come to her or her family.

I glanced at Mr. Rose, who looked troubled. I imagined he was thinking of his own issues he had, and of the debt he owed to a vampire.

The elders huddled at the bench, whispering.

"Elders, may I speak?" Dad asked.

They lifted their gazes and nodded at the same time. I glanced at Tripp, and he shrugged. What was Dad up to?

"Maddox, where're your parents now?" he asked.

She shifted in her seat so she was facing Dad. "I had them leave town a week ago. I spoke to them on break. They're safe."

"Write down the address on a piece of paper," Dad said. "Tripp, get two men to check out the address."

Maddox scribbled on her notepad. Tripp stood then walked over to her. She tore the paper from the pad and handed it to him, then he walked out.

"Guardian, take Ms. Tinsley to a holding cell," Hollings said.

Maddox got up, collected her belongings, and went over to the guardian before he even moved from his post at the side door.

When they were gone, Hollings turned his attention to me. "Jo Mason, even though the evidence presented today leans in your favor, indicating that you operated in self-defense, you are not without fault. You've damaged school property and assaulted a teacher. There are consequences for your actions. Therefore, you are responsible for the cost of the damages. As far as your assault on Ms. Weston, I'll leave your punishment up to her. Is this understood?"

I didn't know which one I was afraid of more. The punishment or the half-million dollars I didn't have. "Yes, sir," I said reluctantly. Where was I going to get that kind of money?

"Very well. This court is adjourned," Hollings said.

All three elders stood and left through the side door. I didn't know what was going to happen to Maddox or how I was going to pay for what I'd done to the school or Ms. Weston, but I was relieved that the trial was over.

IT WAS STILL RAINING as we left Boston. I sat behind Dad while Tripp drove, and Sam sat next to me. I leaned against the window with my phone in my hand, hoping Webb would call. I wanted to tell him about the trial and to brag about Mr. Rose and the great job he did.

Plus, Mr. Rose had been right about Ms. Wallace. She was a great investigator. Maybe she could find out who cut the brakes on the limo. In fact, Dad had asked her if she would be available to take on the task. She said she'd think about it.

I hadn't brought up Ben, although I wanted to. I was curious where he was and what he was up to. But I didn't think Dad would tell me.

I sat up and checked on my brother, who was playing a game on his phone. He'd been quiet since he left the courthouse.

"What's wrong, Sam?" I asked.

He looked over at me and shrugged. "I guess we have to go back to school."

I wasn't sure how I felt about going back to St. Anne's Academy. Could Zea and I still be friends? What kind of punishment did Ms. Weston have in mind? Did I have to pay the damages before I returned?

"Dad, how am I supposed to pay the school back?"

Traffic on the highway was slowing down ahead.

"I'll speak with Ms. Lawrence and work something out," Dad said.

"I'm sorry I've created so much trouble. I'll do whatever I can to help pay." I didn't want to put my dad through hell. Maybe at one time I'd wanted to but not anymore. He was rough around the edges, but inside, he had a big heart. I loved him and wanted to show him I could be an adult.

"Let's learn from our mistakes," he said as his phone rang. "What!" He sounded panicked. "Say that again."

Tripp slowed to a stop. I leaned over slightly and glanced out through the windshield. Blue lights flashed in the distance. I guessed there had been an accident.

"Did you try again?" Dad asked whomever he was speaking to. His voice still held an edge to it. He growled. "Keep trying to contact the pilots."

Sam and I exchanged looks, and I froze. Was he talking about the pilots of Webb's plane? I shook my head as though I were trying to shake off a bug in my hair.

"We'll be back as soon as we can. Call me

when you have further information." Then Dad hung up and hit something.

The sound made me flinch.

"What's wrong, Pops?" Sam asked calmly.

Dad turned in his seat. His green eyes had turned silver, and the water in his eyes made my heart fall out of my chest. Why would my strong, powerful vampire father have tears in his eyes? Steven Mars Mason was always tough, strong, and composed. A leader among humans and vampires.

Tripp kept his focus on the stopped traffic. "Did something happen on the mission?"

Please say no. Please. My breathing increased.

"The pilots radioed in and said the plane was going down. One of the engines had caught fire. Then we lost all communication with the pilots."

I gasped.

"Fuck," Tripp said as he banged on the steering wheel.

Sam ran a hand through his hair as he grabbed my hand.

The blood rushed out of me. My heart plummeted to the floor. Tears clouded my vision. The inside of the car narrowed. The air left my lungs.

This couldn't be true. Webb had texted me not that long ago. He couldn't be—

No. I refused to believe it.

My lower lip trembled. As vampires, we were hard to kill, although I didn't think we could withstand a plane crash. Could we?

My dream of Webb in a coffin tumbled through my mind. Was my dream coming true?

I needed air. I opened the door and jumped out. I ran down off the embankment with my phone in my hand. I dropped to my knees, and with unsteady fingers, I punched in Webb's number. It immediately went to voice mail. I tried again. Same thing.

"Please leave a message. I'll return your call as soon as I can," his voice said on voice mail.

When the beep sounded to leave a message, I said, "Call me, ple—ase." Tears poured down my face. "Please."

"Pumpkin." Dad lifted me off the ground.

I cried against his chest as he carried me back to the car.

"The control room told me they were close to their target jump. That means they had their chutes on. Let's get home so we can find out more." He kissed my hair.

I lifted my head. "Does that mean Webb's alive?"

"I can't answer that. But as SEALs, we're trained for all kinds of situations."

Dad's words gave me hope. I prayed that all sentinels did escape unharmed. More importantly, I prayed that my dream didn't come true.

EPILOGUE
WEBB

We were close to our target landing. I prayed like hell we would get in and get out. I hated to be this far away from life, civilization, from Jo. Every part of me wanted to cancel this mission and stay with her. I couldn't. A life was on the line, and we were under a time crunch to get to our target.

These last few days killed me to see her beautiful face twisted in worry. My fangs slid out as I thought about her. How she smelled of lavender and spring. How her lips tasted sweet and moist. How her skin felt, soft and feathery. How her body molded to mine perfectly.

I squirmed in my seat. I couldn't think about her. I had a fucking mission to complete. There wasn't any room to screw this up. I needed to save lives, to rescue Quade and Crowe. They deserved our complete focus.

Both had vanished on one of our missions in Argentina. We'd been dispatched to extract Bruno Almeida. He'd been on the vampires' most wanted list for years for various crimes of drugs, prostitution, and blood smuggling. Normally, the SEALs wouldn't get involved with hunting down vampire criminals unless the human government raised an eyebrow, and they had more than a raised eyebrow with Bruno's escapades. All over the globe, dead human bodies surfaced, drained of all their blood.

"Lieutenant." Olivia slid into the seat next to me. "The terrain will be tough when we hit the ground. I suggest—"

The plane rocked. I hated turbulence. I didn't have a fear of flying. I did have a fear of dying in a plane, though. There weren't many ways vampires could die, but dropping from thirty-six thousand feet to the earth below... Well, even vampires weren't immune to the impact.

"A storm is on the horizon," Olivia continued when the plane quieted. "Which is why I'm suggesting we look at our alternative route when we land. The Alaskan mountains will be rough even for summertime."

"We stick to the plan, storm or not."

She raised her eyebrows. "But—"

"No. We discussed this. We deviate from the plan, and that's when mistakes happen. That's when the mission fails." I studied a map of the terrain.

"With all due respect, Lieutenant. Do you hear what're saying? You know Bruno was expecting us on that last mission when Quade and Crowe vanished. Maybe the storm is our salvation. Especially if—"

"Olivia!"

"No, Webb. Hear me out." Her voice deepened.

My vision went dark for a mere second before my eyes flashed vampire. How dare she argue with me?

"Get pissed. I don't give a shit. You're wrong on this one," she said.

"Then tell me what I'm wrong about." I bit my tongue to control my anger.

"First, get your head in the game. You've been sulking since we left base. I know you're worried about Jo and the trial. She's in good hands with Tripp. Besides, do you think Sam will let anything happen to her? That pain in my ass has been with her all her life. So let family take care of her."

I growled. I wanted to be her family. I wanted

to be by her side. I loved the bratty beauty. I fucking loved every inch, muscle, and curve on her.

Regardless, Olivia was right. Still, for some reason, I couldn't get Jo's dream out of my head. I didn't want to believe her dream would come true. That I would die.

Maybe deviating from the plan would change my fate, change the outcome of Jo's dream.

Or not.

"Go on," I said through gritted fangs.

"Thank you. Now, command is expecting us to stick to our route." She pointed to the area on the map that I had outlined in red. "You know we suspect a second mole in our organization. We know it isn't any one of us on this plane. So, if the mole is talking to our enemies, then they'll be expecting to cut us off at some point on the planned route."

Olivia was a great strategist, thinking ten steps ahead of everyone. Her unique ability had nothing to do with her vampire powers. She wasn't a psychic, nor could she see into the future.

I thought about this for a second as another wave of turbulence rocked us. I trusted her implicitly. Aside from Tripp, she was one of my best friends. They both had been with me from day one as a Navy SEAL. I couldn't think of a time when she'd ever been wrong.

"How come you didn't speak up when we were in Argentina?"

"What?" Her head snapped my way.

The plane leveled out, and I let out a breath.

"I did speak up to Commander Mason. He was in charge of that mission. You weren't."

"Fifteen minutes to target, Lieutenant," the pilot said overhead.

"Let's get the others up to speed on the change in plans." I didn't have time to analyze why the commander didn't talk to me about what Olivia had told him. We usually discussed all ideas as a team.

We gathered quickly, and Olivia explained the new route using the map. Sloan, Kraft, and Kodiak all agreed with Olivia's strategy.

We readied our gear. We needed more than a parachute at twenty-nine thousand feet. The jump required oxygen and special helmets to sustain the high-altitude drop.

"Five minutes to target," the pilot called.

All of us checked and rechecked our gear. I held up five fingers. Olivia nodded first, adjusting her helmet. Sloan, Kraft, and Kodiak did the same.

As I lowered my hand, one of the engines sputtered. Then the plane dropped sharply.

"What's going on?" I asked the pilot through my earpiece.

"One engine out. Can't get it started. I need you to jump now."

"We're not on target," I responded.

The team could hear our conversation. We were all wired to each other.

"I need to get this bird down," the pilot said.

The door opened, and wind blasted us.

"Engine is on fire! Get the fuck out now!" the pilot shouted.

We didn't hesitate. Kraft jumped first, followed by Kodiak, Sloan, and Olivia.

I took in a breath, the oxygen cooling my throat.

As soon as I jumped out, the plane burst into flames. Parts, pieces, and large chunks of metal fell behind us. One large section of wing was on a collision course for one of the sentinels. Luckily, the sentinel moved at the last moment, and the debris narrowly missed. I thanked the heaven above.

Then something hit me in the back, sending me tumbling out of control. Once I righted myself to maximize resistance, I immediately pulled on my chute. Nothing. I tried again.

The handle broke off.

Fuck.

My life flashed before me as I sped downward, passing my team. I tugged on my reserve chute as the earth drew closer and closer.

I love you, Jo. I vow if I get out of this, I will always listen to your dreams. Forever.

Jo and Webb's story continues in *On the Edge of Misery.* Available now in Ebook and paperback formats.

Turn the page to read a sample.

On the Edge of Misery - Sample

I didn't know true misery until Webb went missing.

My heart is frozen in anguish as icy as the Alaskan terrain we scoured in search of him. Others have abandoned the hunt, convinced all hope is lost. But I refuse to give up.

My dreams warned me of the danger coming for Webb. There's a chance they could lead me to him...

If I only could fall into a restful sleep that now eludes me. The stress is taking its toll on my body and powers.

Until the phone rings...

They say they'll trade my life for his. Warn me that I must come alone. With the watchful eyes of my father and brother, it will be next to impossible to escape.

Still, I will stop at nothing to save the man I love.

Chapter I
JO

I threw off the blankets then swung my angry gaze to the clock on my bedside table.

"Argh," I growled.

Night after night for the last three months, I couldn't sleep. Every time I tried, all I could see was Webb in a coffin. I was numb to the knowledge that he might be dead. I cried my eyes out for the first month. Then all my tears dried up. If I wasn't trying to sleep, I lived in the control room, waiting to hear his voice come over the radio or biting my nails while my dad's team was glued to their computers in the hopes that they too would hear from Webb.

"You have to try and dream," Dad had said.

I laughed at him. The more pressure he put on me, the less chance I would fall into a deep slumber. My vampire powers had grown significantly since Webb's plane went down over the Alaskan mountains. Before then, I could make objects move, manipulate water, air, and earth, and read human minds, but only if I were touching the people. The vampire community considered my father the most powerful of all vampires. But I now matched all his abilities and then some. I'd recently added the fire element to my growing powers. That ability took a great amount of concentration to conjure up fireballs that I could throw like baseballs. Not to mention, I was capable of reading vampire minds, albeit I still had to have skin contact to do so.

The one ability my father didn't have that I had somehow developed was seeing into the future through my dreams, although that power was dead in its tracks at the moment. My dad, Sam, Dr. Vieira, Tripp, and many others were relying on me to find Webb. Again, I'd laughed at them. Aside from my recurring dream, where I was standing in the middle of a cemetery surrounded by coffins, one of which contained Webb, I hadn't come up with anything. If I had, I would have woken up with no memories of the dream world.

Dad hadn't had any luck, either. For thirty solid days, a search and rescue team hunted the Alaskan mountains for any sign of the plane or Webb, Olivia, Kraft, Sloan, and Kodiak. But they found nothing. Dad had finally called off the search.

Through tears, I'd pleaded with him for hours on end. "You're the commander of the vampire

SEAL team. You rule this base. You have to keep looking."

"Jo, the terrain and the weather are slowing us down. I've alerted the military base in Alaska. They'll keep their eyes and ears open. I'm sorry, pumpkin. We have work to do here. We still have to get to the bottom of who stole all your lab data. Remember, Edmund is still out there, working toward building that vampire army. And you are instrumental in his endeavor."

"If Edmund needs my DNA for his plan, then why haven't we heard from him in over three months?" I'd asked Dad.

Dr. Vieira believed that I was the key to Edmund's master plan since I had a unique DNA makeup that no other vampire had. I wasn't so sure I believed that I was the one who could help Edmund build an army of vampires out of humans, at least not perfect ones that could fight against us. So far, Edmund's only experiment that held any substance had been with Blake Turner, the human boy I'd been accused of murdering. But Blake's new genetic makeup had only served to kill him. Still, I didn't want to become a lab experiment.

"If I know Edmund, he's not going to do something on a whim. He's planning. In the meantime, try to see if your dreams tell you anything about Edmund or Webb."

I couldn't dream about Webb. How was I supposed to dream about our enemy? I growled again as I popped out of bed. It was four in the morning, and the apartment was deathly quiet. I tiptoed out of my room and into the hall. I was about to get some water when I noticed that my twin brother, Sam's, bedroom door was ajar. That was odd. He never left it open when he slept. He had this odd sense of fear that someone would attack him in the dead of sleep.

I peeked in to find his bed empty. I wasn't exactly surprised. Like me, Sam had trouble sleeping. Many times, I found him in the training room, venting off steam or in the control room, checking for any news on Webb.

I trudged down the hall and into the kitchen, where I poured myself a glass of blood. After I quenched my thirst, I decided I should try to ease my frustrations. I could stand to shed some anxiety or at least tire myself out so I could sleep. Then maybe I could dream or at least get past the scene of Webb in a coffin.

I changed quickly into a pair of yoga pants, a T-shirt, and tennis shoes then quietly dashed out of the apartment, making sure I didn't wake Dad. The hall leading to the stairwell was eerily quiet. Overhead lights blinked on as I trekked down to the basement. While Webb and other sentinels had their own place to call home on base, Dad wanted to live in an apartment above his office, the control room, and all the other military amenities for the staff. It hadn't bothered me too much, although I would have preferred to have a home where we weren't in the middle of the chaos.

Grunts resounded as I drew close, followed by clanging swords. I smiled as I settled against the doorjamb to the training room. Tripp and Sam were going at it, the air charged with electricity. Surrounded by padded walls, they circled each other with their swords at the ready. Tripp's sandy-blond hair was pulled back into a low ponytail, while Sam's black hair stuck to his forehead. For several months, Sam had sported shoulder-length hair until he decided that short was easier and better. So he had it styled in a cut just above his ears. I loved his new look. It made his green eyes and angular jaw stand out.

Tripp lunged at Sam, the tip of his sword breaking the skin just above Sam's heart. "Pussy."

Sam returned the gesture, thrusting his left hip

forward, sword extended, forcing Tripp's blade down.

"You drew blood, asshole," Sam growled.

"Then pay attention," Tripp countered.

The two stood facing each other, waiting for the other to make a move.

Tripp cocked an eyebrow. "You sure you want to do this, Mason? You know you can't win."

"Ha! You don't know shit, sentinel," Sam spat.

They both circled the mat, muscles bunching on their bare chests as though they were two wolves vying for the alpha spot in a pack. I laughed out loud at that thought.

Both of them whipped their heads toward me.

"Something funny, Sis?" Sam asked.

"Yeah. Be careful or Tripp will shift into a wolf. I mean, he has wolf blood in him."

Tripp crossed the padded floor to a bench, where he snagged a towel, then wiped his face. "How many times do I have to tell you? I am mostly vampire. My wolf heritage has only graced me with the added ability to detect scents ten times more than a vampire."

Sam wiped the sweat off his face with a towel before he plucked his shirt off a bag at his feet and threw it over his head. "Good thing," he chided.

"I'd hate for you to spring claws while we were sparring."

Once Tripp's face was dry of sweat, he switched out the towel for a T-shirt then covered his chest. "Can't sleep, Jo?"

I joined them, sitting down on the slatted wooden bench as a cloud of stinky sweat burned my nostrils. "All I keep dreaming about is Webb in a coffin. I need to get off the base. I need a new venue or something to take my mind off Webb. Then maybe I could clear my head." Dad kept me under wraps, afraid that if I left base, Edmund would strike. He wouldn't even let me go to school, which was fine with me. In fact, Ms. Costner was still tutoring Sam and me on most days at the base library. Dad had said school was too risky. Considering I'd gotten into trouble and killed Blake Turner in self-defense, I agreed with Dad.

Dad was also concerned about Ben Jackson, Sam's human best friend who supposedly had been subjected to Edmund's vampire serum. We weren't sure if Ben was now a vampire or a monster like Blake Turner had been. Ben had escaped from Dad's men when we encountered him at the fundraising gala a few months back. Even Mr. Jackson had been scouring the city, looking for his son. Dad suspected that Ben was probably working for Edmund.

"Good luck convincing Pops to let you off base," Sam said.

"I'm going to ask. I want to see Darcy." She was my best human friend and had been under our protection for a month while her father worked to pay off his debt to a vampire he'd represented in court. "I haven't seen her since she moved back home, and that was three months ago." We'd spoken on the phone, but that was it. Her father wanted her far removed from the vampire world. I couldn't blame him since Edmund had kidnapped Darcy because of her father's poor decision concerning a vampire client of his.

"You need to stay away from the human." Tripp folded his large body as he sat down next to me. "You're only putting her in harm's way. Edmund can use her to get to you. And she's been through enough with him and us."

He was right, but I didn't want to acknowledge that fact. I wanted a friend. I wanted someone who I could talk to about Webb. I wanted a shoulder to cry on. I could cry on Dad's shoulder or Sam's or even Tripp's, but it wasn't the same. They were men, and while they might understand, a female friend understood better, at least to me. Not only that, I wanted to talk about things other than wars, blood, vampires, genetics, and anything else associated with my new world. I wanted to hear all about Darcy's life. She'd started her senior year. Was she dating? Had she decided on college like her father had wished? Or was she still set on beauty school? I could glean all that information over the phone or in an email or text, but I wanted that person-to-person connection, where we could lie around in her bedroom like we used to and giggle or watch a movie or just talk about nothing.

Tripp placed a hand on my knee, his drug-induced touch immediately sending a warm and lazy feeling through my body. "Jo, I don't mean this in a bad way, but you look like shit. Maybe I can help. I can try to put you to sleep."

Sam and I did a double take.

"Since when do you have that ability?" I asked.

"I haven't put someone under in quite some time. I'm not sure the commander would let me do it anyway. The last time I tried was on a family member who didn't wake up for a year. But I think she drank too much of my blood."

"Are you saying you can put someone in a coma if they drink your blood?" I continued to learn something new every day about vampires.

"In so many words, yeah." Tripp swung his

bronze gaze from Sam to me. "My cousin had gotten into a bad fight when she was on the cusp of blossoming into her wolf form. Since she wasn't entirely human and hadn't learned how to shift yet, her mother suggested we try to give her a dose of my vampire blood to see if it would heal her. Otherwise, she would die. The good news was she didn't die and is now a healthy wolf shifter. The bad news was she lost a year of her life. She still has issues with me."

"Does my father know you can do this?" Sam asked.

"Oh, yeah. I had to disclose my abilities when I applied for the vampire SEAL program." Tripp removed his hand from my knee. When he did, the warmth coursing through me turned cold. "At first, your father didn't believe me. So we experimented with a healthy vampire. He fell asleep not long after he drank my blood and didn't wake up for a week. So in emergencies when other vampires need blood, I'm not the one they come to."

My stomach fluttered at the notion that I might be able to sleep for longer than two hours. "If I sleep for a week, then I could dream. Maybe I could find out if Webb is still alive."

"Maybe," Tripp said with a hint of hesitation in his voice. "Your father has to agree."

I didn't see why he wouldn't. If I could sleep, then I wasn't bugging him about getting off base or whining about Webb, and I could possibly help find the team.

No sooner had I jumped off the bench, ready to go in search of my dad, than the sirens blared, the red lights in the room flashed, and Tripp sprang into action, bolting out of the room.

Sam and I followed. When I first moved on base, I'd panicked at any alarm, especially when Edmund blew up a building on base. But now I'd grown accustomed to the chaos. The three of us ran down the hall, up the stairs, and down more halls until we reached the belly of the control room. This was the place where the heart of the military beat, where information came in and went out, and where my father was wide-eyed with his black hair mussed as though he'd flown out of bed, which I was sure he had.

The TV screens lit up on one wall, while vamps shuffled into place, banging on keyboards. As screens changed, showing parts of the base's perimeter, a figure came into view at the main gate. Then three sentinels drew their guns on the dark figure, who held up his hands.

I knitted my eyebrows as I watched the dark hooded figure get down on his knees. Then he lifted his head and spoke. "I want to speak with Commander Mason. Tell him it's Ben Jackson."

Sam and I exchanged a horrified look as my stomach lurched.

On the Edge of Misery is now available in Ebook and paperback formats.

GLOSSARY OF TERMS

Natural-born vampire: A human born with the vampire gene that, when activated, will turn them into a vampire.

Activation process: Those who carry the vampire gene can only turn by drinking the blood of their vampire father at the age of sixteen years or older.

Council of Elders – A group of five vampires who set the laws.

Genetic engineering: Turning humans into vampires through a process of restructuring their DNA.

Cobalt – A vampire's kryptonite. The metal will kill a vampire if staked through the heart. It will also burn a vampire's skin if they come in contact with it.

Reproduction: A natural-born vampire is born by a male vampire and a human female with a rare blood type of Vel negative.

Council of Eternal Affairs: The legal department of the vampire government.

Vampire characteristics: Sunlight doesn't burn them. Their hearts beat at <5 bpm. Skin temperature is ten degrees cooler than a human. Eye color changes to black except for a few chosen ones.

Steven Mason: Vampire and father to twins Jo and Sam Mason. He's dubbed the most powerful of all vampires because of his many powers, including his mind-reading abilities. He can only read minds when touching someone except when it comes to his children. His normal eye color is green. His vampire eye color is silver.

Jo Mason: Turned at sixteen. Powers include seeing the future through her dreams, mind-reading without touching a person, telekinesis, and she's an elemental with the ability to manipulate water, air, earth, and fire. Her normal eye color is silver. Her vampire eye color is violet.

Sam Mason: Turned at sixteen. Powers include feeling what others feel (Empath), telekinesis, and he can compel a person using a series of numbers woven into a magical spell. He's also an elemental with the ability to manipulate water, air, earth, and fire. His normal eye color is green. His vampire eye color is silver.

Jupiter Sentinels: A secret and elite Navy SEAL Team within the military. Their role is to help the human military and guard the supernatural world.

Plutariums: A rogue team of vampires who want power and to engineer an army that would change humans into vampires.

Guardians: Vampires who are equivalent to the human police.

ABOUT THE AUTHOR

Bestselling author **S.B. Alexander** is an independent author with over 20 titles to date. She writes paranormal, new adult, and sweet romances that feature hot heroes stealing hearts.

S.B. or Susan as she likes to be called is a navy veteran, former high school teacher, and former corporate sales executive. She's a lover of sports, especially baseball, although nowadays you can find her glued to the TV during football season.

When she's not writing, she's a full-time caregiver to her soul mate of twenty-two years who got a bad deal in life when he was diagnosed with ALS. Her motto: "Life is too short to waste. So live every moment like it's your last."

You can connect with S.B. Alexander in the following ways:

Reader Group: https://
sbalexander.com/beastsandbitches
TikTok: https://www.tiktok.
com/@susanbalexander
Author Website: https://sbalexander.com
Newsletter: https://sbalexander.com/newsletter
Email: susan@sbalexander.com

<u>**NEVER MISS A NEW RELEASE:**</u>
Sign up for her Author App
iTunes: https://bit.ly/sbalexanderitunes
Android: https://bit.ly/sbalexanderandroid

facebook.com/sbalexander.authorpage

twitter.com/sbalex_author

instagram.com/sbalexanderauthor

bookbub.com/authors/s-b-alexander

goodreads.com/sbalexander

amazon.com/author/sbalexander

ALSO BY S.B. ALEXANDER

MAXWELL SERIES

Upper Young Adult/New Adult Contemporary Romance

Dare to Kiss

Dare to Dream

Dare to Love

Dare to Dance

Dare to Live

Dare to Breathe

Dare to Embrace

THE MAXWELL FAMILY SAGA SERIES

Young Adult Sweet Romance

My Heart to Touch

My Heart to Hold

My Heart to Give

My Heart to Keep

THE VAMPIRE NAVY SEAL SERIES

Paranormal Romance

On the Edge of Humanity

On the Edge of Eternity

On the Edge of Destiny

On the Edge of Misery

On the Edge of Infinity

STAND-ALONES

New Adult Contemporary Romance

Crazy For You

Unforgettable

Holding Onto Forever

Breaking Rules

Rescuing Riley

THE HART SERIES

New Adult Contemporary Romance

Hart of Darkness

Hart of Vengeance

Visit https://sbalexander.com/all-books/ to learn more about S.B. Alexander books and future releases. Please note release dates are subject to change based on reader demand and the author's schedule. Subscribing to the author's newsletter or following her on Facebook is the best way to stay updated with planned new releases.